The Flowers that Bloom on a Dark French Night

Sequel to *The Warmth of Waves*

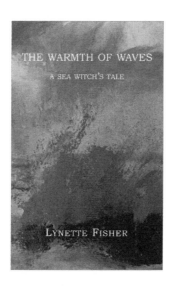

The Flowers that Bloom on a Dark French Night

Lynette Fisher

First published by Le Vieux Four Publishing 2016

ISBN 978-0-9927400-3-0

Typeset by Moira Read, Border Typesetting, Beaminster, Dorset
Printed and bound in Great Britain

Cover image
Mike Jackson www.mikejacksonartist.com

For my dearest father Hervey Fisher, who taught me how to spend a life 'wondering if there is anything worse than being burdened with inspiration without talent'.

With thanks to my friends and confidantes Roddy Stansfeld and Charlotte Delaforce for their endless encouragement. Also for their patient reading and rereading and assassination of my characters.

Also my heartfelt thanks to Mike Jackson (artist) for his inspiration, talent and care in creating the covers for my novels.

Special gratitude to Moira Read, who has put up with me through the publication of four books, her hard work is appreciated on every page.

Thank you to those, who having enjoyed 'The Warmth of Waves', spurred me on to write the sequel.

Down, far below the still blue waters of a normal life,
the Sea Witch lies drowsing, lulled by the wavelets
stirred by the small bright fish that swim above her ...

PROLOGUE

Pinks, proper name Dianthus; a secret message hidden in their scent from the hurly burly of a mother's cottage garden. Wavy petals, like the tutu of some child ballerina who aspires to be a fairy, filling the air with the incense of cloves, as she dances. They continue to appear, day after day, uninterrupted. Long after they have lost their appeal they still fall, silently on her damp, morning doorstep. Sometimes they share the milk crate, but more often they are propped neatly in the opposite corner. Placed, with care, during the dead hours of the night. No one sees. Now and again the heads have no lustre, they are dead, with rotting foliage, musty and insulting.

Hibiscus too. The sweetest of all, luxurious, bewitching, full of the flavours and memories of a previous life in windy sunshine and joy. Manipulative, cunning and clever, they blow secret false promises with every fragrant breath.

Lilies that suffocate and stain. A long box, coffin shaped, sits on the bonnet of her car. Attracting interest, attention seeking, innocent participants in a guileful plan. Quick, squash them with the rubbish, before their menace can escape and drown her with their intimidating, evil beauty.

Springtime brings a complete tray of polyanthus, a bright spread upon her stone steps to greet the early sun.

May Day comes, and the French follow their age-old tradition by offering Merguez, Lilly of the Valley to their loved ones. The adorable aroma of the sweet bell-like flower surrounds her as she finds them; half a dozen bunches stealthily placed on the counter in her shop.

1

Summer brings a hanging basket, too heavy to hang above the door. Reckless and abandoned, he loses all reason now.

Winter frosts herald scentless, paper-like flowers…completely empty of life, piling on the mat outside, proof of madness and abnormality. Rotting blooms, interspersed with layers of paper and cellophane. A grotesque millefeuille on the sad, untended grave of his affection.

A single daffodil lies upon her daily path to the market. How diligently he pursues her now. A bunch against the back door too! How do flowers trespass through locked gates and over walls? Alarm and dismay. How can this be?

"Stalkers feed off any reaction from their prey" … she reads this in a book somewhere, desperate to know, to understand the forces that drive him.

And you know the worst part? No one, but no one, takes her problem seriously. Elle is alone.

PART 1

Avant

"How much better is silence; the coffee cup, the table. How much better to sit by myself like the solitary sea-bird that opens its wings on the stake. Let me sit here for ever with bare things, this coffee cup, this knife, this fork, things in themselves, myself being myself."

Virginia Woolf, *The Waves*

1

Elle

The locals call me simply, *"L'Anglaise"* or *"Chocolat"* the latter nickname being somewhat upside down for an English girl selling the specialties of her native land in France. The whole *"Chocolat"* thing wears a bit thin over time, especially as I bear absolutely no resemblance to Juliet Binoche. Perhaps 'Fruit and Nut' would be more appropriate, given the amount of traditional fruitcakes I sell. My real name is Eleanor, shortened, of course to Elle, meaning *she* in the French language, quite fitting really. After a somewhat turbulent period at sea beginning in my teens and ending in my late twenties, I am now married to a Frenchman, Philippe, and I only talk about my sailing days when pressured. Motherhood has changed me, I have cast aside the Sea Witch title and the sting of her reputation is left firmly in my past. The sale of *Sea Witch* herself broke my heart and I can hardly bear to think of that day now. My precious boat with her gleaming white sides as she graced the water, her cosy stove down below, and the joy of setting out on a breezy day. All are gone.

My life dramatically altered after the twins, and even more so following the birth of my son. Ben was a sickly baby, and taking to sea had suddenly become a risk and therefore an impossibility. My relationship with their father changed too, we had limped along until Ben was born, but the move to bricks and mortar never suited him, neither had parenthood. Finally he left us. My hair has turned a shade darker and the reckless, outrageous nature that drove me to sea is calmed and tamed by my responsibilities as a parent. Philippe is an engineer, sometimes with a job, but more often out looking endlessly for work around the port. I love him, he is there for me, and I understand the difficulties he has with a wife who is the breadwinner. He is a man who wants to be the hunter-gatherer and who loses face when it is not so.

We live above my small shop in a narrow street of an old French town, just around the corner from the market, in a tall building that belongs to a solicitor who lives and works on the top two floors. He has a wonderful roof garden with views across the town and I'm envious. Houses are strange to me. They are not at all like boats for they have many dark corners and cobwebs. I'm shut in now, a prisoner within old stone walls.

Onboard *Galuette* and *Sea Witch* too, I'd always drink my first cup of tea in the morning outside in the cockpit. Whatever the weather, I would listen to the water stirring beneath me, the fenders squeaking against pontoon or jetty, and idly watch the life of the port as it greeted another day. Sanding machines whirred and varnish brushes flew, the smell of anti-fouling as sweet as any blossom on the breeze. I try to be in control of our home, to make it shiny and clean like my boats always were, but it's a battle I can never win. The house was weary with the heavy spirit of previous occupancy embedded in the walls, when we'd first arrived. Now I have made it my own with fresh pastel colours carefully applied to walls and shutters. There is always something that needs painting or repairing and the children's possessions spread all through the rooms like weeds in a garden, always popping up where they shouldn't. On the lower floors, we have no outside space, apart from a tiny verandah attached to the sitting room, which I cram with pots of herbs and flowers. On the ground floor there is a paved corridor area inside the back gate, which seems to collect cardboard boxes and children bicycles. It has become a type of assault course if one wishes access, in or out, that way. I dream of a garden with shrubs and fruit bushes but the beach is only ten minutes walk away, which is some compensation. All in all life is good.

This town is my home, with the hustle and bustle of the joyous morning market just around the corner, tables laden with seasonal fruits and vegetables. In what other place on earth could you find a shrunken old man, who cuts his marigolds as soon as they are in bloom and sells them, alongside his freshly picked tomatoes on a small, makeshift stall? Here is a market full of the taste and aromas of the early summer sunshine of Provence.

I look to the mountains everyday. From the fall onwards, as soon as the Mistral blows a chilly gust across the town, they reappear, as if by magic, from their hiding place during the hazy heat of summer. Through the winter they will become snowcapped and Christmas card perfect, as they appear to slide closer in their winter splendour, to wrap and protect the town.

I'd never contemplate an affair with another man. I'm happy, but we do have our ups and downs in the confines of our second time around, split nationality, marriage. The combination of our five children makes life into a testing challenge of confusing loyalties. My three, from my previous relationship, are the youngest. Their father does not choose to stay in touch, depriving himself of all the joys, (and sometimes sorrows) of their upbringing. The elder two are Philippe's, difficult, surly French teenagers, who would clearly rather have their own mother back instead of this unsatisfactory foreign replacement. I can accept the disappointing moments with my own children; forgiving and understanding is easier with your own. Love is unconditional between true parent and child in almost every circumstance. But his children? Whether their hatred of me is conscious or unconscious, I can't decide. I can feel it, their stubborn distaste hangs in the air like a balloon waiting to burst, leaving the wilted shred of our marriage upon the floor. If I give them a chance to slip in a knife, they will, most surely, turn and push the weapon in to the hilt.

I love my husband, and I try endlessly to please, pasting over the cracks between us that split and threaten to divide.

A typical scenario occurs when Philippe's younger child, Marguerite, comes home from school ... 'Where's Papa?' she says, without actually greeting or even looking at me. She walks straight past me to the fridge, opening and perusing the contents. 'Do we have apples?'

'Yes, there, look, at the bottom,' I reply, and I'm immediately annoyed at my own anxiousness to please.

'I don't like those. They are sour.' Marguerite repeats her former question. 'Where's Papa?'

'Out,' I say to Marguerite's back. She dumps her school bag in the middle of the shop, and heads back out into the street, slamming the door behind her as she always does.

Philippe's children, Marguerite and Yves, the boy being the elder, speak to me, their stepmother, in pidgin English. They know perfectly well I speak fluent French, and to me this feels like another method of alienating me from their life with their father. Shutting me out. Sometimes they speak about me in French to each other in front of me as though I can't understand. My fury simmers. It's pointless for me to say anything to Philippe who staunchly defends them, never chastising them for anything for fear of driving them to choose to spend more time with their mother and her new partner.

These two teenagers bully my own children, especially my little boy Ben, who is only seven years old. I chose the name because of the other Ben that I knew all those years ago in Gibraltar. I would perhaps prefer to forget all that I've been and all that I've done, but I have to remember. Our past is who we are after all.

They stop as soon as I enter the room, but I know their game.

Ben is so innocent of adult ways, their cruel words almost pass over his head but sometimes, just lately, he's looked really hurt and bewildered by Marguerite's sharp comments, and has turned to me to explain. My twin girls, Frannie and Florence, seem to be exempt from their harsh outbursts, probably because they are so busy in their own lives, always out with their friends, and already following fashion, they are oblivious to undercurrents within the family home.

Yves smokes in his room, which is unacceptable and forbidden by both Philippe and myself. When accused he hotly denies it, saying the smell is in his clothes from the company he keeps.

My only consolation is that one day they'll go. Every now and then, but not regularly, Philippe's children spend time with their mother and then the whole house feels different, transformed into a happy, loving home. These are the days that save me from insanity.

I often have to remind myself in troubled moments that my life, however, could be worse. Philippe and I have a large circle of friends, almost exclusively French, as neither of us care particularly for the expatriate community. There are several reasons for this, the main one being our joint annoyance at the lack of effort, on the whole, made by the English people who have chosen to come to France for the lifestyle and the climate, to integrate, and to at least *try* to learn the language. In fact, some of them make me embarrassed to be British. Half of the them are extremely rich and rather pompous, and the rest drink too much, gossip, and hang around outside the English bars, cradling pints of beer, and talking rubbish. There are a few genuine people amongst the large yachting community, but on the other hand there are plenty of complete idiots as well. Philippe has become quite choosy about who he works for, which is probably why he is often out of work. He is a typical

Frenchman, proud and nationalistic, likes his steak on the hoof, and will only eat French cheese. But therein lies his charm, take it or leave it, and I have taken him, quirky French ways and all.

Our closest friends have the shop next door; a Belgian couple who moved south some twenty odd years ago, to pursue their business of selling and restoring antiques. I first made their acquaintance when their small fishing boat was moored alongside my own boat, *Galuette*. I adore this French family for the way they took me to their bosom right from the start, weaving me into the pattern of their days. I was honoured and felt every bit a part of the country in which I was lucky enough to live.

Their shop, even smaller than mine, is packed from floor to ceiling with furniture, paintings, glassware, silver and mirrors. It's an obstacle course for anyone to find their way from the front of the shop to the desk at the rear, where Amelie sits in a dark corner, like a spider at the centre of her web. She is *la maitresse,* the wholesome figure, effortlessly in charge of her family consisting of their four children and Claude, her husband. He is usually in the loft directly above the shop, his mouth full of upholstery pins,(how do they not become mislaid in his beard?) tapping away, mending some little chair or other. He says he doesn't speak English but should a couple of Americans chance to wander in, he leaps to their attention with, "Hello. May I help you? So pleased to meet you," and several other well practiced phrases that make Amelie and I laugh until our sides ache.

Claude says that when he no longer has a wedge of francs in his back pocket, then France is finished. I hope that this will not be soon, as I manage to support my little family comfortably from the cakes that I bake and sell five days a week. My small shop is so different from the French patisseries in the town that I've carved out a niche for myself, with plenty of regular customers, both French and English. The Belgians were extremely helpful when I took over the lease of the shop across the road. How convenient it was when I fell for their good friend Philippe, making us into a firm foursome.

Nothing could be better than piling into Claude's huge, bouncy citroen for a trip to the old town of Nice, to wander in the narrow streets, lingering a while to eat socca and couscous; Claude and Philippe both love these Moroccan style dishes. Amelie is a masterful hostess. A meal *chez les Belges*, is always a special occasion, even in the middle of a busy working day. She bottles fruits and offers a small dish of them around with coffee, but beware for they are steeped in liquor, and one innocent plum, after the feast at midday, can leave you reeling for the whole afternoon.

There's no doubt that the day that I married Philippe was the happiest day of my life, although I didn't realise, until I studied the photos at a later date, how my own children had been pushed into the background by my new husband's attention seeking teenagers. Would it have made any difference to how they are now if I had noticed sooner? Probably not. It's the only thing that Philippe and I ever argue about and each time is just a little worse than the last. I realise now that the die was cast even on our honeymoon, when frequent phone calls from Marguerite began to slightly irritate me. Philippe had left the table at dinner on more than one occasion to speak to her, or worse still imprisoned himself in the bathroom to answer late night calls from his daughter. I've tried to talk about the problem with Amelie but I realise that my friend's loyalties lie with Philippe and his offspring; as of course she has known my husband's family far longer.

'They have had a difficult time, those two,' Amelie says in a firm voice that does not invite contradiction. 'After all, their mother ran off with a horrible man, leaving them to pick up the pieces of their father. Three years she carried on behind his back, you know.'

Of course I knew but I still didn't think that any of that excused their bad manners towards my children and me. I have no one with whom I can share my problem and it gnaws and nibbles at me, day and night.

I spend much of my time asking myself whether my resentment towards them is deserved. Philippe spoils them, never questioning their repeated demands for money, which sadly is in short supply, especially since their father is unemployed. So in reality, if I put two and two together, I'm baking cakes to buy my stepson tobacco. This doesn't please me at all, but if I dare to voice my assumption there would be a huge explosion. The fallout would land on my children, so where is the sense in that? Better to be silent.

There is a hard, sore place inside of me, which festers and spreads with every hour that passes.

Both of the shops, for cakes and antiques alike, are closed on Sundays. I close on Mondays too, my day for catching up on both household and shop chores, before the start of a new week. On Sundays in the summer I love to be invited to join my neighbours with their children, to go on one of Claude's celebrated fishing trips. They are not at all worthy of this name as there are never many fish involved, except for those to be found packed in the picnic, cooked in one of Amelie's cherished recipes. She has a way of conserving tuna fish (during the glut in June) in small jars with olive oil, spices and seasonings that is simply divine. With crunchy fresh bread and unsalted butter, nothing could be better. So deliciously simple, as the best gastronomic pleasures often are.

Their wooden traditional day boat is moored in the old port near the shipyard so it's quite a trudge from the town, laden down with the picnic and drinks in assorted baskets, but Claude declares that we all need the exercise. The berth belonging to their wooden day boat is adjacent to the one where my first boat, *Galuette* used to be moored. This makes every visit one of wistful nostalgia for me as my gaze is inevitably drawn to the spot where I spent so many happy days, varnishing and painting my prize possession. If I close my eyes, I can see her there, her spoon bow proudly protruding amongst the other boats. My past adventures of solo sailing on a Sunday afternoon and my eventual circumnavigation of Corsica are memories that seem as if they might belong to someone else, now that I have a family and motherly duties. I could never just abandon them and take to sea again.

A calm, flat sea is needed, and we all wear huge sombreros to protect us from the fierce Mediterranean sun in the middle of the day. All the children will swim while we chat, eat and finally doze. A relaxing time is had by all ... except Philippe who declines to join us on these most precious of days, declaring that he has things to do. What those things might be I never ask, because I don't really care. If he wants to miss out on a lovely day, it's not my problem. It's my chance to be out on the ocean again, the place where I feel happiest and I can set aside my busy days, leaving them firmly on the shore.

'Maybe he has a mistress?' says Claude looking at his wife and then at me for the answer.

'No, he chooses to spend the time secretly with his own children, whilst we're gone,' I reply, and I feel a stab of anguish that my husband has not chosen to reveal this information to me. Why can't he just tell me? After all it's a pretty reasonable excuse although I imagine him indulging them with a restaurant meal we can barely afford. Anxiety slips in to replace my calm, Sunday mood and I wish we had not spoken of Philippe at all.

The shop, although providing only a modest living, gives me a huge sense of security, and both pride and strength from knowing who I am exactly, within a community, something I had never known during my days at sea. Whatever problems I may have, or sorrows I may feel, they can all be pushed to the back of the stove, whilst I'm busy with my daily baking, serving and chatting to customers. Some days are harder than others, especially when I'm driven almost to tears of exasperation at my unsuccessful efforts to build a healthy relationship with Philippe's children. As I listen to my customers endless joys and sorrows, somehow my own worries are soothed and hope regained.

One day Philippe returns from his job seeking in the Bar Du Port with positive news.

'*J'ai trouvé du travail,*' he announces, and I can see he is about to burst with pleasure and excitement, his face is aglow and not just from the Pastis he has been supping.

'Where, who for?' I ask, not allowing myself to rejoice at the prospect of more money coming, not yet, not until I know for sure.

'It's an Arab boat, a big stinkpot, needs a full time engineer. I might be away a bit as they cruise in the summer, Greek Islands and stuff.'

'So you don't actually have the job then?' The onset of doubt smothers the enthusiasm that was creeping into my heart, a second before.

'No, but I have an interview tomorrow, and the guy thinks I am the right man for the job.'

I have complete faith in my husband's engineering skills. If anything is malfunctioning or not working at all in that field, he has a determined side that will not let him rest until the problem has been resolved. Friends are continuously knocking at our door requesting his services day and night but unfortunately this doesn't pay the bills, just buys Philippe liquor in the bar, which is far from helpful.

'Who does the boat belong to, do you know?' I'll not let the subject rest until I have extracted all the information. I need to decide for myself if there's indeed hope, based on all the facts.

'Oh it's all top security until I know whether they select me, you know what the Arab setup is like.'

Actually this is something that I do know a great deal about. Prior to meeting Philippe in the days long before I had children, I held the position of housekeeper in an Arab owned villa outside Cannes. I was searched on my arrival early in the morning and again on my departure late at night. The work was exhausting, entailing the supervision of a large team of chambermaids, to ensure that the miles of marble corridors, bedrooms, bathrooms, living areas and the terraced lounges around the pool were kept absolutely spotless at all times. Showers had to be wiped down as soon as they were used, toilets cleaned if they'd been flushed, and cushions plumped if they displayed as much as a tiny dimple. The in-house laundry operated day and night, washing towels and sheets from beds that were changed several times in one day. The Arabs shopped for more clothes than they could possibly need, and demanded all their purchases to be washed before they would wear them. The work was not only hard, but somewhat demeaning as we were never allowed to look or speak to the occupants of the villa. The salary, on the other hand, was more than I had ever earned in my life, and the food at midday was a feast of delights, a banquet, the like of which I'd never seen. After discovering a cache of guns under one of the guest beds however, I resigned, a quick decision based on pure terror. Oh yes, I know about working for Arabs.

We badly need a second source of income, both for the health of our finances and the stability of our marriage. I'm crossing my fingers that whoever is in charge of the hiring will take a shine to Philippe, and that his arrogant French demeanour will not rise to the surface.

The shirts are flying in and out of the wardrobe, like a girl dressing for a party.

'Iron this one for me, Elle, please, you do a much better job than me.'

I give in, and pull out the ironing board while he shaves with the accuracy only a Frenchman can achieve, dragging his cut-throat razor along the edge of his designer stubble. This is followed by carefully administered Chanel. Not really what one would normally expect of an engineer at all, but this is Philippe, my engineer, with the cleanest fingernails I've ever seen in a man.

He's gone for two and a half hours, during which time I begin to suffer butterflies of nervous expectation in my stomach, as I am well aware that the outcome could improve our circumstances a great deal. At last he comes back into the shop, setting the bell jangling with his slam of the door.

'Steady,' I say. 'Did you not get it?'

'Of course, I did,' he shouts with a grin, throwing his arms wide for an embrace. I run and bury my nose in his shoulder to hide tears of relief. 'I'm sorry I stopped at the bar for a quick celebratory drink so I was a bit longer than planned.'

This admission almost spoiled the moment but I let it go. 'Come on then, let's fix some lunch and you can tell me all about the job.'

'*Naima*, that's the name of the boat, means calm. It's also the name of one of the owner's wives or children; I can't remember what he said now. Too much to take in at one sitting.' Philippe is talking at the same time as stuffing pieces of bread into his mouth, he's so excited. I sincerely hope that this job will be secure and life changing for us both.

'We will be cruising a fair amount though, from Easter through to the end of the summer so I don't know how often we'll be back here. But you'll be all right won't you? You have the kids to keep you company, and the shop to keep you busy. I don't suppose you'll even notice I'm gone!'

I'm subdued, wondering how life will be. Will Marguerite and Yves go more often and stay with their mother? I pray silently that they will. They don't even like me and with their father gone, surely there could be no reason for them to stay with me all the time. I can only hope; time will tell.

Amelie (four years later)

The proud French woman named Béatrice walks down the street towards the abandoned English cake shop with a purposeful stride, but as she reaches the door, without so much as a cursory glance, she turns her back on the flaking paint of the white frontage and rings the bell on the front door of the antique shop opposite. Amelie answers the door and regarding her visitor as if she's not entirely surprised to see her, ushers her inside. There are gaps Béatrice has to fill, as a prosecutor must see all the evidence in any case. She has to see the whole picture before her, and there she hopes to find the calmness of spirit she so desires, and banish any fears of her own culpability. Driven to research every tiny detail, she sits down now, and raises her open hands above her lap, a signal to the woman before her, one of Elle's closest friends, to tell her all that she needs to know.

Amelie takes a deep ragged breath, and begins to relate to her all she can, understanding the woman's need to piece together the events that had led up to the event that had irretrievably changed her life forever.

'*Au sujet d'Elle? Je me souviens notre premier impressions de cette petite fille. One day Claude and I arrived at our boat to go fishing. It was a long time ago, perhaps fifteen years or more, she was standing on the little wooden boat next to ours. She had taken down the sign which hung between the back stays saying "A VENDRE." We found it an extraordinary idea that this*

17

petite, flaxen haired English girl, the colour of a hazelnut, had purchased this yacht (si mignon), from the rather bizarre French owner who had never spoken a word to us during the several years we had been tied up alongside. She bravely made our acquaintance immediately, with her attempts to speak French making me die laughing for at that time, her command of the language was shaky'.

Béatrice cannot help but notice the affectionate way that Amelie speaks of her friend.

'Claude said I was rude and that she was admirable for making the attempt. She changed the name of the boat to Galuette, the original launching name, as she disliked the one the Frenchman had chosen because it referred to a submarine. Claude said that Galuette, the name of a small herring gull in the local patois in Breton where the boat was built, suited both owner and craft.

She was the cook on a big yacht moored in the shipyard. We knew there were several men in her life one after the other, back then. One of her suitors was Antoine, who we knew well. He was a security guard in the port, we also knew his wife so the whole affair was rather awkward for us.'

Béatrice opens her mouth as if to interrupt the Belgian's story but thinks better of it, gesturing for her to continue. She is eager to reach the part that might concern her.

'We assumed it ended badly although we never really knew what happened. I was pregnant with our first child at that time and the second followed swiftly, so I'd no chance to embroil myself in port gossip although Claude made it his business to try and keep up. I think she sailed away again after all the carry on with Antoine. She occasionally reappeared to see us in the shop, she'd sold Galuette and was working all over the place. Claude found out she'd bought another boat, a bigger one called Sea Witch, so our little gull had matured and become the Sea Witch, another name to suit both girl and boat.

18

A decade passed before we saw her with the twins and Ben looking at the shop opposite ours and we struggled to comprehend how much time had passed, for we had not noticed the years flying by, being so adsorbed in our own family life, I suppose.

We encouraged her with her shop, she was struggling with single parenthood as the children's father was gone who knows where and we knew better than to pry. Elle had not changed much and although her hair was several shades darker, (she said it was something to do with a hormonal change after the birth of the twins) she was the same girl. She still had a fiercely independent streak about her, but at the same time she gave the impression that she was determined to do the best for her children. She was forty years old and I believe she understood that her time to live recklessly on the sea was over. We both wondered if she'd manage to leave the freedom of the ocean behind her and become content with her family, steady work, and maybe a little fishing le Dimanche.

We were always having dinner parties and we rarely left her out, feeling sorry for her continuously working and stuck in her house with the children. She had virtually no contact with the English yachting fraternity, they were no longer a part of her life, almost as though she tried to block out the past by disassociating with her countrymen. She preferred to be thought of as French but she will always be "L'Anglaise" to us. In her single days, when she came to eat with us the children came too so she had no need for a babysitter; the twins amused themselves with our children and she would carry Ben home asleep at the end of an evening. One night she met Philippe at our table, he was really a friend of Claude's more than mine, one of the boys, but you could see throughout the evening he only had eyes for Elle. I had made les boules d'agneau with garlic, I will never forget it, she was horrified when she realised what they were. Philippe found the situation a source of tremendous merriment, so much so that

I wondered if Elle would ever speak to him again. Not only did she speak to him she married him, and he moved in above the shop within a few months.'

2

"She loved him absolutely, perhaps for half an hour."

E.M. Forster

Six weeks have passed since my husband took up his new position and I take a moment, sitting with my cup of tea at the end of a busy day, to reflect on how our lives are subtly changing since Philippe moved aboard *Naima*. For a while he had been able to live at home but now the season has begun with the Monaco Grand Prix and he is obliged to settle into life onboard ship. For a ship she is, an enormous floating palace of luxury, with two speedboats on the top deck and a helipad. There's plenty to keep Philippe busy. The salary is more than generous, but I know how hard he has to work, for his life is no longer his own. He takes meals with the rest of the crew, while they're still in port, so I rarely see him before I've eaten and am thinking about retiring to bed. We've not had a chance to speak of anything other than the details of his new job and experiences, since he joined the ship. He's masterfully taken centre stage in the family, dressed in his important white uniform, with epaulettes on his shoulders. But now the yacht has been summoned elsewhere and in a whirl of frothy engine power, he must leave. Off to cruise the Greek Islands, via Italy and anywhere else the owner might choose to go. A life literally following the whims of the idle rich, I remember what that's like.

The house does feel a little strange at first, but I realise that I'm actually enjoying the calm all around me since I've been on my own. The children are happy, particularly Ben, as they have my undivided attention with Philippe absent. I eat earlier with them in a new routine, help them with their homework, and then I'm able to coax Ben to bath and bed, without feeling torn between spending the time in the evenings with my children, or with my husband. Marguerite and Yves, have virtually moved back in with their mother, just as I'd hoped, except for sudden, surprise visits. These always coincide with a demand for money, or food from the fridge on their way home.

I spend time trying to analyse the situation but I never arrive at a clear conclusion. I love Philippe, and being married, but this sudden freedom makes me feel like myself again, instead of being an accessory to someone else. Does marriage inevitably come with a loss of identity? It's exciting to be liberated and independent, to make my own decisions concerning my daily life and work again. Like I did before, when I was single.

We speak on the phone in the evenings everyday.

'Hi cherie, how are you?' It's good to hear his voice.

'I'm fine, a little tired,' I reply.

'Busy in the shop today then?'

'Yes of course, its Saturday,' I say, impatient now, how could he not realise what day it is? 'Where are you?'

'Portofino.'

'Sounds good.' What else can I say? 'I miss you.' Am I being honest, is it true?

'You seen my kids?'

'No, not today.'

'Ok, must go, *je t'aime*,' he always signs off the in same way.

'I love you too,' I say, and replace the receiver gently with a heavy heart. His call has knocked me off balance and confuses me.

After the first week the phone calls gradually dwindle.

Amelie and Claude worry about me being on my own. 'Nonsense,' I say, 'I'm fine,' and this is the truth, for that's exactly how I am, "fine".

Married life without my husband is ideal, in a number of different ways. I can add up the plus points. I have the sense of security that marriage provides, yet none of the duties and restraints that a husband imposes merely by his presence. I revel in the luxury of watching my favourite detective programmes in bed, reading my book, or simply falling asleep when my day is over. No one to answer to, no guilt over services I'm too tired to provide. I'm able to spend more quality time with Ben, Frannie and Florence, without having to justify myself. I bear no resentment for having to undertake all the household tasks because there is no one else to whom I can delegate. Maybe I miss his body neatly curved around mine, well, just a little, but as each day passes, the big bed all to myself is delightful.

The financial relief of our new situation is almost over-whelming. Philippe takes a small part of his salary in cash and the remainder is paid into our bank account. For the first time since we were married, I can, if I'm careful, begin to amass some savings, instead of ending up at rock bottom again after paying all the monthly outgoings. I never had any money worries until I had the children, who forced me to put down some roots on land. The shop thrives better too, without Philippe dipping into the till to pay his bar bill and other sundries. The weekly food account for the children and myself is negligible.

Do I feel lonely? Between the children and the shop, I barely have a minute to think about Philippe not being around. From the moment I open my shop early in the morning, I'm not only obliged to lend a sympathetic ear to the wide range of worries from my regular customers, but also to make polite conversation with strangers who wander in from the street. By the time the children return from school again I'm quite ready to close the door and shut the world out for the evening. Peace.

'Do you think she's all right?' Claude enquires of Amelie over dinner.

'She says she quite likes it,' his wife confides.

'*Eh bien*, well, I think it's not at all normal for a husband to leave a wife, she is an attractive woman and should not be left to her own devices.'

'They have no choice,' Amelie replies with a typically French shrug of her round, comely shoulders. '*Enfin*,' she concludes. 'It's only for the summer months this separation, and then he can work from home.'

I've built up a reliable list of suppliers for everything I need for the smooth day to day running of the business. Free range eggs are delivered, (I use at least two dozen a day) the local wholesalers deliver butter, cheeses, finest Belgian chocolate and all the different flours and sugars I require for my daily baking. A company named *Le Carteaux Blanc* (the name derived from an amalgamation of the two words, *'carton'* and *'gateaux'*) supply me with pretty cake boxes, ribbons, paper bags and eclair cases. All of my packaging comes from this one warehouse. The suppliers all call me during the course of a week, so that I may place my order with ease. This has become a well-oiled system, which means I rarely have to leave my busy kitchen to fetch things.

For several months now, the voice that calls me from *Le Carteaux Blanc*, has been that of a pleasant young man. I'd guess him to be about twenty-six or seven, not more, full of the jaunty authority of youth. Probably a bit of a know-it-all, to be honest. And then, suddenly, today, a different voice on the other end asks for my order. This unusual intonation of the exact same enquiry for my weekly requirements completely takes me by surprise. Surely I've heard this man before, his way with words is undeniably most distinctive. Ah … I have it now, it's his voice that I hear on the answer machine when I call late to add something I've forgotten.

The following week I start to wonder; his soft local vowels

beguile and fascinate me. What might he look like? Such a cheery note, like a smile, detectable behind his tradesman's banter. Our conversation lasts just a fraction longer on each occasion. Is it me that prolongs our exchange or is it him? May the heavens blush at the thought that I would encourage this peculiar form of flirtation! After all we are just playing a harmless game for we've never set eyes on each other. Just chatty phone calls that come and go. Quickly forgotten. He asks me, 'What do you do in your free time?'

'I haven't any,' I reply, with a chuckle, considering I have my three children to care for, and a business to run, my answer is undeniably, absolutely true.

Philippe calls me from somewhere at the bottom of the boot of Italy, announcing the news that he has a weekend of leave and is about to jump on a train and try to wend his way home. It's a long way and a complicated journey but he is determined to come. I can sense he is homesick. Like many French men, he's not a man who enjoys leaving his home town for long. I go to the market at six on the Friday morning before I have to dress the children or open the shop. With the fridge bursting with good food for the weekend, I'm prepared. I pop in to tell Amelie, and to say that neither I, nor my family will be able to join the planned Sunday fishing trip. I will devote my day off to Philippe, he might want to go somewhere special to eat for the occasion of Sunday lunch *en famille*.

He arrives at the station, late, tired and understandably grumpy. The children are already asleep but they are happy and surprised to discover him at home in the morning. The conversation is easy between myself and Philippe, and I wish it could always be like this. We discuss the possibility of a proper family holiday when he returns in the autumn. While I'm working in the shop he disappears to catch up with his mates and on his return his good spirits, after a sound night's sleep, are infectious.

25

We're just sitting down to dinner when Marguerite and Yves bowl into the house.

'Would you like to join us?' I ask them. 'There is plenty, I'll fetch some plates.'

Marguerite peers at her father's meal. 'What sort of meat is that?'

'Lamb, it's roast lamb.' I try not to snap. Stress begins to creep towards me again, like an unwelcome insect crawling across the table.

'Oh, we won't then.' Apparently Yves shall not be given the choice by his younger sister.

Marguerite stands at her father's shoulder and proceeds to pick morsels off his plate, whilst chatting with him. He accepts this show of bad manners as if she were five years old. I struggle to contain my anger. My three children are quiet, barely daring to look at me, sensing the situation that is brewing. Yves has disappeared outside to smoke.

I try bravely to move on, suppressing my fury at Marguerite's behaviour. 'What would you like to do tomorrow, Philippe?' I ask.

'Shall we drive out to the country? It would be refreshing to be away from the sea and to drive into the hills for a few hours,' he smiles and takes my hand across the table. But the surge of relief is only temporary, for my stepdaughter interrupts, destroying our intimate moment.

'But Papa, I need you to come with us tomorrow to look for a car for Yves, because the one we choose for him will be the one I learn to drive in as well. All the garages are open on Sundays and we can have a good look around before you go back.'

I am crestfallen and horrified. I hadn't seen this coming. I may as well go fishing with my neighbours after all, even though I'll probably not see my husband for the rest of the summer. I wait, hoping that just for once Philippe will prioritise spending time with me instead of his children. Of course he turns immediately to Marguerite and placing his arm around her waist, he says, 'Now there's an idea, you don't mind do you Elle? If we set off in reasonable time I shall be back early and we can go for a drive in the afternoon.'

I know he won't be home before nightfall. Speechless and hurt I slide off my chair and start clearing the dishes. Perhaps he'll spend a lifetime endeavouring to compensate for the breakup of his marriage. I'm not sure I can bear to contemplate the way things are so obviously set in stone for the rest of our days.

Philippe has gone, and the memory of our brief time together takes on a dream like quality, as if he was never here. Finally I succumb to the sadness of our parting and bury my nose in his pillow to try to inhale some small trace of him. There were some cross words when he had finally returned with Marguerite that had soured both our nighttime relations and his departure. How can I accept second place in his affections without upset? I felt so excluded when he had chosen to spend his only day at home with his daughter. I remember the occasion of his birthday when he said he was going to the bar with his children to celebrate without me. I'd not been welcome at my own husband's birthday drinks! My children accept their new extended family unconditionally but this will never be the case with Marguerite and Yves. It's almost as though I must carry the blame for their mother's indiscretions and in my eyes this can never be justified or indeed, fair.

Life resumes the unproblematic normality that I'd become accustomed to before the disruption of Philippe's weekend at home. Ben plays with his toy cars and trucks after school, quietly giving the drivers the ability to converse in little, squeaky voices, and the twins complain continuously about my restrictions concerning the hour of their return later in the evening, always pushing their boundaries.

On Monday, whilst I'm cleaning the shop ready for opening

next day, I spy one of the *Le Carteaux Blanc* vans driving up the road to the other bakery at the end of my street. I quickly decide to swop brooms and sweep just outside so I can perhaps see who is in the driving seat. Of course, as he is the boss, the chances of my new friend doing a delivery round are fairly unlikely, but I still must investigate. No crime in knowing what he looks like. I try to spy without being obvious, but any observer would definitely notice my frequent, surreptitious glances towards the top of my road. Unfortunately the van itself blocks my view of the front door of the other shop, but I do catch a glimpse of the figure unloading from the rear of the vehicle. The driver certainly looks taller and better built than their usual young, gawky delivery boy. He goes to the passenger door for something, probably the paperwork, and I take in the back of a sandy haired man with a stripy sort of sweatshirt, tucked into khaki trousers. Yes, this could be him! I scurry back indoors for fear he should turn and catch me looking.

Philippe (four years later)

Béatrice had met with Philippe on two or three occasions since the end of it all.

They sit now in a cosy bar in the back of Nice, away from the probability of meeting anyone they might know. Ironically it crosses her mind that this would be how lovers would meet, secretly sharing confidences. But this was not the reason for their rendezvous.

'It was so marvelous to be employed,' her companion begins. 'I felt like a man again instead of a sniveling worm, always *having had to answer to my wife because she was the provider of everything. Life is not healthy for a man in that situation; it's all upside down, the wrong way round. I do love her and miss her though, watching her standing on the quay when we pulled away and out to sea wasn't easy. But she's always been a strong woman and quite capable of looking after herself. It was only for the summer after all, and I knew I could come home for the odd weekend here and there. I was more worried about the children, my two that is, they had been through such a difficult time. It broke my heart to see Marguerite traipsing between her mother and I, living out of a small bag. I'd have done anything to make her happy again, except of course, reuniting with my ex, something every child of separated parents dreams of, whether consciously or subconsciously.*

And Yves, he was becoming something of an uncontrollable tearaway … but I still can't take the blame, it was after all their mother who had the affair and took off with someone else, otherwise we'd still be together, a normal family.

I thought they would adapt, that the relationship between Marguerite and Elle would strengthen when I was not around and they'd ceased to compete for my affection. Of course I loved my wife but I will always put my children first. What man wouldn't?

The two stewardesses onboard were stunning, did I say? And I was a married man. But we were so far from home and how would Elle ever have known? I can't say I wasn't tempted which made me just as guilty as her, did it not?'

Béatrice sighs and looks away from him, focusing, and yet not seeing, the traffic in the busy street outside the café. There were so many sides to it all, like some sort of Chinese puzzle, complicated and unsolvable.

3

"But there was more to it than that. As the Amazing Maurice said, it was just a story about people and rats. And the difficult part of it was deciding who the people were, and who were the rats."

Terry Pratchett, *The Amazing Maurice and His Educated Rodents*

In the following days, I find out how a couple of fairly minor occurrences can completely knock my sense of confidence and well being, setting me spinning, uncomfortably amidst a new fear, that of being alone. I am woken one morning by the most alarming sound of gnawing, somewhere in the region of my bed head. There seems to be no sign of penetration through the wall, thank goodness, but the sound is unbearably loud and in spite of my banging on the area adjacent to the noise, the wretched intruder continues to work, chewing away. I can imagine it there, threatening and uninvited.

I throw on my dressing gown and rush to the floor below, careful not to wake the children; the girls would add total hysteria to my own mounting concern. Ben will be calm because he has a touching affinity with rodents! Of course, I know what's happened, the wretched beast has gained access to the small space created by the lowered ceiling in my office, which is full of electrical wires and insulation. God help me if it should munch at these, it could cause a fire, never mind anything else. And if the rat, (I can hardly bear to think the word let alone say it) should descend through the walls into the shop, or heaven forbid, find it's way to the kitchen, this could be a disaster! My mind races on through the list of catastrophes that could occur if the vermin was not apprehended.

There is a small hatch in the ceiling through which I could climb if I absolutely had to, but the idea of joining the rat up there in the roof, isn't a pleasant one. I study it thoughtfully for a moment, before diving into the cupboard under the sink in the kitchen, furiously looking for mouse and rat poison. I locate the black packet, right at the back; I'd put it behind everything else so it couldn't be retrieved in error by anyone else. I bought it last year when I thought I saw some mouse droppings in the entrance hall, but it turned out to be a false alarm. This time, however, was a different story and just for a moment I wished Philippe was at home to deal with the problem. What happens if the rat dies in the roof space and then rots causing a terrible stink? Ben is small enough to wriggle through the hatch but I don't reckon he would be at all chuffed at being given the job! First things first, I cut up an old butter tub to make a tray, fill it with the poison, and wobbling on a step ladder, I carefully place it just inside the hatch, closing it quickly for fear of meeting the animal head on. To my absolute horror, as soon as I slide the hatch back into place, I hear the mad skittering of tiny feet and the unmistakable sound of something crunching the food, with obvious enthusiasm. The idea of this most unwelcome, disgusting creature a mere couple of feet away, is almost too much for me to bear. How I'd coped with large cockroaches on the boats in the Caribbean I'll never know. I go back in the kitchen to make a cup of tea, consoling myself with the thought that I've done all I can for the moment. Nothing but a waiting game now.

'What are you doing Mama? Is it time to get up?' A sleepy Ben appears, half wrapped in a trailing blanket.

'No, my darling, I just needed a cuppa, you go back to bed,

and I will come up in a moment.' With a quick glance at the hatch, I follow my son up the stairs with a sigh.

Philippe calls the same evening and I recount the whole, sordid tale of Mr Rat.

'Not exactly a danger to life or limb then,' he says, clearly amused.

'More of a threat to the business and a fire risk, I would say,' I'm instantly hot and angry that he should find it funny. 'I don't suppose for one minute you'd be keen on climbing through the hole and sorting it out.'

'Probably not,' he says and a heavy silence falls between us.

A few nights later when the rat was no longer to be heard, or smelt, (dead perhaps, but not yet decaying) the second incident occurs. Fridays are often the busiest day of the week, the shop bustles with trade and there are orders to prepare for Saturday. This particular one is as hectic as any, and I am exhausted when I finally retire, not long after the children. I know that a time will come soon when I go willingly upstairs before my offspring. Already they've caught me dozing off whilst they are watching their favourite programmes at the end of the day.

'Mama! You are asleep,' shouts a triumphant Frannie.

'Well, I was,' I reply. 'Until you woke me up.'

'It's always a good time to ask for things when Mama is half asleep,' remarks Ben. 'Because she always says yes.'

'You are so cheeky,' I say, lurching across the settee to give his head a playful smack, amazed at the canny mind of my seven-year-old boy.

'Missed,' he says triumphantly sliding to the floor.

I adore my children more than anything in the world.

'Bedtime,' I say.

I'm suddenly wide awake, a noise in the street below disturbs me perhaps. I listen hard, not sure if I dreamt a sound or actually heard one. Surely not the rat again! There, I definitely heard something. Just footsteps maybe, on the pavement, quite a normal sound on a Friday night. I glance at the clock, struggling to focus with sleepy eyes on the bright green numbers. *2.30*, I need to be asleep. Then comes an explosion of breaking glass. Leaping from the bed, my legs threaten to give way beneath me as I shake with fear. The children are already running to my room and I pull them down on the landing where they sit, huddling close together, in silent panic. I can hear her my own heart beating. I'm still not sure if the broken glass is my window, of course it could be on the other side of the street. Until I hear another sound from the shop downstairs, and I know in a flash, that someone has broken in to steal whatever they can or worse. I encountered a thief once before on my boat in Gibraltar but I was braver then. Now I have children to protect. I hug them tighter, placing a finger to my lips to quiet them.

A voice, and the sound of someone opening my front door, next to the shop, with a key.

'Elle!' It's Claude, thank goodness. He is half way up the stairs now to save us.

'Where are you, cherie? Are you okay. I heard the glass go!'

I crawl along the landing to meet him at the top of the stairs, with all the children still clinging to me, hampering my progress. 'There was someone in the shop, did you see?'

'I'll go and take a look, whoever it was probably scarpered when I came in the house door.'

I looked at the ageing Frenchman in his tartan dressing gown and slippers. Hardly a deterrent for a determined robber. 'Be careful, please. Should we not call the gendarme straight away?'

'*Oui, bien sur,*' he said, 'but I have to go downstairs to fetch the phone anyway so I'll take a look around.' He seemed calm and fearless and I was so glad I'd recently given him a key to the property. 'Stay there with your children and I will bring the telephone.'

He disappears and moments later I hear the low murmur of two voices and realise that Amelie has followed her husband's path in the front door.

Resplendent in another tartan dressing gown, and a particularly strange form of bonnet, the pair resemble a drawing from some old seventeenth century journal. Amelie joins me on the landing, '*Ca va maintenant?*' she says, 'Claude is talking to the gendarme and there seems to be no one in the shop. But there's a lot of broken glass so the children should go back to bed, while we tidy up as best we can.' She firmly takes control and I feel tired and blessed.

Once Ben and my protesting girls, (who want to stay up to see the gendarme) settle to their beds, we clear the glass and Claude comes back from his own shop with a board that he nails in place over the gaping window.

'I don't think anything has been stolen,' I look around the shop and the burglar doesn't appear to have reached as far as the kitchen before being disturbed. 'I had the cash box upstairs anyway.'

'He must have seen me at the front and gone out the way he came in,' says Claude.

'*Bien sur,*' says his wife, 'one look at you in your dressing gown is enough to frighten any burglar!' They laugh and I begin to feel safe.

'*Merci,*' I say, 'thank you both so much, where would I be without you.'

Claude shakes his head thoughtfully. 'Alone, I think,' he says.

I tell Philippe the next evening, but I don't reveal how scared I was, for in the light of day, I feel better and can see the episode for what it was ... a petty burglary. Probably a drunk, staggering home, the gendarme had said. A chancer looking for a cash box to fuel his habit. The window has already been replaced today.

'*Mais mon amour,*' Philippe protests at my calm words, 'I'm not sure you are safe on your own all summer. I shall ask Yves or Marguerite to come back with you while I'm gone. I'm sure I can persuade one of them with the offer of an increase on their living allowance.'

'No, no,' I assure him quickly, 'I most certainly don't want you to bribe your children to nanny me, thank you. I am perfectly safe on my own, and of course I have Claude and Amelie within shouting distance. It's not as though something like this happens everyday.'

'Well if you're sure?'

'I am adamant. I would rather you didn't even mention it to them. I certainly don't want anyone fussing about me, and that is my last word on the subject.' If I am honest with myself I know I would be equally scared if Philippe or anyone else for that matter, were in the house with me. What difference would it make, simply an even bigger pile of terrified bodies on the landing. I will make sure we have a telephone upstairs, in future.

'You can be so stubborn,' Philippe replies.

'And that is why you love me,' I laugh, switching our conversation, with these few words, to a far lighter note.

Patrick, yes, we've been on first name terms now since his call the previous week, phones me on Tuesday morning for my order. Even before he comes out with his usual cheery *"Bonjour,"* he asks, 'Are you okay, I heard through the grapevine that you had a window smashed on Friday night?'

'Yes, I'm fine. It was just an opportunist drunken fool, the gendarme said. No harm done, just some glass replacement needed.'

'But you must have been terrified surely? And the children?'

Children? Have I spoken of the twins and Ben to him, I must have done, My mind is racing now trying to recall the details of our last conversation. It's quite a few days ago now and it's all a blur.

'We are all absolutely recovered now, thank you. It was scary at the time, but thanks to my close and caring neighbours in the antique shop, who turned up just at the right moment, we were saved.'

'Were you there on your own with the children then?' I can see where this is heading.

'Yes,' I say, there is surely no harm in telling the truth? 'My husband is away in Greece at the moment.' I didn't say why, or how long he was away, best not to reveal too much to this man I don't really know at all, if I haven't already.

Changing the subject I asked, 'Was it you I saw delivering up the road the other Monday? I didn't realise your vans come down here more than once a week?'

'Yes, that was me. I nearly popped in for a cake, until I realised it was Monday and you were closed.' I think of him now in his stripy shirt and casual trousers, and wish I'd seen his face.

Daringly I ask, 'Maybe you'll bring my delivery sometime soon? We could shake hands and meet formally.' I can sense my colour rising as I speak and I think maybe I've gone too far.

'I will, maybe even this week, I'll surprise you, you'll see.'

With a laugh and an "Au revoir," he hangs up, and I realise within seconds that I've dumbly forgotten to place my order and he had forgotten to ask! I'll call again later and hopefully speak to someone else to save embarrassment.

I replace the receiver thoughtfully and turning around I see to my horror and shock that Marguerite is standing leaning against the doorpost.

'Oh hello,' I say, trying desperately to stop the blush that threatens to claim my cheeks, I stutter on. 'How long have you been there?' I try to sound offbeat and casual but I feel the opposite.

'I just came down to see if you were ok. Papa phoned and said the shop windows were smashed or something? Who were you talking to just then?'

'The packaging company,' I say, desperately trying to remember word for word exactly what I'd just said to Patrick, whilst totally unaware that Marguerite was eaves dropping. *How dare she?* Their conversation had been totally innocent surely? Why should I worry anyway? Regaining my composure now, I continue. 'Yes, we had some drunk break a window on Friday.' (I'd asked Philippe not to tell his kids.) 'Terrible noise it was too, we were frightened at the time but it's all fixed now. Nothing was stolen because Claude and Amelie turned up in their pyjamas and saved the day.'

'That was lucky then,' Marguerite said, heading towards the fridge, and the awkward moment passes. 'Do you have any cheese for a sandwich?'

'Yes I will fetch some bread,' Relief washes over me, but why I feel so guilty over an innocent conversation with my new friend is beyond my comprehension. I am and always will be a free spirit, making friends with whomever I choose. I'm sure Philippe is surrounded by charming stewardesses who share confidences with their handsome engineer, and I'll never even know. We are married but such relations are not betrayals by any means. If we are unable to have such friendships then our marriage will surely become a prison where each of us will lose our own individuality forever. I've never been a girl's girl and I draw much pleasure from conversing with men from all walks of life. I have no intention of changing my ways now I'm married.

'Well, if everything is okay? Papa said to check … then I shall go home and see you later.' Sandwich in hand, Marguerite departs. I think about the word "home", which is apparently now her mother's house, but when her father is here at the shop then this is "home". Life must be complicated and emotionally destabilising for children of parents who have settled with a new partner. I understand Marguerite, but her exhibitions of bad behaviour I cannot tolerate, or endure without comment. For this reason we won't ever be close. I shrug my shoulders at my step-daughter's habitual slamming of the door. She never goes quietly.

Marguerite (four years later)

Béatrice was aware that talking to Philippe's daughter probably was not a particularly good idea, because at the time when it all happened, she would have been full of teenage anxiety, muddled with the grief of her parents separation. She had no wish to stir up the past for this young woman who now appeared to have changed her stance somewhat concerning her stepmother. The part she had played in preventing any reconciliation between her father and the woman he loved, was obviously the cause of some remorse to the girl, now that her life had moved on and some other aspects of the story had come to light. She catches up with her, (having asked Philippe's permission to do so) in the gardens of the Lycée she attends, one lunchtime.

'Chienne, Putain, I remember the terrible names I called her ... I hated her back then, what was my father even doing with her? He could've chosen someone much younger and prettier than her. There was no way I was hanging around there when Dad wasn't there, pretending to like her when I didn't. And as for her insufferable spoilt brats, she could keep them out of my way as well. I thought Mum's man was not half so bad, he bought me stuff at least, and he didn't have any children, well only grown up, left home type ones, and they weren't likely to be much of a problem.

When Dad was worried about her and wanted me to go and stay there sometimes when he was away, I threatened to take all my friends with me and stay up all night partying. She couldn't say anything to Dad because I would have said it wasn't true, and he always took my side in everything anyway. I could tell she hated that, well, I thought she had to learn her place in my family if she wanted to continue being a part of it. She thought she was so special, "L'Anglaise", with her perfect shop and her perfect children. Even Claude and Amelie thought she was wonderful, it sickened me. I really wasn't a nice person at all back then, I suppose I was extremely jealous and messed up too. Well, I decided to keep a tight eye on her, and if she slipped up, even just once, that would be enough and I would tell my Dad and he would find out what she was really like and leave her with any luck. Then we could have our own house just Dad, Yves, and me.

So I helped her to incriminate herself, I regret that now and I knew at the time it was wrong but I just couldn't stop myself. I'm sorry, that's all I want to say really, just that I am sorry, for you, and for my Dad. If I had left well alone then it all would, most likely, have just fizzled out.'

4

"In a word, I was too cowardly to do what I knew to be right, as I had been too cowardly to avoid doing what I knew to be wrong"

Charles Dickens, *Great Expectations*

Patrick arrives on Thursday to deliver my paper bags and cake boxes. I still wonder why the owner of a fair sized company such as *Le Carteaux Blanc* would be out on the delivery round.

We shake hands formally, as if we have misplaced the frequent, friendly banter we've shared on the telephone in previous weeks. Tongue-tied now, I study his features as he carries my purchases in and places them neatly on the nearest table. His tanned face is on the rugged side, not in the least like the perfectly groomed good looks of my husband. Slightly pock marked even, but full of character and with a smile to charm all his customers. There is no doubt about that. He's wearing a different coloured striped shirt to the one he wore the other day, but with the same trousers, and heavy style work boots, Philippe would never wear such footwear. His shirt is open at the neck revealing a glimpse of his tanned chest as he bends. I draw my eyes quickly away, realising with a start that he has just asked me a question and I have no idea what he said.

'Sorry what did you say? I missed it.' How stupid I sound and I know I'm blushing like a girl.

'No it's my fault, I mumble. I just asked if the shop has been busy today?'

A small, awkward silence. I take a breath, and ignore his question. 'Can I make you a coffee?'

'That would be wonderful,' he says.

'You are quite brown,' I say, braver now, 'I imagine you are an outside sort of person who hates being behind a desk?'

'You're right,' he's smiling again. 'Are all English ladies so astute I wonder? Actually my brother has a small shipyard down on the port and I spend all my free time helping him hauling out boats and spraying them down. In fact, I prefer his line of work to my own, perhaps not so profitable, but definitely a better way of life. And what gave you the idea to sell British cakes to the French?'

'I had a hunch they might like something different and they do, luckily, so I prosper!'

'And how come you speak such perfect French?'

'You flatter me. It's not that perfect by any means, but I manage. I used to work at *l'aeroport de Nice* for a French company, sometimes I would be in the office in the back end of the town answering the phone all day, so my French had to improve. It's much harder to understand people on the phone than when they are in front of you, I learnt quickly. There were no English speakers in the office, and it was, or still is, old fashioned in a traditional French way. I had to take the cash box up to Grandpa in the attic at lunch break! A "do or die" situation really.' We both laugh at my observation of old habits that cling in a modern world.

'That's typical sort of practice for a few old businesses I could name,' he says, adding quickly, 'but not mine, I assure you!'

'Sometimes I worked at the *Palais du Festival,* in Cannes for the big exhibitions as well, that helped my language skills, calming arguments between French and English contractors. That was a long time ago, before the children were born. Taught me all the swear words I could ever need. I met their father there.'

'Was he English?'

'Yes, he was working for a French broadcasting company. We were never married, just sailed and lived together and had children, until he met an air hostess when he was waiting for me to finish my shift at the airport one day. And that was that! He went back to England with her and I took the lease on this place ... and then of course I met Philippe. He's brilliant and the children adore him.'

I meet his eyes with my own. In them I can see the depth of his genuine interest, not only in what I'm telling him but in myself as a person. I think he is wondering what makes this English woman tick. He looks fascinated. I won't tell him about my life before, on the sea, there's time enough for all of that. I try to remember for an instant if Philippe had ever looked at me in a similar way.

'And what about you? Are you married, do you have children too?'

The bell on the shop door makes its customary tinkle, announcing an intruder, '*Monsieur Dames,*' the man says, forcing them back into the real world with a bump. I sell him two, fat fruitcakes and he departs with a cheery, '*Bonne Journée,*' leaving the two of us grinning at one another. My visitor shows no sign of taking his leave and I know I should be baking and organising my day. Oh, where's the harm I work hard enough.

'Where were we then?' he asks, 'yes, I know, you just asked me if I am married and if I have children. Firstly, I'm not married nor ever likely to be, as I see no advantages in the married status at all.'

I think that sometimes the French are so flowery with their choice of words, and I struggle to concentrate on the point he is making so firmly.

'Secondly I have three boys that I'm not sure I wanted at the outset of our arrangement, but of course I love them now. My boys, where would I be without them! Their mother and I tend to live more as brother and sister as we've had many differences of opinion, over the years. I suppose we hold together for the children but the situation is far from ideal.'

I'm surprised and taken aback that a man who has only just met me can be so candid about his family. I'm not sure how to reply to this outpouring, I myself, having only provided him with scant details of my separation from the father of my children.

'Oh, how sad,' I say, sounding less than sincere. 'Philippe and I sometimes fall out over his children's behaviour, but apart from that, I think we are pretty solid, excepting of course finances, they are always a strain on any marriage, I think, don't you?'

'Not for my partner, she doesn't want for much.'

'Well, she's extremely lucky then.' I'm still wondering how our conversation can have sailed into such personal waters in the space of half an hour. I decide I must try to draw our chat to an end without being rude, and I pray silently for customers, but the day is still young and this is not on my side. Luckily the telephone rings, a startlingly ferocious sound to interrupt our quiet talk. A lady requires a cake in a couple of hours.

'*Eh bien*, I'd better get on with it then,' I say, hoping my friend will take this last comment as a dismissal.

'Do you have a pen handy?' he says, and spying the one on the shop table, he proceeds to write a number on an empty paper bag. 'Here's my mobile, if you need something when the office is closed, or you just want to chat I'll always answer and phone you back if I'm busy or you can text me if you want. You do have a mobile, don't you?'

I nod, trying to think where it might be, I'd rarely ever used it, and certainly had never sent a text message before, but I wasn't going to admit to that. '*Merci*,' I say, putting the bag to one side. '*Á bientôt*.'

'I hope so,' he replies and he is gone with a firm and final jangle of my bell, which always has the last word in my small world of comings and goings.

My busy disorderly, life slips on through another week, until the day when I must speak to Patrick again to place the order. I have flutter in my belly, partly from excitement but also from dread and trepidation. I pull myself together, I'm good at that, no reason to feel like this, just another acquaintance, part of my working life after all. But I know in some way that this time it's different. I am free-falling into unknown territory and I'm scared where I might land.

Philippe is coming back for the weekend of his friend's fortieth birthday and I'm both glad he's coming, and happy as I think about him. I seem to spend a good deal of my time these days gazing out of the window and dreaming. Perhaps we do need a holiday this winter, some quality time as a family, to weave us tightly together again as we were when we first met, before we had to face the pressures of money and children together, as a couple.

Patrick rings early on the usual day, either eager for my order, or to speak to me again, I wonder which? 'You didn't message me then?' he says and I can sense his grin.

'Why? Was I supposed to?'

'No of course not, I just thought or hoped you might send me a piece of interesting town gossip or something. You must hear everything that goes on from your shop.'

'Probably not as much as you do on your delivery round,' I say and we laugh together, our cheerful chatter resumed.

He makes a proposal. 'We should meet for coffee one day, on a Monday when you are closed, then we can have a proper talk in comfortable surroundings.'

'I always have so much to sort out Mondays, it's my only time to catch up on so many things, but maybe one day, in Nice or somewhere, if I have some shopping to do.'

I knew immediately that I had suggested Nice because I didn't want to be seen drinking coffee with a man other than my husband on my own doorstep. Not that it should matter, it was the same as meeting up with one of my girlfriends surely? Well, perhaps not quite the same on reflection.

'Anyway the children break up next week so I shall have my hands full.'

'As will I, but I'm sure there will be a day.'

'We'll see,' I replied, terrified to commit to anything, my mind wavering back and forth between what would be considered normal behaviour within my marriage and what would not.

The end of term dawns and the children are at home for the long summer holiday. A difficult couple of months are ahead for me for I must cope with a busy shop and having my three, demanding children under my feet. Most of the time, being accustomed to the situation, they are reasonable and easy going, although watching their friends going away on holiday, must be tough for them. Florence and Frannie have a social whirl with their school friends, and at eleven years old they expect the freedom of adults. Ben, (bless him) is content to play at home with his lego with the promise of an outing to the beach at the end of the day.

Philippe is due home for a long weekend to incorporate the party to which we have been invited, and to complicate matters further, his elderly mother will arrive for a few days on the same weekend. This means that Philippe and I must move into the spare room so that she can have our room with the ensuite bathroom, not a problem really, but I'll have to move our clothes and toiletries. Popping into my mother-in-law's room at five in the morning to find clean underwear is not an option. I'm sure Philippe has not considered these sort of issues at all. At least I won't have to find a babysitter for the night of the party, for the children adore their step-grandmother and do not find her half as intimidating as I do myself.

Philippe arrives just before his mother on the Friday, just as travel worn and cross as I had anticipated. The tourist season is kicking off with the start of the holiday and the coast is flooding with Parisian holiday makers. The weather is humid already and stiflingly hot. My mother-in-law appears in a taxi with enough baggage for a month and is moaning even before she is properly inside the front door.

'Are Marguerite and Yves here? Are they coming to eat with us? I hope you told them I shall be here for a few days.'

'I am sure Philippe will have told them, don't worry I expect they'll come and see you and their father tomorrow. After all they haven't seen him either for a while now.'

'Yes, well, I suppose it's too much to hope that they might come especially to see their Grandmère. Philippe! Where have you gone, not too far I hope, I need you to take my bags to my room so I might freshen up, I feel sticky.'

Philippe emerges from the kitchen where he has been pouring himself a cold beer.

'I'm here, at your beck and call, Mama,' he says, winking at Elle.

'I saw that,' says his mother. 'There is no need to be cheeky.'

I am secretly terrified of her. Suzanne, nicknamed "Zanne" by all the family, is a typical French lady of her generation; immaculately dressed, with a style that betrays her nationality. She has perfect hair, youthful makeup and perfectly manicured nails. Her hair would have been jackdaw-black with the sheen of velvet in her youth, like her son, highlighting her startlingly, bright eyes, the colour of murky brown-green waves on a windswept beach. She fades now but the fire is still smouldering inside her, sometimes dampened by the confusion that comes so often with old age. She has ruled her family over the years with a rod of iron, and now in her widowhood, given half a chance, she will continue to do the same. But this is my house and she must play by the rules of her hostess.

'Philippe will take your bags in a moment, Zanne. Just let him have a swig of his beer. Would you like a cold drink?'

Zanne looks me up and down before replying. 'You look thinner than I remember. Are you all right?' This was more of a statement than a question needing an answer. 'Yes I will have a white wine with some sparkling water, a long drink, that's what I need in this heat.'

I knew the old lady could become tyrannical with a few glasses of wine so I mix a weak concoction out of sight in the kitchen, and carry it through to where Zanne has now turned her attention to Frannie, who gazes at her adoringly. She's probably thinking about the pocket money that is usually forthcoming from her step-grandmother.

'They are pretty little things, your daughters,' she says. 'You should be proud.'

'And so I am,' I reply, giving Frannie a glancing kiss on the top of her head as I bend to place the drink on the table next to our guest. 'But don't flatter them too much or it will go to their heads.' All thoughts of Patrick have vanished as I prepare for a busy weekend with work and family.

Saturday is an exhaustingly busy day in the shop. Thankfully Amelie and Claude invite us for a meal in the middle of the day after I close. Eager to escape once the meal is over, the children and I decide to go to the beach for a swim, allowing Zanne and Philippe some quality time with Marguerite and Yves, who are due to appear to see their father and grandmother. We don't have to go out, it just serves to make things less complicated. Marguerite so likes to be the centre of attention where her father is concerned. I love to swim in the sea, and my children are happy having me all to themselves, away from customers and their house guest.

Philippe and I, his "English rose", as he calls me, make light conversation as we dress for the party, slightly distanced from each other in a way that I struggle to fathom. Probably because I have rediscovered myself in his absence, and unconsciously I continue to stand alone in my thoughts. I can't help but watch him with affection as he stands looking out of the window. Impulsively I put my arms around his waist from behind, leaning my head on his shoulder.

'I have missed you,' he says.

'And I you,' I admit, for I have, in my own way.

'You look lovely,' he adds, turning to survey me in my long, Mediterranean blue summer dress, 'Are you ready? We should go.'

'I'll just settle Ben and remind the girls to behave for Zanne and I'm ready.'

The house of Philippe's friend is just a few minutes away on foot; an attractive villa in the centre of the town but with a delightful garden hidden behind high stone walls. All the food and drinks are laid out on tables outside, a buffet style affair, with couples sitting at small tables and some reclining picnic style on blankets on the grass. Wonderfully informal, and I can't help but heave a sigh of relief that I will not be stuck between people I hardly know, as I would undoubtedly have been in a sit-down dinner situation. One never knows with the French, it could easily have been the latter. Philippe appears overly attentive, keeping his arm firmly around me, as he introduces me to groups of people that I do not recognise.

The figure standing just inside the double doors leading into the kitchen, catches my eye. My mind goes into a whirl and my knees feel weak. Why would he be here? Surely it can't be. As he turns slightly, deep in conversation with another man, I can see him clearly. It is most definitely him. I was quite cool until this point but now I am most uncomfortably hot.

'Shall we find a drink Philippe?' I steer him, purposefully

away from the house towards the drinks table, postponing the moment when Patrick will inevitably notice me.

There is no chance of escape, for he has seen me and is making a beeline for us.

'Elle,' he says, 'What a pleasure to see you outside of work, and you must be Philippe. I've heard so much about you. My wife is here too somewhere, you must meet her.' (I register the word wife, although I know perfectly well they are not married.) Philippe looks completely baffled.

'Sorry, yes', I stammer, 'this is Philippe.' I know my cheeks are aflame again beyond control, they always let me down. 'Patrick and I do business together, cherie, to do with cake boxes and paper bags and things, mundane shop stuff.'

'Mundane they may be, but extremely necessary for your line of work, I would say.' Patrick laughs at his own comment, looking far more at ease than me, although he talks loudly which could, I think, be a way of disguising his nerves.

'I shall go and look for Béatrice,' Patrick announces and following his glance I spy a tall, blonde with a small crowd of attentive men around her. Surely that can't be her! She is more distinguished than I could possibly have imagined, and she certainly doesn't look like someone who has borne him three boys. But yes, he is walking towards this life and soul of the party, and he is pointing back towards Philippe and I, so it must indeed be her.

I make a quick decision. We need food so I navigate Philippe towards the spread and firmly give him a plate, hoping to ward off more introductions.

'You seem to know that guy pretty well?'

'I expect I do, I see him every week, and he takes my order over the phone,' I reply, slightly irritated now. 'I have to talk to plenty of different people, suppliers and stuff. Would you like salmon?' I serve him and brush the subject away focusing my mind, (and hopefully his as well to distract him) on all the delicious plates and bowls of food spread before us. 'Look new potatoes, and proper hollandaise sauce, I love that combination.'

Just as we are about to wander home, Patrick catches up with us again with his partner on his arm. 'Ah there you are, this is Béatrice.' We all shake hands, shyly. 'Philippe, you work on yachts, I believe,' Patrick strives to begin a conversation, searching for some common ground between two men who quite obviously live completely different lives. 'Béatrice and I thought we might charter a small yacht in Greece with the boys next year. Might be a fun family holiday?'

'I don't know anything about flotillas, I work on a huge motor yacht so I have no idea about that kind of holiday, but I know people who have enjoyed them,' replies Philippe, 'it's Elle you need to talk to about sailing boats, she's the expert.'

'*Sans blague,* you're joking, I had no idea,' Patrick is now unashamedly staring at me.

'Oh I would love to go on one of those super yachts,' enthuses Béatrice.

'I am afraid the owners, well mine at any rate, are extremely private people.' And so Philippe effectively kills the conversation giving me a clear chance to make our excuses to leave. Grabbing the opportunity, I start by casting forth my doubts about the capabilities of our elderly babysitter, suggesting this to be the main reason for our abrupt departure. In truth I'm exhausted and long for my bed. I feel happy and relaxed as we wander back down the road towards home. 'It's lovely to go out, but even better to go home,' I say, reaching for Philippe's hand as we walk.

'Do you mind if I watch the football for a while in bed?' he says.

'Not a bit,' I answer.

How was I to know that this would ruin our evening?

Philippe puts the volume quite loud, and I toss and turn beside him unable to shut out the noisy commentary and the screams of the crowd. I'm so tired.

'Do you think you could turn it down, just a little?'

'*Salope'*, he says.

'Excuse me?' Have I misheard?

'Bitch, I said you are a bitch. What a fuss you make about such a small thing.'

I can't believe what I am hearing, and I turn away from him rubbing my eyes lest he should see me cry. The wine is talking, it never fails to turn him into a beast, or does it simply release the real Philippe?

Philippe (four years on)

Béatrice turns her head back towards him again to pick up the thread of their conversation. 'So you were tempted to have an affair on the ship then?' she asks?

'Well of course I was, especially when I didn't always feel Elle was particularly happy when I did manage to come home.'

'Why did you think that?'

'I will never forget when I walked down the quay towards her, I thought she might run to greet me, having not seen me for quite some time but instead she lingered as she came towards me looking almost baffled.

I had come all the way home to spend the weekend with my wife but she turned away from me at the slightest thing that upset her. Like my choice of television programmes. Was it too much to ask that I might be allowed to enjoy the football in my own home? Or perhaps it wasn't really my own home because it was hers. She paid all the bills with her shop money after all and

I was just a hanger on, a sponge. I bet that's what she told all her so called "friends" Like your high and mighty Patrick, with his cardboard box company ... some achievement that is!'

Béatrice had already decided before their meeting not to argue with Philippe about their respective partners. Becoming embroiled fighting against each other would be time wasting, upsetting, and bring her no nearer to the truth.

Philippe disregarded her lack of comment and steamed on. 'Do I love her still I ask myself? Of course I do, I just wish she hadn't been so bloody good at everything, running the house, looking after the children and earning money all at the same time. There hardly seemed room for me in her life, she managed perfectly well without me, even managed to poison a rat by herself. She's been half way around the world on her own so what could she possibly need me for? What have I done but spend most of my life in the same town ruled by my overbearing mother and my ex-wife?

I often wonder what it would be like to have a wife whom I could support so she would have no need for a business of her own. I suppose a woman like Elle could never have been happy with that kind of life so it was a waste of time my even trying to imagine it, especially as her independent streak was the thing that attracted me to her in the first place ... life and love are so complicated, I hope we all make it through and find some kind of happiness in the end.'

5

"Friendship is really the finest balm for the pangs of disappointed love."

Jane Austen, *Northanger Abbey*

As I pack his bag again the next day, I know there is no point in mentioning the events of the night before as he won't remember, and he will deny it if he does. To speak about it would be like poking our marriage with a sharp stick.

'I am sorry I have to go back, will you cope with Mama?' he asks.

'We shall be fine, it's only a couple more days, and she'll eat with Amelie and Claude at lunchtime when I am busy.'

'Thanks, I will make it up to you I promise. We should try and plan that winter holiday you wanted.'

Perhaps he does remember and he's trying to make amends, I hope so, knowing that it is not the first, nor will it be the last time that he has upset me with a ferocious outburst when he has been drinking. Why do I always make the same mistake? So many of my relationships have been haunted by the demon drink. I have always imagined myself to be an adequate judge of human nature but I have failed miserably time and time again.

I rummage through the drawers of my desk. Somewhere in here I have a mobile phone, I've never really used it; I only acquired one to please Ben but even he had quickly lost interest. Ah ha...

I have it now, buried at the bottom and luckily the charger is there too. I drag them out, the charger wire pulling all sorts of other junk with it, you name it, I have it all in these drawers. I plug the phone into the charger and set it at the back of my desk where it is fairly well concealed so as not to attract attention. Ben notices everything to do with equipment; he homes in on it automatically. Such an inquisitive boy. "An inquiring mind is a sign of great intelligence," my mother said, "it's the children that sit about like potatoes you need to worry about."

I have been planning this ever since Philippe went back, I have decided I'll send a short message enquiring if Patrick and his "spouse" enjoyed the party ... just to see if the phone works. Innocent enough, but I do seem to be giving the project more thought than one single text message could possibly merit. I have no need to order any packaging supplies this week, so there is no reason for a call.

It is still fairly early in the morning and the phone has been charging for an hour or so. Ben is playing in the living room, the television blaring with cartoons that he is half watching. The twins, having eaten breakfast quickly have already gone out to meet their friends, close by in the market (they are forbidden to go further). A typical morning in the school holidays, except that before I have any customers demanding my attention, I intend to send a text message. I nervously press the key with a picture of an envelope and the screen changes to prompt me to enter the number of the recipient. Feeling pleased that I've managed to reach this point, (I'm no expert as far as technology is concerned) I copy the number from the cherished paper bag into the box. The screen now asks if I would like to save this number to my contacts. 'Oh my goodness, no I don't want that,' I mutter aloud. And now for the message, *"Did you both enjoy the party on Sunday?"* There, that will do. I hit the 'send' button and the phone beeps loudly to indicate that my message has been sent successfully. Immediately I am overwhelmed with guilt at this simple contact and quickly place the phone back in it's hiding place, as if it has suddenly become too hot to hold.

The shop bell clangs repeatedly announcing customers and I settle into the rhythm of my working day, almost forgetting about the message, until, to my horror, I hear a loud succession of three or four beeps, which spin me into a panic. I'll have to sort the volume out on the phone, I don't need the whole world to know each time I receive a message. Luckily today there is no one else to hear. I resist the temptation to look at his reply for almost two hours, but finally in a quiet moment I decide to read what he has written.

"Thank you for your txt, yes, I enjoyed the party, and I thought you looked lovely in your dress."

I blush as I read, well, I hadn't expected such a compliment. It's not right for him to flatter me, but it has been a long time since Philippe has said anything that has this effect of restoring my confidence and making me feel feminine and attractive. "Salope," he had called me on the evening of the party and his words still sting as I turn them over in my mind.

I won't reply, not now anyway.

I sort out the mobile phone instead, to eliminate the sound when a message is received, just in case. I find myself looking at it from time to time, half wishing for another message and half dreading that he should contact me in that secret fashion again. It is exciting though, I have to admit; having a secret makes me feel buoyant and alive.

Patrick texts me again early on Friday morning, I have a feeling there will be the sign of a message on the screen and on close inspection there it is, flashing in one corner. He has written, *"I know you start work early, can I call you?"*

I reply immediately, I don't want him to call, the children are already up and about and I am busy. His call would be an inconvenient intrusion on my routine at this time of day. He is thoughtless, pushing boundaries. *"Not a good time to call,"* I type the letters quickly, making errors, flustered in case he decides he will phone anyway.

Another message from him. *"What about that coffee we planned?"*

"Imposs during holiday time." Surely he must understand that!

"Oh. Disappointed." I'm not going to reply, what does he mean 'disappointed'? It must be obvious that I am not going to disappear to meet him for coffee abandoning the children to their own devices. He has no right to dare to expect that I might behave so irresponsibly. I regret the first text message now. I shall not speak to him again until work makes our contact inevitable.

A few days pass and as I'm busy baking and entertaining the children as best I can, it's easy to put him out of my mind. Then I see him walk past, right in front of the shop with two of his children in tow and he doesn't even glance towards my window, not a wave, nor a smile, complete indifference. What does that mean? Surely a friend would look and wave at least? He must be still sulking about the coffee thing. What does it matter, I don't care anyway. So if I don't care why do I feel so miffed? I can't explain why, I just do.

In the evening I take the children to the town pool, to swim away the stresses of the day and wear the children out sufficiently to make for a peaceful evening. They play together squeaking and jumping, Ben stays in the shallow end supervised by his sisters so that I am able to swim quiet lengths losing myself in the motion and ripples of the blue, comforting water. As I turn at the deep end, I spot a blonde head swimming breaststroke, steadily towards me. I know the face, where do I know her from? As I swim I try to place the features I saw in that quick glance. Maybe the woman has been in the shop, I see so many faces from day to day. When I reach the shallow end I turn again just in time to see her pulling herself out of the water, exiting, almost running, towards the changing rooms. Of course, I recognise her now, it's Patrick's wife, or partner or whatever she is. To swim without her children in holiday time doesn't make any sense. Béatrice, that's her name, such a regal name, it suits her, she is such a haughty looking woman. I wonder if she has left the pool in haste to avoid having to make polite conversation with me. Fair enough, I don't really feel like talking to her anyway, I would be embarrassed, I know that much. Listening to my children chatting away in English, for once I feel like an intruder in this environment, especially without Philippe's protective French arm around me. Béatrice's hasty departure only exacerbates my uncomfortable sensation; perhaps the French woman doesn't want to mix with the English, unlike her partner. I appear to hold a special fascination for him and I know he won't give up easily, even though his attentions towards me are inappropriate given our joint circumstances.

Patrick calls for my order the next day, apologising for not coming in when he was in my street. He must have guessed I'd seen him then. 'It's difficult when I'm out and about with the kids,' he says.

'Yes, that's exactly why I can't agree to meet you for coffee until the holidays are over,' I reply. Men can be so stupid.

'*Je sais, je sais,* I know, I know,' he says. 'I enjoy our chats that's all, it's wonderful to have someone to talk to, it brightens my week of drudgery.'

'I'm sure it's not that bad,' I say.

'You would be surprised, I'm more stressed when I can't talk to you.'

I am again taken aback at how personal he is becoming, when we have only really spoken on a handful of occasions. But he flatters me and seems to need me. It's tempting to take this to heart.

'We will have that coffee, I promise, when term starts again,'

I say, knowing that I will go to meet him somewhere away from shop and home, where we can be two individuals with time to share, without pressure, but maybe not without guilt.

Summer passes like an enormous wave, plump with visitors enveloped in heat, rising up to crash onto the warm sands of a September beach, leaving the smell of suntan oil, rancid in the air. I'm exhausted but pleased with my season of busy trading. Philippe is not due back in port until almost the end of the month, so here I am wandering in the old town of Nice passing the time before meeting Patrick for a Monday morning coffee and chat. Nothing more complicated, just coffee with a friend. I keep reassuring myself of the ordinariness of this event, although the butterflies are back, trapped in the pit of my stomach. What if I should bump into someone I know? Hardly likely when all my friends are at work. Just relax, I tell myself, and enjoy some time out for once. My steps, across the cobbles, become almost a skip.

I'm the sort of person who is always early for a rendezvous, be it for work or pleasure. The extra time allows me to present an unruffled appearance which would't be achieved by tardiness. I wander in and out of the small shops in the narrow streets delighting in the surprises I find there. The old town is full of different influences and cultures, a little piece of Italy on one corner followed by slice of Morocco on the next. There is Claude's favourite place to eat Sauerkraut in one restaurant and he has introduced me to the best Couscous I've ever tasted in another. Claude is such a gourmand; I can't help smiling, as I remember all the meals I have shared here with my friends. I've arranged to meet Patrick in a small Italian restaurant with a courtyard and a rather rude fountain, as far as I can recall, a statue of a small naked boy with the water descending from a particular part of his anatomy. Perhaps I'll stay awhile with him and eat pizza, why not? The day is, after all, my own.

I dally down narrow, stone stairs into a shop full of Provencal fabrics, no wider than a corridor, the materials rub against me as I wander through. The fabrics have a distinctive fresh smell. They are so charming, but so expensive. I glance at my watch and see to my satisfaction that if I make my way to my assignation now, I'll be six or seven minutes perfectly late. Satisfied with this calculation, I wend my way to the café. Bending under the arch at the entrance to the courtyard, I scan the tables. He's not there apparently. I choose a table with a clear view of the door and plonk myself down, my calm mood subtly altered to one of slight dismay.

'*A votre service Madame?*' The waiter approaches me straight away with normal Italian efficiency.

'*J'attends quelq'un,* I am waiting for someone,' I say, and he bows and leaves me to my surveillance of the archway.

Another ten minutes or so pass before Patrick comes, bearing the most enormous bunch of tightly closed, green lilies.

'I am so sorry, I am always late,' he says laying the flowers on the spare chair at the table. 'You will, when you know me a little better, realise that something always crops up to disrupt my day, however hard I try to be on time!' Glancing at the flowers, I forgive him instantly. Philippe rarely buys me flowers and when he does they are obviously carelessly gathered from a corner stall. The lilies are magnificent, and will last for days as their colour is not yet evident.

'They are white with a shot of pink, I believe,' he says, reading my mind, then adding, 'I think a house should always be full of the sight and scent of flowers.'

'Me too, thank you, it's so thoughtful of you,' I say and I mean this wholeheartedly.

All men are different, my husband, ever the engineer has only a tiny compartment in his brain assigned to romance, indeed so small, I rarely see evidence of his powers to charm and woo me, or any other female on the planet for that matter. But I must stop these comparisons, they are two different characters altogether and Philippe has other exceptional qualities or I would never have fallen for him. Sitting face to face with Patrick, I have the chance to examine his features and I decide that I'm not attracted to him physically. Perhaps it's the way he appears to be so enamoured of me that draws me to him. What greater flattery could there be than for a man to turn his back on his busy life, in order to worship me with his eyes and to choose me flowers of such perfection. It is as if a strong arm has plunged through the layers of my worries, pulling me through, up to the surface where I'm able to breathe the fresh breeze of excitement again, filling my sails with optimism and hope.

Patrick interrupts my thoughts, 'Why are you looking so solemn, have I upset you?'

'No, no,' I reassure him, 'just thinking, that's all, about flowers I suppose. Shall we order coffee?'

'Yes a large cappuccino for me and what would you like?'

'*Chocolat chaud, s'il vous plaît,*' I answer without hesitation. Hot chocolate is something I only allow myself when I am out somewhere. A special treat, an indulgence of frothy, hot sweetness.

'I saw your wife, Béatrice, at the pool the other day.' I offer this information just for something to say, but a small, most unnerving, silence falls after I speak while we wait to be served.

'She is not my wife and I am not aware what she does with her days. It's none of my business.' His reply is gruff, I was not expecting his change of tone.

'I only thought ... ' I begin.

'Well don't,' he says taking my hand across the table. 'I am here to spend a pleasant hour or so, finding out about you, no one else is of any interest to me at this moment.'

I redden and pull my hand back a little, although not completely, my fingers still lie under his and I notice how much larger they are than my own. Philippe has delicate hands. There I go again! Strictly no more observations of their differences now, that's enough!

'Tell me about your three boys,' I say and he does, and the mood is lighter and we laugh as he recounts their latest antics and I understand that his children are as important in his life as mine. This is a sentiment we share without a doubt.

I watch him closely while he is talking, his body language changes as he speaks, but his eyes look into mine intently, and in their depths I see something else. I look away as I don't understand what I see there. I can't describe it, it's almost as if he is saying one thing but his thoughts are of a different nature entirely. Fascination draws me back to meet his eyes again, braver now.

'Shall we stay awhile and eat here?' he asks, what time do you have to go?' I glance at my watch and see that the day is flying by. Already after one, how can that be?

'My Ben will be home at three today so I must be back before then. A friend of mine walks him home with her daughter, it's a perfect arrangement as I'm stuck in the shop most days.'

'But not today,' he says with a smile. 'A quick pizza to share then and I shall let you go.'

I like the way he takes control and makes the decisions about simple details. From this I perceive him to be a strong character who always does exactly what he wants to do. The people he loves are taken care of but he stands alone, apart from them, in his own space.

While we eat I tell him a few stories from my shop, amusing him with descriptions of the variety of characters I encounter daily, and how I'll never cease to be surprised by their delight in my simple English recipes. I've always been in awe of French patisseries with their perfectly presented, ornate and extremely complicated creations, perfectly placed on shiny glass shelves with never a smear or fingerprint to be seen. My Dundee cakes and chocolate brownies come from a parallel universe but have won their place nevertheless in the shopping baskets of many of the residents in our small town. I'm proud of this achievement, however insignificant it might look to others.

'You have every right to be proud,' he says, 'there are a good deal of English people here, who come and do nothing and make no effort to add something to France as you have done.'

I glow in the shadow of his praise, Claude and Amelie have often voiced the same sentiment, although Philippe would prefer (although he never says) that I just cared for the children and never worked at all. Such is his pride, he desires the status of unique breadwinner, but sadly this eludes him.

I don't want to go home and face the transition back to reality. We rise, he settles the bill and with a French style embrace, a light kiss on each cheek, I inhale his aftershave and perhaps the aroma of his work place, a foreign odour to me but not unpleasant. I wonder if he can detect the smell of baking through my own perfume. I'm sure it must linger in my clothes and hair.

'I'll text you,' he says and he vanishes into a stream of ambling tourists flowing by, he's not able to walk with me, as we have parked at opposite ends of the town, and he too is tied by time. Bearing my lilies I wander in a trance to the car, reluctant to step back into my ordinary routine of work and children.

This lunchtime has been like a brief holiday, both refreshing, and stimulating for me. I'm alive again, I'm Elle, the mischievous Sea Witch of old. I know I would like to repeat the experience, and my lilies, adorning the empty fireplace of my home with their silent beauty, promise me that I will.

6

"Men know that most women want to have an emotional connection with someone before they sleep with them. Men know that a lot of women think it's romantic to be friends first, and then the friendship blossoms into a relationship. Men know that they have to jump through all these hoops, before they can get laid. And that's really all romance and courtship is to a man; hoops he has to jump through to get laid."

Oliver Markus, *Why men and women can't be friends*

My eyes are repeatedly drawn to my phone for the rest of the afternoon, making me nervous and uneasy. I almost want this new friend, this unexpected complication in my tidy life, to disappear, but then again, I privately delight in my secret. The children are squabbling their way to the tea table when my phone vibrates in my pocket; I turned the beep off some days ago.

I resist the impulse to rush into the kitchen to read his words immediately. I'll look later when the twins and Ben are settled into their own pursuits. Safer that way, they're so nosey.

Amelie comes round when she closes her shop, just for a chat before she begins preparing a meal for her family. *'Bonjour, ma petite,'* she says settling her wide girth into the carver chair at my kitchen table, 'Did you have a fun day off? Claude said he thought he passed you on your way out of Nice earlier.'

Blimey, did no one miss anything around here? 'Yes, I felt like a wander in the old town this morning, so I met up with a friend for a coffee and we had a good time.' Best to be straight and normal about things, just not say exactly who I had coffee with.

'Hmmph,' Amelie sort of snorts and I'm wary of any observation that may be about to follow from the lips of my motherly friend. 'I suppose you don't really manage to have a break like that often do you? I expect you need to be reminded now and then that there is world outside your shop and kitchen.'

'Yes,' I reply, relieved at Amelie's own justification for my presence in Nice, 'you're absolutely right. I feel trapped sometimes, what with kids, and work and everything else.'

'Oi, Mum,' Florence butts in, 'We don't trap you do we?'

'No, of course you don't my darling. Don't pay so much attention to what we grownups have to say, it's all nonsense really.'

'Perhaps not so much nonsense,' Amelie mutters, and raises herself to leave, planting a kiss on Ben's blonde head as she passes towards the door.

'*A toute a l'heure,*' I shout to her departing figure.

With the children upstairs at last, I take a peep at my phone. Two messages!

"*Thank you for a most enjoyable lunch.*" This is the first. Well, that's a trifle stiff, but yes, we did have an "enjoyable lunch" I suppose.

"*Miss you already.*" The second one, has quite a different tone. What peculiar things text messages are! Trying to understand the sentiment of the sender in a few clipped words is almost impossible. Sighing I put my phone back, high in a secret place in the kitchen. I don't know how to respond. Perhaps tomorrow, I shall sleep on my reply.

Patrick telephones her in the morning, on the pretext of taking her order.

'Did you get my texts?' he asks.

'Yes, but I was busy with the children and stuff you know how it is.'

'I must certainly do,' he agrees.' Do you need anything for this week. We have a new driver who will come to you, Daniel, he's a good chap and will put everything away for you I'm sure, especially if you give him a cake or two.'

'Sounds good to me.'

'But don't chat to him too long or I shall be jealous.'

'You? Jealous? I can hardly imagine that,'

'Oh, I can be, remember you hardly know me yet.'

No, I don't suppose I do,' I think about his last comment, trying to recall exactly how many times we have been in each other's company now. Is it really only three or four times?

He shifts the subject. 'Your husband will be home any day I should imagine. Shall we try and squeeze in a Monday picnic in the hills? I don't suppose I will see much of you once Philippe comes back.'

Instantly his tone has altered, it has become possessive, even whinging.

'Maybe we could, to the first part, and I expect you will still see me sometimes, to the second. I can't commit to next Monday yet, I shall have to see what happens, I have a lot to do here.'

'You think I don't?' His voice has changed yet again, almost cross now. What right has he to pressurise me?

I stand firm. 'Like I said, we shall just have to wait and see, Okay?'

'I suppose so. Let me know. *Chow!*' He has hung up without waiting for me to say goodbye. Infuriating, men can be so odd!

I walk back into the shop and Marguerite is sitting at one of the tables, having served herself a coffee. 'I shouted but you were on the phone,' she says without a smile or greeting. 'Was it Papa on the phone? It sounded like your "talking to Philippe" voice.'

Do I have a particular voice for certain people? If I do I certainly wasn't aware.

'No it wasn't your Papa. Just one of my mates.' Marguerite couldn't have heard exactly what I was saying through the thick wall so there was no need to worry. I wish she wouldn't sort of sneak up on me though. Maybe I'm overreacting, she'd stayed in the shop after all, and not disturbed me, whilst I was talking.

Philippe calls me later the same evening, full of the grumbles of the long season and tales of guests blocking toilets, and the endless misbehaviour of generators. He longs to come home so he can leave the vessel at the end of his working day and return to creature comforts; to reinstate his routines with time to relax and no surprises. I understand and make sympathetic noises to calm him. I remember the trapped feeling of a yacht after endless days at sea or on charter. 'You will soon be here,' I say.

'Not soon enough, another three weeks seems like an eternity,' he moans.

'Chin up, at least maybe we can afford a winter break.'

'I can't wait,' he says.

Two whole weeks with just my children and my husband. No contact with Patrick. On reflection I too, would welcome a holiday.

In the end I agree to the picnic idea for the last Monday before Philippe's return. I still have some reservations about going but Patrick persuades me in the end, tempting me with his plan to drive me in his open top car to my favourite village, a few kilometres inland from Nice. A place where the peace is only broken by the tinkle of the goat bells as the animals graze, speckled across the rugged terrain. I've not been back there since my single days, when a few friends and I used to drive up there regularly for Sunday picnics, making our way with big baskets, laden with food and wine, through the village and onto the mountain path that leads to the grove of olive trees. This place was a favourite haunt for the crew from *Sea Princess* in the days when we had time to escape from work. There in the shade, we would lie in the rough grass for hours, chatting and munching bread and cheese washed down with warm rosé.

Peillon, the name would always hold a certain magic for me.

We meet on the bright, sunny morning in a back-of-town Nice car park having made a special effort to escape early, so as to have as much of the day as we can possibly steal. We both have restrictions on time for the same reason; we need to be home for when school finishes. I dread the scenario of driving like a maniac through the busy traffic of Nice to beat Ben home, so I will not allow myself to be late. It is, after all, supposed to be a relaxing day out, with nothing to spoil our time at the end.

We walk stiffly, apart from each other, and I wonder if he'll take my arm. We buy a ticket for my car, which will stay here for the three, or four hours until we return.

'Would you like a coffee or something before we head off?' he says.

'No, let's just go.' I scan the car park, half expecting Claude, Amelie or worse still, Marguerite or Yves to pop out demanding an explanation of my presence in this place on a Monday morning.

Once we are safely speeding along the long winding road alongside the river gorge, through the outskirts of Nice, I slip into a new state of subdued excitement. The sensation of the breeze on my face is delicious after the leg-achingly, hot days spent in the kitchen.

I can sense Patrick's glance falling upon me, from time to time, but my eyes are shut, allowing my mind to rest from the turmoil induced solely by his company.

'You can open your eyes now, here's the turning!'

I do just that as the car swings round the corner and there is the sign. "PEILLON 3KMS."

'I love this road,' I say.

'Well, you'll have to be my guide because I don't think I've ever been up here before.'

'It's often the way isn't it, that we never, or rarely, visit the most wondrous places that are closest to home.'

'You do have a point there.'

We come to another sign, which directs us onto a smaller single-track road that begins our steep ascent up into the hills. 'I suspect there might be grass in the middle of the road in a minute, I hope my old car can stand the pressure.' Patrick laughs a nervous sort of chuckle, peering around each bend with obvious trepidation.

'It'll be worth it, you'll see shortly.'

Another half a dozen corners, each more hair-raising than the last, and the village comes into view at last. The sight gives me goosebumps, a fairy tale indeed, a special place like no other. Perhaps he wouldn't feel the same or worse, think me silly. I wait for him to react.

'You're right. Well worth the climb, but I shouldn't like to live here when it's icy in the winter months.'

I nod in agreement although I would adore to live here, ice or no ice. The village is perched right on the top of a mountainside, with small windows peeping out from the rock, being the only proof that there is indeed habitation within the stony rock face. The chapel spire is just visible at the highest point. The last part is the steepest and we lose sight of the village for a moment as we climb, and then suddenly the road levels off and we pull up outside a small restaurant with an enchanting terrace shrouded with vines. The central square lies a few yards in front of us with a stone fountain bubbling. This trickle of water and the goat bells in the distance are the only sounds to be heard.

Patrick takes me by the hand as we amble towards the steps up into the main block of dwellings. 'Did you really never bring Philippe up here?'

'No, I haven't been back for years. It's part of my other life, before the children came, even before I met their father.'

'Don't bring him here please.' I detect the other character in him sliding to the fore, the jealous, angry side that I catch a glimpse of every now and then. Like Jekyll and Hyde.

We climb the narrow footpaths that serve for streets, between the houses, all the way to the chapel at the summit. The doors we pass are wooden often with rounded tops, and brass plaques with the name of the owner or resident. They are all beautifully maintained with polished knockers and shiny varnish. They remind me of Hobbit holes or perhaps Mrs Tiggywinkle is in residence somewhere near. No cigarette ends or chocolate papers on these miniature streets. A door slams somewhere and the sound echoes. Around one corner or another we come across stone steps to higher doors, with pots of brightly coloured geraniums layered along the sides. But we don't see a soul.

'I suppose a lot of these places are holiday homes,' Patrick says, stooping to read a plaque by a door.'

'Yes, some, I had a friend who had an Aunt with a flat here, we went inside once, it was on the left hand side, so the view was out over the olive groves at the back. It was stunning but she didn't live here all the time, like you say, it was a second home.'

'It would be too quiet to be here all the time, and so remote.'

'Beautiful though, I love the quiet.' I know I sound wistful, but given the opportunity I would jump at a chance to have one of these front doors as my own.

We reach the top at last, a walled courtyard outside the chapel building. I try the door but to my disappointment, it's locked.

'Well they wouldn't leave it open, would they? Probably some valuables in there, and tourists can be vandals.'

'I suppose you're right. Shall we go back down to the restaurant and see if they will serve us a coffee before we wander off with our picnic?'

'*Bien sur.* A sound plan, it's still only early after all, we have plenty of time yet.'

As we reach the bottom of the initial flight of steps I notice that the huge wooden doors to the right that were previously padlocked have been thrown wide revealing a cave full of wooden sculptures and other hand chiseled items obviously for sale.

'Their ears must have pricked up when we walked past. They think we're tourists.' He laughs, at my comment and the harsh, human sound of it breaks the sleep of the courtyard. The only other audible noise is the trickle of water over stone.

'I expect they open about now everyday in the summer in case of visitors more like, not especially for us! Come on let's take a peek.' He drags her inside, taking her hand again, more firmly this time than before.

There are magnificent salad bowls, breadboards and cheese boards with olive wood handled knives, smaller bowls for olives, and all types of lovingly carved utensils. I flip over a price tag and raise my eyebrows, angling it so Patrick can see. After a quick glance he shakes his hand in the typical way the French have of expressing their view of an expensive item. A woman steps out of the shadows at the back of the shop and we know we have been spotted. She explains that her husband is the woodworker and that he makes everything there, '*sur place,*' as it were. 'But today he has gone to Nice to pick up some materials. If you want to know anything about the sculptures I will be happy to help.'

'Oh don't worry, we are just wandering, *merci quand même*', I sound as stilted as I feel.

'Ah, you are English, I detect a small accent there *n'est ce pas?*' My husband is also English, it's a shame he is not here,' and with this she retreats into the gloom behind her, disappearing like a ghost.

I'm glad to step back into the sunshine as we wander down to drink coffee under the canopy of leafy green in the Auberge where the car is parked. There is only one other couple seated in the corner. 'I bet the days are long here when nobody comes,' Patrick observes 'and imagine the winter, it must be deathly.'

'Well I think the place has a wonderful calmness about it, after the hurly burly of the coast. Trust a man to find fault.'

'I didn't say I didn't like it, just wouldn't want to be here everyday that's all.'

We fall silent while we drink our coffee and I'm slightly uncomfortable under his continuous gaze. It's such a bizarre situation to be here with this man I barely know and I'm swept by regret and a sudden longing to be home, back in my own environment.

'Shall we fetch our picnic from the car before it melts and I will show you where we used to go in the valley behind the village.'

'No rush is there?' he says.

'We mustn't be late back,' I insist now by rising from my chair.

'Okay, come on then.' Taking my arm he steers me back down the steep steps to the car.

'I can manage,' I say, wriggling out of his grasp.

Patrick retrieves the picnic basket I'd prepared early that morning from the back of the car, adding a bottle of wine that was concealed under the driver's seat. 'We shan't want much of that, it will only make us sleepy.'

'Nothing like a nap in the sun after a picnic.' I'm slightly unnerved this time by the way Patrick asserts control.

We stroll back into the village square and as we enter, I take an immediate left turn to rediscover the small path leading down behind the houses. Everything is exactly as I remember, and I'm amazed to find that my favourite property that stands alone looking across the olive trees is completely unchanged, with another stone drinking fountain next to the gate, just as it always

71

was, all those years ago. I wish I was the same girl now as I was then.

'This is the only house here with a proper garden and a place to sit outside. Definitely my favourite, I could live here and be content.'

Patrick makes no reply and we progress on down the winding stony way, until we are among the grassy ledges covered in olive trees, with a view up towards the village from the other side. There is a pool at the base of the steep cliff-like drop beneath the dwellings, but it looks green and untended. 'I wonder who owns the pool,' he says, at last.

I shrug in ignorance and point to a place beneath a tree where the grass is not so tall, and where we would have some shade. 'Shall we picnic there?'

'Good plan.'

I see something now I hadn't noticed before. He had placed a rug over the basket he was carrying, which he now proceeds to spread on my chosen spot. He's right, I decide, much better than having our legs prickled to pieces by the rough grass, as I'm in a skirt and he in shorts! Although I'm not entirely sure this reasoning was in his mind when he packed the blanket.

We settle comfortably, in spite of the somewhat stony ground beneath us and I lay out the food, cheeses, paté, baguette, some olive oil spread which has gone runny in the heat already, tiny Italian tomatoes on the vine, and finally a large punnet of strawberries. I've remembered a bottle of water and two paper cups but he immediately fills them with wine. 'We can drink the water straight from the bottle.' He grins. 'Thank you for all this, it looks marvellous.'

'Thank you for driving me all the way up here.'

'At least we're not likely to bump into anyone we know.'

'Do you worry about that too?' I ask him.

'I suppose I do, not for long though, I soon forget. Distracted by your mesmerising company.'

'Tease,' I say.

'Oh I'm not teasing. I feel so relaxed. I'm so stressed at work most of the time, by staff and other problems. I have a number of other business deals going on apart from the packaging company, and then there are the boys, always some problem or other with them. I had no one to talk to before I met you.'

'Nonsense, you have Béatrice.'

'I don't talk to her about business at all, I don't really want to involve her, I never have done. I paddle my own canoe, and make my own decisions. Of course we discuss the children, they are about the only thing we have in common these days. We often argue. She has her career although she doesn't need to work as I pay for everything. I have no idea what she does with the money she earns, I certainly don't see any of it.'

I am beginning to feel more comfortable with him; the wine and the sunshine are soothing my anxieties like a soft, cosy blanket, protecting me from sharp, uncomfortable thoughts. I think I'm beginning to know and understand this strange Frenchman, who is so different from my husband. I use the olive oil spread as a dip for my piece of bread before perching a slice of brie on the top.

'You eat so delicately,' he says.

I ignore this comment and begin to reveal a few small details of my own marriage.

'I've never had anyone provide for me, even the children's father was a poor one at maintaining an income. I wouldn't mind trying a more leisurely life for a while and seeing what it's like to be "a lady who lunches" as the saying goes. Philippe hates me being the breadwinner. This job he has now is the steadiest one he's had since we were married. When he has no work he is depressed and argumentative, and he spends too much time in the bars on the pretext of looking for work, and that makes me angry. His children are not supportive of me at all, of course they would rather have their parents back under the same roof, but they have to accept that's impossible and stop making me and my children suffer because of their unhappiness. I never thought it would be easy, but I never imagined it would be this hard either.' (Why is it I have total recall of all the bad bits about my marriage to Philippe but none of the good?)

'Regrets then?'

'Some I suppose, yes, but I do love Philippe, I know I do.'

'Who are you trying to convince? Me or you?'

I feel disloyal now and confused, unsure of how to answer him. Maybe I'm pouring my heart out too freely to Patrick, why would he understand? But I need someone to talk to sometimes just as he does.

'It's a tricky one,' he says, 'I shouldn't like you to work all the time if you were my wife either. Come here.'

Elle raises her eyebrows.' No, no, I don't want that.'

'Want what? I am not suggesting anything, I just want to give you a hug, that's all.'

I move across and lie next to him resting my head on his chest, and he rubs my arm as we look through the branches of the tree at the perfect blue sky above us, and we're quiet now.

I think he may have fallen asleep until he says, 'We can just be good friends who are there for each other can't we?'

'Yes I'm sure we can, that would indeed be the best arrangement, confidantes, nothing more.'

'If I ever do make love to you the setting would have to be perfect ... *un hôtel exotique sur la plage avec une bouteille de champagne.*' I turn my head sideways to glance at him.

'You Frenchmen always over romanticise.'

On the drive home, as we wind through the busy traffic of Nice, Patrick makes a firm statement, 'I can't not see you all through the autumn and winter just because your husband is home again.'

'There will be times, I'm sure.' I know my voice lacks conviction.

'There had better be,' he says.

7

'With a quick lip and a fierce tongue, the sort of tongue that draws you in with charm and words of praise, awkward silences and desperate worships.'

Coco J. Ginger

After our day out together in the hills, Patrick begins to text me everyday. A couple of times in the morning and sometimes in the afternoon too. I read his messages eagerly now, they make me warm inside; I have a special someone who cares for me, and who is interested in my problems day after day.

The colours of my life are somehow brighter, sprinkled with the glitter of suspense, and with a curious sensation of hope. I know he needs me too, as he pours out his worries concerning his business and family, although he rarely mentions Béatrice. He has his new delivery man now so he can find no excuse to deliver my order anymore. I know this is probably for the best as someone else might remark upon our friendship. For although this is all we have, and I've no intention to take him as a lover, others might not see our relationship in quite the same light and jump to a much more serious conclusion. I'm scared when I imagine the possible scenario of losing both my husband and my friend, over a misunderstanding. I shall be prudent and say nothing to anyone. I shall only consult my phone when absolutely no one else is around.

One afternoon within a few days of Philippe's imminent arrival we arrange to meet after I have closed the shop, in the cafe at the back of the market. I can safely leave the children while I pop up the road, I've often done the same in order to pick up something for dinner. But our plan is sabotaged when Ben comes home from school sick and feverish. After tucking him in bed, and leaving the twins firmly in front of their favourite programme, I go to the kitchen to send Patrick a message.

"Can't make it Ben poorly." No need to say more than that.

Immediately my phone vibrates with a reply.

"Not a good excuse see u in 5."

"I mean it I won't be there." My stomach begins to churn, he has that disagreeable physical effect on me, of course I can't go if the children need me. This is one point we have always agreed on; the importance of our respective children.

I see his van drive past the shop, but he doesn't look in. His features look set and grim. No more messages arrive. Studying his last, clipped text doesn't help me understand at all. What on earth has changed to make him place such pressure on me? Can five minutes with me be so important? Ridiculous, as if life isn't difficult enough! I reach up and chuck the phone back on the shelf and likewise Patrick out of my mind.

The next morning however, his good humour apparently restored, he texts me. *"Good morning"*

"Phil home later" I reply, to remind him straight away that today is the day. I don't want anymore of yesterday's nonsense.

"Are you telling me not to text?"

"No, only my replies might be slow."

That's fair, I decide and the phone goes back out of sight again. I don't want to think about him today.

Patrick's driver Daniel delivers my order mid-morning and I'm so glad he's not Patrick. I need to be calm and ready to welcome Philippe home, and I have Ben upstairs, still poorly, distracting my attention from work and my customers. I'm torn in two at times like this, I want to shut the shop and concentrate on being a mother, but I can't afford to do that.

Daniel is a personable sort of a man, reliability shining forth like the shoe polish on his brown, leather shoes. I gave him a chocolate brownie on his first visit and with his mouth bursting with chocolate he had said, "Will you marry me," and we had giggled at such foolishness, like old friends.

I consciously intend to build on this friendship in order that he might share confidences with me about his employer. Handled carefully he could be my spy and informant. The house and warehouse on the outskirts of Cagnes-Sur-Mer that calls itself *Le Carteaux Blanc*, holds a fascination for me, as does the owner. I need to find out what he is like day to day, and also about his true relationship with his partner. I'm not sure I trust him. Perhaps things are, in reality, a little different from the picture he paints.

Philippe calls me at midday.

'Where are you?' I ask.

'We just finished tying the stern lines. We're here!' Close up early and come down if you want. We are having a few beers naturally to celebrate.'

'Okay, I will in a bit.'

'Give us a call when you leave and I will walk part way to meet you.'

'All right,' My head is muddled with thoughts of how my life will alter again now my husband is home, and not just the with the loss of the freedom I've enjoyed all summer. Marguerite and Yves will be back on the scene again disturbing the smooth family life I've reestablished with my three. A frown creases my face as I begin to tidy the shop in order to close and go to meet

Philippe. I have just enough time to go down and have a quick drink with him before I have to be back to make supper for the twins. Ben is considerably better and assures me he will be fine snuggled up on the sofa. I shan't be long. I pick up the phone to call Philippe.

'Will he be home tonight to sleep?' Ben asks.

'Yes, of course, I mean I reckon so, after he finishes for the day. I expect he can't wait to sleep in a normal bed again.'

'Do they have bunk beds then, on his boat.'

'I'm sure, although I haven't seen his cabin, I expect it's probably quite luxurious on that size of motor boat.'

Appeased now Ben turns his gaze back to the television as I dial Philippe's number.

'I'm on my way,'

'I will set out and meet you half way, if you want?' he offers.

'No, that's crazy I can find you there, just keep an eye out for me at the gangway or they might not know who I am.'

Grabbing a light summer scarf, I realise that I've put no thought into perhaps changing my outfit to greet my husband home from the high seas. Too late now. I always put a huge amount of consideration into what I'll wear when I go to meet Patrick, but then he always remarks upon my dress. Philippe never compliments me in that way. It's both a waste of time, and of energy trying to look special for him. "I love you as you are," he has said in the past when I've chastised him for his indifference.

I wander along the quayside enjoying the sights and sounds of the harbour. I don't come down to the port often enough, I shall bring the children for a walk here at least once a week, especially when the beach weather is over.

I can see a figure walking steadily towards me. There's something familiar about the shock of black hair in the sunshine and it slowly dawns on me that this man in uniform is Philippe. I thought we had agreed that he would not walk to meet me, so

I'm surprised to see him. I continue to amble along, the sun in my eyes, until we are face to face.

'*Ma cherie,*' he kisses me lightly on the lips and places a proprietary arm about my waist. 'How have you been? I am so glad to be home.'

'I hardly knew it was you, I thought you weren't going to meet me?'

A little strange with each other, we walk back to his boat and I gaze at the splendour of the polished white topsides in awe. 'Are you sure it's okay for me to come onboard with you? Am I invited?'

'Of course you are, all the crew have their partners or wives coming down this afternoon. It's a special day.' We make our way along the side deck to the stern where pretty stewardesses are ladling a summer punch into tall glasses. Philippe places one in my hand. 'Relax for once and enjoy.'

'You know me, I'm not good at social gatherings with people I don't know.'

'*Bien,*' he whispers, 'try for me okay, just this once.' He propels me around introducing me to the rest of the crew and I struggle with small talk, feeling suddenly rather tired. How could I possibly have anything in common with any of them, I'm a sailor at heart not a motor boat person at all. Of course they probably all know my husband at least as well, if not better than I do. I eye up the sun-tanned girls, there seem to be so many of them!

After half an hour I plead to Philippe to let me go, 'Ben isn't well at all, I shouldn't leave him any longer than I have to.'

'You go on home then ... I won't be long behind you, I promise.'

He escorts me back to the gangway and gives me a reluctant hug, maybe because he is under the watchful eyes of his crew mates, I'm not sure, but I'm glad to make my way up the quay away from the boat, where I know I have no place. The yachting world is not my scene anymore. It's different now, I'm on the outside, looking in. Philippe will be waylaid in the Bar du Port. I know how it works. After all he has to walk right past the door on his way home. I knew I would definitely not see him before supper time, and I wish, just for once that he would tell me how things will be, instead of always "promising" me something else. Annoyingly he always says what he thinks I'd like to hear, but not the truth.

He finally climbs into bed next to me around ten. I'd been dozing but I'm instantly wide awake. He snuggles up to me and puts his arms around my waist, burying his face in my hair.

'Mmmm, you smell good.'

'Like cake and croissants you mean?' I say, turning to face him as best as I can within his grasp.

'Yes, those, and you as well. Your smell. I've missed you. You didn't seem overjoyed to see me today though. I expected you to run down the quay when you saw me.'

I choose my words carefully as I don't want to argue with Philippe when he has been drinking all afternoon and evening. 'You said you weren't coming to meet me, and with your uniform and the bright sun in my eyes, I wasn't even sure it was you.'

'Not a magic homecoming then.' This didn't seem to be a question so I didn't answer and within a few minutes I knew by his deep breathing that the alcohol had taken its toll and he was asleep.

Lying beside him, I slide into a sleepy, downward spiral of wondering why I'd married him. I was smitten at first and flattered, hoodwinked perhaps by my friend Amelie's admiration for the tall, spirited, Frenchman. I should have been wiser and looked further to examine precisely what we had in common, but is anyone as analytical as they need to be when caught up in the whirlwind that heralds a new romance? I had my doubts on the eve of my wedding, for I saw my children being pushed aside by Philippe's offspring during the preparations. I should have seen this as a warning sign of things to come. I was so swept up in the moment, that I stupidly ignored the signs. I honestly thought that we needed a man in our lives to strengthen and protect us, but this summer alone has shown me that we can be solid band of three who have no need of anyone. And now there is this other man, violating my thoughts. Where will that lead me if anywhere? Or does this new friendship merely serve to show me that I'm not truly in love with my husband.

On the first Sunday after Philippe's arrival, we decide to go out for the day and find a restaurant to eat somewhere near St Tropez. The children love the town and the beaches there and as the bulk of the tourists have now disappeared, it will be quite pleasant. Marguerite nearly ruins our plans by asking if I might be cooking Sunday lunch for everyone, but Philippe is firm for once and tells her we're going out, but she is welcome to join us. She declines. What could be worse than a situation where she is forced to share her father all day? She is so predictable.

We are all up early, the children touched by the excitement of being a whole, normal sized family again. Usually this means more treats as Philippe often takes their side when I put my foot down. He is happier now we've have reached the weekend and he can put work aboard ship aside for a couple of days, resuming family life at home. I know it was bound to take a few days, or maybe more for us to adjust, for although he's home he still has to go to work in the week, he's not on holiday. I go outside with a cold box full of cans of drink, to sort out the boot of the car. As I stand in the road I glance up the street and I'm sure I see the back of one of Patrick's company vans disappearing around the corner. Why on earth would it be down here on a Sunday? The bakery up the road is closed today as well, so they can't be calling there. I shake my head at myself, thinking I must have mistaken the van. What a suspicious detective I have become! Of course there must be others similarly coloured with white writing. Patrick would have no reason to spy on my shop. Nevertheless I go back inside feeling just a little uncomfortable.

I take a sneaky look at my phone in the kitchen. No messages. We had agreed after all, no texting at the weekend. 'We are ready, Mum,' Florence and Frannie burst in like puppies, panting at my feet, I can smell they've been using my perfume again.

'Okay, okay, where is Philippe?'

'In your office still going through all his letters.'

'I'll tell him we're ready.' I walk to the doorway and watch my husband for a moment as he scrutinises his mail. Do I love this man? I know I was captivated when we first met, but am I still? Each time he hurts me he erodes another piece of my love away and I'm not convinced I can reach back and find those pieces again. Life is not that simple, although I would like to try.

'We're ready and only waiting for you, cherie,' I stand behind him now with my hands resting softly on his shoulders.'

'I'm coming right now.'

We take the motorway to avoid the traffic on the busy coast road; a much quicker way to reach our destination, although this choice is not the scenic route. At the *peage,* I think I see the blue van with the white writing again in one of the far queues, but when I look back it has vanished. I must be imagining things. How silly! As if Patrick would have nothing better to do than to follow me on my day out with my family. What would be the point?

On such a bright windy day with a touch of Mistral in the air, St Tropez is not too busy as we make our way down to the quay to have coffee. Philippe likes to see which boats are moored stern to the wall. He knows many of the crew members on the big powerboats and he loves to chat about the problems they have all had to face during the summer season. A couple of guys that he knows are sitting on the terrace outside the bar and he greets them joyously with much back slapping and laughter.

I move away to reserve a table with the children, giving him some space to talk to his friends. I know he will rejoin us shortly, but standing in the shadows waiting for him makes me feel like a wallflower. Better to sit with the children and order hot chocolate. This is my place, enjoying my children's chatter for I'm not a part of my husband's working life. It's when I start to relax and look around that I see him. He is leaning against a lamppost about fifty yards away, talking on his mobile phone. At first I'm not quite sure it's him, but as he moves engrossed in deep conversation I know by the way his body shifts, and the way he kicks at stones idly with his right foot. There is no doubt in my mind now; Patrick has followed us here, it can't be a coincidence. He is watching me with Philippe.

My stomach hurts with nervous fear, and I try to locate a toilet. What can he be thinking of to spoil my day out with my family? What have I done to deserve this? I'd never dream of doing the same to him. To approach him now would cause a scene, he knows I won't risk that, so the best thing to do is to simply ignore him and to move on as soon as possible.

'Philippe, your coffee is getting cold.' My tone is fiercer than I intend.

'I'm coming.' Philippe excuses himself from his friends, with further hand shaking, and finally comes to sit us.

'Shall we drive on and find somewhere sheltered from the wind where we could eat lunch outside?' (Surely Patrick will not follow us further?)

'Yes, if you would like, your choice, I know how little you have been out and about this summer.'

This comment from Philippe pierces me, a knife of guilt concerning my secret day out in Peillon. I regret every part of it now, with this latest behaviour from Patrick. How could I have been so stupid? Would he try to justify following us in this way when I have a chance to confront him? I utterly blame myself. He'd better not try to deny it, for I saw him plainly, and he made no attempt to hide whatsoever. The gall of the man! Although the rest of our day passes without event, I find myself looking over my shoulder and inspecting the cars behind us at every traffic light. Luckily Philippe doesn't appear to notice.

Discussing our winter holiday is a favourite topic between us.

I desperately want to take the children to the Windward Islands in the Caribbean.

'*Tu blague,* you are joking,' Philippe retorts, 'for one thing we can't possibly afford it, and for another, there are masses of biting insects out there and you know I don't like being bitten.'

'I bet going anywhere for winter sun costs about the same when all is said and done, and that's a bit selfish of you, not wanting to go because you are scared of mosquitoes. Where do you suggest we go then?' I shrug in exasperation. 'I love the Caribbean I was so happy there.'

'I think the Canaries will be fine; Fuerteventura is brilliant for windsurfing. I will be content to have a go at some water sports while you and the kids relax on the beach.'

I look it up in a guide book for the Canaries later, for I had been there but not to that particular island. 'Looks a bit like a lunar landscape, not much vegetation.'

'Does it matter as long as we have blue sky and beaches?'

'I suppose not, it's just not exotic that's all.'

'We can't afford exotic and look at where we live, one of the best holiday destinations in the world!'

'I'm not at all sure what that has to do with anything, a holiday is surely best spent away from home?'

'Come on, cherie, we can only go for a week and that's just not enough time to go traipsing off to tropical islands.'

'I know, I know, perhaps we will one day.' She is giving in and moves across to lay her head in his lap.

'We will, maybe when the children are older, it's a long flight for them, across the Atlantic.'

'They aren't babies anymore.' I have the last word as usual.

As soon as Philippe leaves for work on Monday morning I grab my phone.

"Why did you follow us yesterday, not fair, completely unacceptable behaviour."

"Follow you? I went for a day out. What makes you think I was following you?"

"Because I saw you, idiot."

"I was not aware that you and your family had exclusive rights to St Tropez."

'Don't try and tell me it was all a coincidence because I don't believe you."

"You are being silly now. When can I see you?"

"You can't." Furious and shaking now with this exchange, I delete all the messages and shove the phone back in the tray upon the shelf, determined not to look at it again for the rest of the day.

Patrick walks into my shop the following morning, looking pleased with himself as if none of the cross words of the previous day had ever passed between us.

For once I'm annoyed that having a shop with an open door makes me so accessible.

'Are you on your own?' he half whispers.

'Not entirely, Philippe is at work but the children are upstairs and anyone could come in at anytime.' I was thinking more especially of Marguerite and Yves, who would spot anything out of the ordinary.

'Does that matter? We are not doing anything wrong are we?'

'I'm not, no, but goodness knows what you might come out with.'

'Oh come on, that's hardly fair.'

'Don't tell me what's fair after yesterday.'

'That was yesterday, and now it's today and I thought I would pop in to say hello as I am passing.'

'Philippe could easily come home.'

'Yes, well, I met him didn't I at the party? I'm not a stranger.'

'No, I suppose that's true. As long as he doesn't find you here too often.'

'I have to see you sometimes Elle, Philippe or no Philippe *ça marche pas sans te voir,* nothing goes well if I don't see you.'

Another typical French habit. Exaggeration. I sigh; I'm flattered and unable to stay angry with him for long. 'Soon you will have to be without me for a whole week. No texts or anything.'

'Why is that?'

'We are going to go on holiday for the mid-term break. To the Canaries.'

'So are we, but we are going for two whole weeks to Cuba. I don't know how I shall survive it.'

This news hits me like a bombshell. The fact that Patrick might go away "en famille" has never occurred to me. He has told her so many times that his relationship with Béatrice is distant; a thing of the past that has left them with three children who need both of them to be around. For one awful instant I acknowledge a surge of jealousy mixed with annoyance, that Béatrice would be at his side, and their destination didn't help much either. Cuba isn't exactly where I want to go but it's a lot closer to the mark than Fuerteventura. I barely hear his next remark; I'm so lost in trying to cope with the thought of Patrick and Béatrice walking romantically arm in arm on some Cuban beach. Surely the holiday would rekindle their feelings for one another.

'I will try to phone sometimes,' he says, taking my shocked look for one of horror at the thought of his absence.

'No, no, you don't need to do that. We can exist without each other, all friends can.'

'Yes but it will hard to be so far from you, I'm used to our chats and texts now, I don't want to be without you.' He comes close to me in the back of the shop, cornering and holding me for a second until I pull away from him.

'What do you think you are doing? Anyone could look through the window and see!'

The bell on the shop door announces the arrival of a customer, and I spring to place some distance between us. The elderly lady customer, one of my regulars, glances at each of us in turn, perfectly aware that she is interrupting something. A confidant lady, and sharp, right down to her tightly laced shoes. She removes the top of the ancient tin that she uses to transport her cakes, refusing to succumb to the use of cardboard cake boxes which she considers harmful to the environment. An enemy for Patrick. She chooses three cakes and watches intently as I arrange them in her tin, and I hear her customary, sharp intake of breath at the price, although the sum is always the same.

Out of the corner of my eye, I can see that Patrick is struggling to contain his amusement. This intrusion has at least served to release the previous tension between us.

'Why will she not take her cakes in a box and have done with it?'

'Habits die hard amongst the elderly, you must realise that.'

'I must go,' he says.

'Yes you must.' I look at him and my heart yearns to hold him back, to tell him other things, to shout at him perhaps, mad nonsense from the depths of my conflicting emotions. All best left unsaid.

8

"I always want to know the things one shouldn't do"
"So as to do them?" asked her Aunt.
"So as to choose," said Isabel.

Henry James, Portrait of a Lady

The most shocking thing that has happened to me since Philippe's return, must be that I no longer have any physical desire for him. He doesn't exactly repulse me, nothing like that, I just want to be left alone to think. I feel as if I've already betrayed him when in fact I've done nothing of the sort. Or have I? Does seeking the companionship of another man outside my marriage count as infidelity? Have I been unfaithful in my mind already? Philippe senses something, I know he does but maybe he just puts my distance from him down to his long absence from me. Our independent lives have driven a wedge between us. But I know the situation is worse than that, a whole lot worse.

I lie awake at night while he snores, churning all this around in my mind, like my mixer in the kitchen, adding more reflections like ingredients, as they spring to mind, seasoning and stirring. Philippe constantly accuses me of not listening to him, of not being interested in his work, and of being too focused on my own business to recognise his achievements. He always comes back to this after a few drinks in the evening. Like a tape recorder, so repetitive, hurtful the first time, but by the second or third time around I simply cease to listen. He relishes picking holes in my parenting skills as well, that's his other favourite gripe. "You must realise that you spoil Ben, making him into a mummy's boy, and you always favour him above his sisters." I will admit sometimes I am over protective of Ben, he is only seven years old, and will always be the baby of the three, but I love my children equally. They are my life and I despise his unjust criticism. He should look at his children and measure his own parenting skills, although I would never dare to voice this thought. Even though it is only the drink that brings these unkind comments to the surface, I know they are always there, simmering beneath his polite, sober exterior and I hate him for that.

Does he not notice that it's me who keeps the household together? I pay the bills and stagger back from the market, often with food for his children as well as my own. He has been salaried all summer, tips as well, I shouldn't wonder. We had agreed that his wages would go straight into the bank but I've not had a sniff of his earnings. He says he has opened a savings account for us, but I've seen no evidence of this and I worry now, about our future.

Yves and Marguerite bowled up looking for cash and he scuttled off and produced wads of it, yes, literally wads, joyfully handing it out like Father Christmas, but none came my way for the housekeeping. Ha ha, that's a laugh! He even puts his hand in the till every morning for change for his coffee at the Bar du Port on his way to work! I don't dare say anything for fear of the row of all rows, and where would it end? Like launching a skyrocket. Light the blue touch paper and stand back! I will talk to Patrick about it, he will see it from a man's point of view and tell me if I'm being unreasonable because I'm simply not sure anymore.

The texts come regularly again now after our near falling out over the St Tropez business. I have forgotten about it, (well not quite, but almost). I need an ally, and a friend, this is the justification for our friendship. Just, *"Bonjour, how are you today, I wish I could see you on this glorious morning,"* from him, that sort of stuff but it's comforting and reassuring and I hate the thought of my phone screen being blank and silent.

We manage to arrange to meet on a Monday, in a remote car park at the back of town for fear of being spotted. I sit and wait, accustomed now to his habitual lack of punctuality.

He jumps into the passenger seat of my car tossing a bunch of freesias into the back seat, taking me unawares as I sit, with eyes closed almost dozing. I breathe in the heady scent of the flowers for they are truly delightful.

'Why do you always look at me like that?' I ask him.

'Like what? How do I look at you?'

'I can't explain it. Sort of as though you are both surprised and relieved when you see me.'

'Well I am, both. I want to see you so much and I'm always worried you might not come.'

'If I say I'm coming I will, I'd tell you if I wasn't.'

'I know that. You asked me a question and I answered it, okay.'

'Yes, well here we are.'

'I have a present for you,' he says with a sly grin, producing a small, brown paper bag.

'What is it?' I try to snatch it from him but he dangles it out of reach, playing with me.

'Go no then, *voila,* you can have it.' He chucks the bag into my lap.

I peer in holding the bag almost to my nose, for I suspect the contents might be edible, and then I'm puzzled. 'It's a key.'

'Yes, it's a key, well spotted.'

I make a playful gesture of slapping him now for his teasing. He catches my hand and holds it to his mouth until I pull it away.

'What does it open anyway?' I feign disinterest. 'Are you going to tell me or shall you continue with your game?'

'It's not a game,' he says, serious now. 'There's a flat above the Tabac in Rue d'Albert, belonging to a mate of mine. He used to let it furnished but it's empty right now, he's only there occasionally. He said I could use it if I ever needed a bolt hole.'

I grimace, I can't help it, the flat just sounds, for want of a better word, sordid.

'Why the face, what's the problem with that idea?'

'I thought I had made it clear, I love having your friendship but an affair is *hors de question,* not on the cards. I am married to Philippe and you have Béatrice.'

'Yes, of course, but I just thought we could go there, away from prying eyes, have coffee, chat, eat and talk as much as we want.'

'I suppose so,' I say hesitantly, slowly imagining how it might be if we had somewhere to be instead of a car park like this.

'Anyway, I don't have Béatrice remember.'

'Yes, but you do live with her, and she would, I am sure, be unhappy about our friendship in the same way that Philippe would, should he find out.'

'Maybe, maybe not who knows. Shall we meet there sometime? It's only just up the road from your shop.'

'I am well aware of where it is, I shall give the idea some serious consideration.'

'*Merci Madame,*' he says mocking my both serious tone and my choice of words. 'Perhaps when you can meet me there you will let me know?'

'I will, but I don't know when. We are both going away soon anyway.'

'That's four weeks away!'

'Yes, but the time will go fast, and my Mondays are busy. Sometimes I must meet Philippe for lunch as well, he's been moaning that on my day off I could, but I never do.'

'Oh Philippe, this and Philippe that, he's much too old for you anyway. You need someone a bit younger and more fun.'

'Like you, I suppose?' I can't help but laugh at him.

'Of course! And now I have to go back to work, so I shall see you soon.'

'Maybe,' I blow him a kiss as he closes the car door.

He mouths the words, 'Text me!'

I sit for a while, after he has driven away, going over and over our conversation in my mind. I often do this, trying to analyse exactly why we enjoy each other's company. He said Philippe is too old for me. I can list many reasons why Philippe is unsuitable but age is not one of them. He is only four years older than me, he had married young first time around, and had his two children quickly. His wife had been his first love; they had been together since their school days, a recipe for disaster. We grow up in our twenties, and then a young marriage risks to be burdened with the added pressure of children and finances. Things can often go wrong.

As it happened Philippe's wife had an affair and then left him, dramatically, to live with the "other man". I believe he suffered enormously from the humiliation, and loss of face. I know I've helped to rebuild his confidence and that his ability to attract and marry a younger woman has vastly infuriated his ex-wife. But Philippe is still full of the bitterness of the split, making the job of being his new partner incredibly hard. And then there is the money thing, a worry that always prays on my mind these days. As for Yves and Marguerite, their blatant distaste for me, their new step-mother, is just the last straw.

Patrick is my escape, both in my mind and in our hurried meetings when he becomes, for an hour or so, reality. I know our friendship is a betrayal of both of our partners, but I'm not going to give him up, not for anything. What a mess our lives have become. Something has to change.

As I predicted our respective holidays are looming on the horizon and I'm actually looking forward to some quality time with Philippe and the children. Luckily his two have made no suggestion that they might want to come and I'm more than a little relieved.

Patrick is texting me two or three times a day, but we are too busy to meet. I'd forgotten how stressful it can be making holiday preparations. I need to organise someone to stay in the house for I hate to leave the property empty, especially with the shop closed. It will be obvious to everyone that we have gone away. Also, our old cat is always happier if someone is around even though Amelie has offered to feed her. I find a girl who works at the *Vétérinaire,* at a price of course, but she appears to be reliable.

I create my own tidal wave in the shop each time I close for a holiday, as my customers are determined to stock up as if a terrible drought of cake is about to be imposed upon them. I have to sit and down and make sure all my bills are up to date and make a few batches of things for the freezer so that I don't come back to a blank canvas; there is so much to think about to facilitate a worry-free week in Fuerteventura. By the tone of Patrick's texts he is becoming increasingly stressed as the mid-term break draws closer.

I know I am spending far too much time deliberating on love and relationships these days. Every song I hear, all the books I read, I look for answers everywhere but find none. Is Patrick merely a symbol of my mid life crisis? Is this the beginning of my menopause at forty-three and all the strange hormonal twists and turns that accompany the change? Or could this be the start of something real and life changing. In my mind I'm able to float away with Patrick to a new situation where I'm adored and appreciated and of course he would love my children too and never criticise my skills of motherhood. Ah such dreams, dangerous to hold on to and even more dangerous to believe them.

Patrick rings me on the landline in the last few days before our departure. He has taken to doing this lately and it does not please me at all.

'If someone comes you can just say ... no thanks I don't need an order today ... hang up and no-one will be any the wiser.'

'That's all very well but I don't like play acting, it's almost as bad as telling lies and I don't like doing that either. Why can't you stick to texting me?'

'Because I prefer to speak to you, and in a few days I won't be able to do that for two whole weeks. Please take your phone away with you.'

'No, I definitely can't because it would look suspicious. Philippe knows I barely use my mobile phone so to take it to Spain with me would be extraordinary behaviour.'

'So I can't even text?'

'You can after the first week because I shall be home again, but why would you even want to when you are sitting on the beach in Cuba.'

I shan't be sitting on the beach because I hate sitting around in the sun. I shall leave the others and go exploring on my own.'

'You always have an answer, don't you?'

'Nearly always yes, I'm glad you notice.'

'I have to go, I have things to do.'

'Ooooh, things to do.' He was annoying me now; he irritates me in this mood. I know it's the stress of our imminent separation. It brings out the worst in him. When we are together he never winds me up like this.

'*À bientôt,*' I say firmly, and hang up.

I go straight upstairs to examine the children's swimming costumes in case they need new ones before we go away; I have a feeling that the girls have almost grown out of their suits during the summer, they are turning into young women, changing shape. The phone starts ringing again. I decide to leave it, the answer machine will kick in after a few rings. The ringing stops and I hear a voice.

'No, I don't know what you are talking about. This is Marguerite, who are you?'

'Elle? Yes, okay I will tell her.'

My heart seems to be trying to explode in my chest, it's beating so hard it hurts.

What has he said to her? It has to be Patrick of course.

Marguerite is thumping, heavy footed up the stairs. 'Why does every one think I'm you when I answer the phone?'

'Probably because you sound like me and they expect me to answer, it's my house.'

'It's annoying.'

'Who was it on the phone anyway?' I try to keep my voice calm and normal.

'Just some bloke said he hadn't finished talking to you or something, a bit weird, but he said he would phone another time.'

'Fine. I'm just trying to sort out swim gear for the holiday.' I change the subject hoping that the phone call will lose importance and be forgotten.

Marguerite still looks puzzled and turns on her heel and goes down into the kitchen. I can hear her opening and closing the fridge, her usual trick. I breathe out slowly, with relief; the moment of danger has passed. I hear another beep from the phone; perhaps she didn't replace it properly the first time.

'Flo, you are turning blue, for goodness sake, go and put your wet suit on please.'

'But Ben isn't wearing his.' My child protests.

'Ben isn't blue or shivering he's like a seal, cold blooded. Now don't argue.'

The sun is hot, and the pool is clean and blue, but colder than expected. I have tested the water already with one toe, but pulled it out again quickly, I'm a warm water swimmer. The breeze across the sun bed is keeping me at the perfect temperature, I hate to be too hot or too cold, no extremes for me. I lie back with my book, absorbed. I know I'm selfish sometimes, as I love to read whilst on holiday immersing myself in a fictitious world. Philippe doesn't read at all and I think I'm probably dull company. I watch him as he comes down the steps from the apartment; he has a bottle of Rosé on a tray with two glasses and some olives in a bowl. He has been the perfect husband since we arrived, pampering me and playing endlessly with the kids. How much better life is when we are away from all the pressures at home.

Yesterday we went to the best windsurfing beach at the end of the island and he thoroughly enjoyed himself. It was so windy on the dunes that the sand blew in our eyes and almost made the day unpleasant so I'm glad to stay at the apartment today. Everyone seems content and apart from the chilly pool, it's perfect. Philippe pours me a glass of wine, ruffles my hair and kisses me. I love my husband anew in our breezy island paradise.

Settling back into my book, the sensation of Patrick lacing his hands with mine the day before we left springs to mind without warning. Our fingers fitting together tightly, was an over-whelmingly touching sensation, almost as if we were committing a sexual act. His strong hands enveloped my small fingers, squeezing them hard almost cruelly. I try to banish the thought of it, with a shake of my head, but the memory lingers.

'What are you shaking your head about, *mon amour*,' Philippe turns towards me and is studying me intently, from his sun bed alongside my own.

'Nothing, just something in my book,' I say, 'sorry to be reading. You know how I am on holiday, such a bookworm.'

'That's fine as long as you are happy.'

'Yes, I'm happy,' I answer and this is the truth.

We drive around the island on the next day and I'm saddened at the lack of vegetation. Every palm tree or flower bed has to have a complicated visible irrigation system of ugly hose pipes in order for the plants to survive which makes the landscape appear artificial. Fuerteventura is a barren island of dunes and rock, windswept and dry.

We stop for fuel at a small petrol station and the attendant tries to short change me. I retaliate with a tirade of angry Spanish.

'Wow Mum,' Frannie says, 'You sure sorted that guy out!'

'Impressive!' says Philippe, putting his arm around me, and I'm taken by surprise by the rush of affection I feel for my husband.

As the week draws to an end and we begin to start throwing clothes back into our bags instead of pulling them out, I know what I must do. I will end my friendship with Patrick at the first opportunity before our amorous play-acting becomes a serious threat to my marriage.

9

"I cannot fix on the hour, or the spot, or the look or the words, which laid the foundation. It is too long ago. I was in the middle before I knew that I had begun."

Jane Austen, *Pride and Prejudice*

Patrick telephones me from Cuba, like he promised he would. His call comes in the middle of the day, but of course where he is on the other side of the Atlantic, it's the middle of the night. I find it hard to picture him sitting outside his holiday apartment in the dark, but I can hear tree frogs and I'm sure I can also hear the sea. I don't ask, as the idea of his perfect holiday with Béatrice swamps me with unreasonable jealousy.

'We have to talk when you get back,' I announce, keen to prepare him for the decision I've made.

'That sounds ominous.'

'I've had plenty of time to think, while I've been away, to work things out.'

'I hope you are not going to say what I think you are.'

'We will meet at your friend's place and talk it over in peace and privacy.'

'And what if I don't want to listen.'

A moment of panic now. What if he does stubbornly refuse to understand my reasoning and won't give up. Worst of all what if he says something to Philippe in the anger of rejection. 'We need to talk it through, before we hurt everyone, especially ourselves.'

'Now you have me really worried. You know that film, "Bridge of Madison County" with Meryl Streep where the guy is left standing on his own in the pouring rain?'

'Yes I saw it twice.'

'I'm that guy, I'll be the one left out in the rain, you'll see.'

This time I notice the apartment, last time I had barely looked around me. I'd been so excited at the prospect of private time with Patrick that the surroundings had melted into the background, as scenery for two actors in an unfolding drama. The decor shrieks of the masculinity of the owner. No feminine touches here, no ornamentation, magazines precisely arranged on the side. The owner's unseen presence hangs in the air, his aftershave sits on the bathroom sink, his toweling robe hangs on the door. I can imagine his bed linen, a dark colour or check, but I will not look at the bedroom.

Of course Patrick brings flowers for me, three bunches. I can be another person here with him, a different Elle, not the one who is married to Philippe, a pastry chef and a mother.

'I can't take all of these home, I can explain I bought one bunch, but I wouldn't have bought three!'

'Leave them here then, I am sure we can find a vase, and they will be here for next time we come. Then we shan't be able to leave it too long or they will be dead. Anyway, have you missed me?'

I notice that in two weeks he has achieved a dark tan. 'Yes and no. That's what I need to talk to you about. Cuba was obviously hotter than Fuerteventura, look at the colour of your skin compared to mine, I'm like a snow drop! Is there coffee we can use here?'

'In the bag on the table, I bought some, there is milk there too.'

'You think of everything.'

We sit with our coffee, formally opposite each other at the small table in the kitchen.

'It was good to be away from here, for the children obviously, but most of all for Philippe and I. We were better with each other, so much more relaxed and I want that now. I want my marriage back on track and that won't happen if we keep meeting like this.' There, I've said my piece.

'So I must lose my confidante and my best friend? I'm not your lover so how can I be damaging your marriage.'

'Believe me you are. Didn't you become closer to Béatrice with me thousands of miles away?'

'No, because I didn't want to be any closer to her, that's the difference. Did you make love to Philippe while you were away?'

'I really don't think that's any of your business.'

'Of course it's my business, I need to know all the details about your relationship with him, not just the parts you choose to tell me.'

'That's totally off limits. I don't ask you about your sleeping arrangements with Béatrice.'

'We don't sleep together, not even in the same room. She would like to but I'm not interested.'

'I don't want to know, that's between the two of you.'

'But I want you to understand.'

I can see I'm not achieving anything like this. The conversation is going round and round, and he's not accepting the point I'm trying to make, because he doesn't want to try. 'I mean it, Patrick, I would like to bring, whatever it is we have, to an end before anyone is seriously hurt. We both know the trouble it would cause if someone saw us together, overheard a phone call or if, God forbid, Philippe should find my mobile and read all the texts you keep sending me every day.'

'Don't you delete them?'

'Yes, of course I do but I would only have to forget once and sure as hell that would be the day he finds the phone.'

'This is the first time I've seen you since I got back. I was so looking forward to this day, so much to tell you, and all you want to do is argue.'

I'm uncomfortable now, I want to go home. 'I just know it would be for the best.'

'And I "just know" it wouldn't be.'

'I'm sorry Patrick, it has to be this way.' I pick up my basket, place one bunch of flowers carefully inside and walk out of the door, leaving him sitting at the table, shaking his head, half smiling in sheer disbelief.

'I will try not to text,' he says and I look back at his face for a second, shocked at this glimpse of his vulnerable side. All of his arrogance has fallen away for an instant.

I step back inside my front door and see the sight I have come to dread. Marguerite's collection of bags and holdalls are littered in the hall, her jacket lies upon a chair.

She emerges from the kitchen. 'I'm back for a bit,' she says. 'I told Dad. I need a change.'

My stepdaughter is an expert at playing one parent off against the other. If Mum and her new husband were not giving her enough rope then she would appear on our doorstep, confident in her ability to talk her Dad into giving into her latest plan, whatever that might turn out to be.

'Where have you been anyway? Are the kids not home yet?' She peers into my basket. 'Nice flowers.'

This is the closest thing to a conversation that we have had in a long time and I'm suspicious of her motive. 'They will be home shortly.'

'That's lucky then, you are home just in time.'

I decide to ignore this comment, but the unnerving sensation that Marguerite has come back with the sole intention of spying

102

on my movements after that wretched phone call, creeps over me. Maybe she has even discussed it with Philippe. No. I'm being ridiculous now, worrying over nothing. The girl has probably dismissed the call from her mind long ago. It was nothing, unimportant, and it's over and done with.

I put my mind to thinking what to cook for supper. It's simple with only my children and Philippe but now I have to try and cater for this girl who treats both me, and my cooking with nothing but disdain. And she gets away with it because Philippe never, ever reprimands her for her rudeness.

After a moment spent holding my phone in my hand and staring at the screen, I turn it off. No more messages and no more Patrick, it has to be the right thing to do, even more so now that Marguerite is skulking around watching my every move, waiting for the phone to ring so she might snatch it before I have a chance. Imagine the humiliation of being accused of having an affair when I'm not! I'm sure Philippe will side with his daughter if push comes to shove. Best to blow out the flame before it burns me.

Nevertheless, I find myself watching out for the van. No sign. One of his employees calls me for my order. I am longing to turn on my phone to see if there is a message hiding there, but I manage to resist all week long. I'm cut off, and bereft. The days have the flavour of Autumn and I throw myself reluctantly into the preparations for Christmas ... so much baking to do; the French love my Christmas puddings and hand-crafted fruit cakes. A few days of rain and then a chilly October wind reveals the mountains in all their splendour with a fresh topping of snow. How I love it here, life anywhere else could never be the same.

This evening, being Saturday night, (I can have a lie in on Sunday) I have invited Amelie and Claude to dine with us. More work for me but I enjoy the company of my friends and if we dine at home it avoids the problem of babysitting. Philippe always volunteers Marguerite's services but I have a horror, (based on past experience) of leaving her alone with them. Marguerite likes Amelie and Claude, they are friends with her mother as well, and have known her since she was a little girl. So we are five around the table, the little ones having eaten earlier. I try to be at ease in the presence of my step-daughter who I know would rather her mother was sitting in my place, like things used to be before her parents separation.

'*Alors les vacances sont bien passé?*' Claude begins, jovial as ever.

'Yes, thank you, we had a marvelous break. Windy, I have to say, but the sun was warm and I think we all enjoyed the change and the rest,' I pour the wine, as I speak.

'And it's good to have your husband back where he belongs for the winter?' asks Amelie, 'no more lonely nights.'

'Yes it's lovely to be a complete family again,' I rest a hand for a moment on Philippe's shoulder as I fill his glass.

Marguerite gives a sort of a snort and we all look at her.

'Do you have something to say?' Philippe asks his eyebrows furrowed with concern.

Marguerite is on the spot now. She looks around the table. 'Nothing important. Just that I don't think Elle was too lonely, she does have quite a few friends.'

I feel my face flush. How dare she! My words tumble out in a rush. 'Of course I do, and customers, and a business to run to keep me busy, I'm never lonely.' I look directly at Marguerite. 'Do you have a problem with that?'

'Not if Papa doesn't?' she says turning now to her father.'

'Of course I don't, silly girl, Elle has to have a life whilst I am away, just as I have made friends on board ship and on my travels.'

'*Bien,*' she says, and noisily pushing back her chair, she stands up. '*Excusez moi,* but I have to go and meet my friends.'

Amelie intercedes, 'but you haven't eaten, cherie?'

'No matter, I will get something in town.' Moments later the front door slams.

'I am so sorry everyone. Teenagers!' says Philippe.

I shake my head and begin to serve the first course.

Before bed I go to Ben's room and stroke his smooth, corn-coloured hair as he sleeps. A few days before he had said, 'Why doesn't Marguerite like us Mummy?'

How perceptive he is for a seven year old. 'Because she thinks you might steal her Papa I think. She probably doesn't mean to be unkind, she's just no good at sharing her Daddy with a new family.'

'I see. But I would like a big sister, I really would.'

'I know that, my sweetheart.' I try to reassure him. 'I am sure Marguerite will feel better in time.'

I resist the temptation to turn on my phone until Monday. At six a.m. when I'm the only one awake, I press the power button and then replace it quickly as though it might bite me. It vibrates furiously and repeatedly, revealing a queue of messages. So much for no texting! Thank goodness there was no one around.

The first one sent on Thursday is just two words. "*Je crack*"

He cracks? I have too by turning on my phone when I had promised myself I wouldn't.

"*Are you okay? Can we just go back to texting every now and then?*" Text number two sent on Friday.

And then, "*I miss you. I know your phone is off but I shall text in case you turn it back on.*"

Sunday morning. "*Elle, every day I hope that you will TURN ON YOUR PHONE.*"

It vibrates in my hand giving me such a start that I almost let it fall.

Another text. He must have realised I've turned it on already! Was he sitting watching his phone waiting for his messages to be delivered? He has to be.

"Enfin, how are you?"

"Too much to say in a text," I type thinking about the threat of Maguerite's words at the dinner table.

"We must meet then."

"Maybe soon." I press the send button and then panicked by a moment of fear, I delete all his messages and my replies and turn the phone off again, hiding it carefully. It would spell disaster now if anyone else turned it on, for sure.

We arrange to meet at the apartment, I feel safe there behind closed doors. For once he can't be late because I have no key and hanging around on the doorstep would not be wise. Patrick is already brewing coffee when I arrive. He throws his arms around me, holding me tightly, and all I can think of is how much taller he is than Philippe, my head only just reaching the crook beneath his shoulder. He has never attempted to embrace me like this before. He pulls me in front of the mirror that hangs in the small hallway. 'Look, that's us, you and me!'

I glance at our reflection and then move away with embarrassment. I am pleased to see him but confused by his apparent emotion.

He sits at the table. 'What's been happening then? Tell me.'

I sit on the other chair, facing him, our coffee cups between us.

'Marguerite has been really suspicious of me ever since you made that unfortunate call that she answered. She sounds exactly like me on the phone, which is hard to believe as I am English and she is French but it's true. Everyone mistakes her for me. You must be careful, or preferably never call the landline as she is staying with us now.'

'My fault, I am so sorry. I didn't mean to make problems for you, I just wanted to talk to you that's all.'

'We have to be so careful if we want to continue being friends. Can you imagine the pain and disgrace I would suffer if I were to be accused of an affair I'm not even having. And no-one would believe me, least of all Marguerite and Philippe. They would never understand the simplicity of needing a friend.' Patrick takes my hand and I leave it in his, resting my chin in my other hand with my elbow upon the table. I look deep into his face trying to guess what he's thinking.

'You are my tonic. I honestly have no one to talk to in the way I can share things with you. Please don't say I can't text or see you again,' he says.

'It will be Christmas soon and we will both be busy so we have to be calm and patient and extremely careful. No rash phone calls.'

He is like a small boy now, reprimanded and full of remorse. 'I promise I'll try,' he says. 'I brought you lilies.'

'Oh no! How am I supposed to explain those away?'

'Say you bought them.'

'I never buy such extravagant flowers.'

'You do now.'

Allowing him to embrace me with a peck on each cheek, I leave him carrying the enormous lilies wrapped in my arms, my head full of their scent and the memory of the look on his face when I had walked in the door of the apartment.

I place them in a vase, declaring brazenly to all who should enquire that I'd bought the bunch cheap in the market because they were fully open and would not last. Only a small white lie and it was not questioned even by Marguerite, who burying her nose in an open flower, is wounded by a smear of bright, red-orange pollen upon her cheek.

10

"Cause it takes something more this time
Than sweet sweet lies oh now
Before I open up my arms and fall
Losing all control
Every dream inside my soul"

David Gray, *This Year's Love*

Patrick resumes the daily text. I seem to be his lifeline, stabilising him in some way. He never brings my deliveries but will sometimes pop in to the shop in the middle of the afternoon taking me unawares. This makes me uneasy. Marguerite could easily come home early as she has a flexible timetable and although she would find us chatting innocently, she might easily pick up on an undercurrent of familiarity between us.

We talk about Christmas, and the separation it will inevitably bring. Zanne is coming to stay for the festive period and Philippe has a long break off work. I'll be surrounded and madly busy with the shop and the household with little time to myself. No chance to be the other Elle, Patrick's Elle. 'Probably best just to forget about one another until it's all over, simpler, and much less frantic,' I tell him.

'And what if I don't want to forget about you?'

'I don't think you have a choice. Christmas is a family time after all. We just have to accept our obligations. It's all about the children.'

I've worked something out now, I have recognised over time

the trigger that changes him from being an agreeable friend whose company I value and enjoy, into an ogre of non-negotiation and stubbornness. I hate this other side of him, he transforms like a werewolf under a full moon, whenever I attempt to place a restriction to limit our time together, to avoid risk and damage to our families. The most worrying side to this is that he doesn't seem to care if our world were to explode around us, almost inviting such a scenario; he often dances dangerously close to the possibility of exposure.

'I shall text you and then you can tell me when it's safe to call, I am sure you can manage to be on your own at some point,' he says.

I hate the thought of our lack of contact over Christmas as well, but the continual pressure from him is worse. 'I can't promise,' I say.

On Christmas Eve, exhausted as I am, I drive out to *Cap Trois Mille*, the giant, out-of-town shopping centre where I can finish all my Christmas shopping in one place and pick up last minute groceries as well. I wander around trying to calm myself now that the shop is closed and done until the second week of January. My head is spinning and impulse buying in a tired sort of frenzy is a serious risk, one that our finances cannot support. Philippe wanted to come with me but his tendency to overspend is even worse than mine. So I've left him with his mother and the children, making old fashioned paper chains and organising the tree. He has the best part of the deal for I hate shopping, especially amongst the mad crowds on Christmas Eve.

I spot Patrick's car on the way back with my parcels and an extremely, heavy basket. Instinctively I fluster, what a mess I must look, tired and burdened. He has parked a couple of rows down from me, and I'm sure he must have seen my car. I smile in anticipation of a chance meeting, and after loading up I decide to sit and wait a while, watching families pile their cars high with exciting, brightly wrapped presents. The French wrap so beautifully at the point of purchase, such a brilliant idea that the British have never mastered.

I doze for a minute or two, feeling warm and comfortable in the car, at last a few moments of peace after all the rushing around during my day. As soon as I walk in the door at home I'll rejoin the chaos of my family Christmas with the twins working Ben up to a feverish level of excitement. I open my eyes as they walk past. They too are laden down, and as they pass they are deep in conversation, their bodies close as they stop beside their car. Patrick doesn't even glance towards me, not once, not at all. Surely he must know I'm here. I had not for one moment envisaged him shopping with Béatrice. How stupid I've been, how blind! He has of course painted the situation exactly how he wanted me to see it but I'm beginning to realise that his description of his relationship with his partner is possibly a long way from the truth. I want to go home now as quickly as possible, back to my family where I belong. I drive right past them, on my way out, and struggle to focus in the glare of the oncoming traffic in the dark, tears blurring my vision.

We speak only once over the festive period. One afternoon, when I find myself briefly alone while Philippe takes the children for a walk around the port to see his boat, I send him a text to say he can call. The children have been begging to look onboard *Naima* and with the owner away and most of the crew on leave, Philippe seizes the opportunity and takes them all, Marguerite and Yves as well. When I'm not with them, I know the dynamics of the group are different, for the older ones become more accommodating of the younger. Marguerite is altered in my absence, taking the twins proudly under her wing, as an older sister should. It's me holding the position of wife and mother that she hates and not my children.

I'm contrite and cold with Patrick when he calls me back. I don't explain why, I'm hurt and distrusting of him, and he is mystified and desperate. So be it, he deserves to suffer.

'What's the matter Elle?'

'Nothing.'

'I really need to speak to you.'

'You are.'

'No, I mean I need to see you.'

'Well it's not possible, is it?'

'What's the matter, is it just the pressure of Christmas and family?'

'My family are not a pressure,' I say defensively. 'I must go as Patrick's Mama is downstairs and she will be wondering where I am.'

'*Quand?* When can I see you?'

'When the holidays are over, maybe,' I say.

Patrick continues his texting, sometimes I answer and sometimes I don't, my mood is variable, swinging like a pendulum, for and against. The shop is open again but I don't need a delivery of packaging because I stocked up thoroughly before the rush. I have a birthday early in February, such a miserable time to celebrate. Why could I not have a mid-summer birthday when everyone is more in the mood? I'm convinced that having a birthday in February has cast a spell of melancholy over my whole life, for I so hate the winter, the short dark days and the cold. I think about birthdays spent basking in winter Caribbean sun. It rains incessantly on the coast here while the snow falls in the mountains above us, and the children and I are fractious in our imprisonment.

Patrick books a table out for my birthday dinner, which he does almost routinely, every year. The children's gifts amuse and enchant me. Ben offers me one candlestick, which should definitely be part of a pair and he has made me a sort of a rake at school, miniature, quirky and ornamental; a feat of his early engineering days, the forecast maybe of greater things to come. Marguerite gives me a trashy novel of the kind I never read, (I have only to look at the cover to know this), and Yves gives me nothing which is probably the most genuine gesture of them all. Zanne gives me money and I'm really grateful and declare immediately that I'll buy new boots. 'What do you need boots for?' Philippe asks. Such is the understanding of men in some instances. Patrick is in ignorance of my birthday, thank goodness or he might do something stupid like send me flowers. An innocent ticking bomb of colour surely destined to blow my life apart on my birthday.

The dinner starts well with Philippe being attentive and loving, but as the evening wears on, and the wine disappears from the bottle (never mind the two gin and tonics he had on arrival), he becomes argumentative and on the attack, picking as usual, on my most tender spot, my parenting skills. We walk home in silence; I'm blinking back tears. With a brief '*Bonne Nuit,*' to Zanne, causing the old lady to have her suspicions that all might not be well, I go straight upstairs to bed without a word to my husband. I can hear the low murmur of their voices below me, Zanne accusing and Philippe wriggling, but I no longer care. Birthdays! Just another day and another wine bottle to exacerbate the deep problems that lie beneath the surface of our marital ocean. I want to talk to Patrick, I want to cry long and hard on his shoulder, and feel his hand upon my hair.

It is Philippe's fault, I tell myself as I'm on my way to the apartment to meet Patrick on the next Monday when the children are in school. If he had been a bit kinder to me, I'd never have agreed to this rendezvous, however persuasive Patrick had been, and he had certainly seemed keen to see me.

I had come back downstairs, to look for Philippe, to cancel the bitter words and try and find a better end to my birthday, but he had raised his whisky glass to me and peered at me through the cut glass. '*Pourquoi?* Why did we marry, oh Elle mine? You never listen to a word I say or take my advice on anything.'

He was still in the same vein, so I turned and went to bed. He must have slept downstairs for I never heard him come up and in the morning he had disappeared to the bar probably for early coffee and a hangover cure.

Patrick is my sun on the horizon this Monday morning; he is the breeze that fills my sails with optimism. In reality there is no sun for the rain is falling horizontally, and the clouds are dense and grey. My footsteps echo the windscreen wipers endless rhythm on the cars that pass me, sending the spray high towards the bodies that trudge heads down, upon the pavement. I watch my feet, claiming independence from the rest of my body and my mind. The rain stings my face encouraged by the north wind. I could still turn round, but I know that would be impossible. My course is set. I rehearse how I will be, unhappy but controlled, not weepy. He's there already and the coffee steams on the small, wooden table that has listened to all our conversations here, in this borrowed place. When I see him everything changes. For the first time I want him closer to me, to feel his strength and protection. His aftershave envelopes me as I step off the edge of my world and into another.

Patrick raises his hands palms toward me, a silent signal for me to place my hands against his own. He links our fingers as he did before but this time he has a purpose, an end in sight, and he walks backwards leading me into the small bedroom behind the living room.

I allow him to undress me, and then I watch while he strips. He rarely takes his eyes from my own, as if he is looking for my

113

protestations, waiting for me to verbalise all the doubts that fly around in my head. But I stay silent, and he takes me forcefully with no thought of my pleasure, he is dominant and I fear him. I close my eyes to hide the greed in his own, and in this darkness I see only Philippe wearing the twisted countenance that the wine has stripped of all decency, his mouth releasing a stream of ugly words across the dinner table.

When Patrick is spent I rise, feeling slightly nauseous, and locking myself briefly in the bathroom, I wash and dress quickly.

'You could have lain with me a while, I want to talk to you,' he says.

'No, I should go home, I have things to do, and I will be missed.'

Full of remorse and confusion, I leave him then spread-eagled on the bed. A naked middle-aged man is not a pretty thing, and I marvel at the absence of his modesty. Glancing back as I go to the door, I see the stranger in him, a man who I still know nothing about, and my heart swings back towards the familiarity of my husband, suffocating me with sadness.

11

"And we were left alone
As love's own pair;
Yet never the love-light shone
Between us there!
But that which chilled the breath
Of afternoon
And palsied into death
The pane-fly's tune"

Thomas Hardy, *At an Inn*

Marguerite

I've kept the scrap of paper with the telephone number of the man who mistook me for Elle in my purse, so I can't possibly lose this precious item that fills me with suspicion. Although quite dogeared over time it is still legible, and I take it out now, smooth the creases carefully and scrutinise the digits, as if they can reveal the answer. The winning number that could quite possibly, if I'm right, remove my stepmother from our lives forever, and her brats will go with her too. Even better. I've made a plan to lay a trap, and all I need is the right window of opportunity. I know I have a chance today and I'm determined not to let such a perfect opportunity pass me by. I've even taken the day off school, I can catch up on the work, this is so much more important. I have to save my father before his life is ruined. I've already discussed the idea with my mother who immediately offered to assist me with undisguised relish. Although she discarded my Papa, she's not particularly happy with the fact that he has married someone younger, and who, she believes, is way more exciting than herself. She still wants to protect my father, after all they were married for ages and they have Yves and I to join them forever. Anyway I consider it her duty to help me to save Papa.

Ben has a hospital appointment in Nice and Papa has taken the day off work to accompany them. He has to see a consultant regarding his heart so the problem, (although not life threatening) is of quite a serious nature. Papa is completely unaware of my plans. I imagine, if I warned him, that he would be horrified and fiercely protective of Elle's virtue. Elle's virtue! That's a joke! I know all about her chequered history during the period of her life spent cooking on yachts and what I don't know I can easily guess. Everyone will soon realise what she is really like, she hasn't changed just because she has married a respectable man. I am reassuring myself, turning things over and over in my mind, until I'm absolutely certain I'm doing the right thing. My mother is coming for back up in case the man at the centre of the storm turns nasty when cornered. I bite my nails as I wait alone in the bakery for her. She finally arrives all bluster and foundation as usual.

'You don't need so much make up Mama,' I jump in to criticise. 'You actually look better with only a touch.'

'I am not here to listen to your personal comments, lets just get on with it,' she says obviously even more nervous than me, if that's possible.

'You can sit in the car if you want, I'll give you a shout if I'm in trouble.'

'No, I'll sit in the other room, you don't even know who this guy is after all.'

So saying she plonks herself in Elle's armchair in the living room. 'I recognise this chair, this used to be my chair!'

'Now is not the time to be worrying about past history, be

quiet will you while I call the number. It's no good if he hears you jabbering away in the background.'

'Calme toi,' my mother says, a comment which adds to the strain of the day, almost driving me to violence.

'Quiet now, I'm going to call.'

I dial and after a moment Patrick answers his mobile phone. 'Hello.'

I hesitate for a second, as he does not say more, how can I be sure it's him? Too late I must carry on regardless, I can't change tack now. 'C'est moi, Elle, I'm in trouble, you have to come, please, right now, quickly.'

Of course he won't doubt the identity of the caller, he didn't before so why should he now? My heart is beating hard and fast.

'What's the matter?'

'I can't tell you on the phone, just come, please ...'

'To the shop? Or to the house door?'

He obviously knows his way around then, I register this before replying.

'To the house door, I'll leave it on the latch.'

'Okay, see you shortly.'

I take a deep breath, and put the handset back in the slot. Now all I have to do is wait. I leave the front door ajar, hoping he will walk straight in, reinforcing his guilt.

Fifteen minutes pass, an eternity for us who are waiting.

Unsure of what he might find as he comes through the door Patrick calls out nervously. 'Il y a quel q'un ... is there anybody there?' Bewildered now he clears his throat, 'Elle!'

I wait hidden behind the sitting room door, I can see him through a crack as he pushes the front door to behind him, just as he turns back towards me I pounce. 'Elle isn't here!' I take two pictures of him on my phone, my hands shaking uncontrollably, before he has time to protest.

'I am Marguerite, Philippe's daughter. You remember Philippe? He's the man married to Elle, or have you forgotten

117

about him? I have proof, I know you are having an affair, you and my horrible, cheating stepmother!'

My mother peeps out. 'Ça suffit Marguerite! Let him go now.'

'Not before he explains himself. Come on Monsieur whoever you are!'

'My name is Patrick,' he says quietly and turning he walks out, slamming the door behind him.

'I'm going to call Papa.' I'm hot and red in the face in my triumph.

'You can't he's in the hospital with Elle and Ben,' states my mother firmly, 'and are you sure this proves they are having an affair? Any friend would react like in the same way to such a cry for help. Just think a while before you stir a hornet's nest and ruin everyone's lives. I expect he has children too, and there's Ben and the twins, they don't deserve this.'

'I've seen other signs; she's always out or on the phone when I get home. I have to tell Papa.'

My mother shrugs, 'I'm going home I want nothing to do with what you decide to do now, I have said my piece and supported you as far as I see fit. Just remember that your father loves Elle. Do try to put his happiness first and not your own.'

I slump down on a chair in the hall, humbled by my mother's words. The door closes with a soft click, and I listen to her heels striking the pavement as she walks away, testament to her strength of character.

I go over and over all the information I have gathered in a flustered frenzy. Is Elle guilty or not guilty? Best thing to do is to put all the evidence in front of my father and let him be the judge. Taking a deep breath, I dial my father's mobile. He answers immediately. 'Papa, it's Marguerite.'

'I know, your picture pops up as soon as you ring me.'

'Okay yes, I forgot.'

'What's the matter, you know I'm at the hospital with Elle and Ben.' He sounded put out already.

'Yes. Is she with you?'

'Not right now I just popped out to find some coffees.'

'Does she have her mobile with her?' It occurs to me that Patrick might try to contact Elle, to warn her or to collaborate on the story they would tell.

'I don't know! I doubt it, she hardly ever uses it. Why?'

'I did something Papa, there's this man that Elle knows and I called him pretending to be her and he came to the house. I think, well I'm sure, almost sure that she is having an affair.'

'What man? What on earth are you talking about? Just wait until we are home and then you can explain it all to me. We've had your games before and I don't like the sound of this one.'

'It's not a game Papa, I honestly believe she is having an affair behind your back.'

'I will hear you out when I'm home I promise. Right now I must support Ben.' Philippe presses the 'off' button and makes his way back through the corridors to where his small family are sitting, his head a whirl with unanswered questions.

Philippe sits back down beside me with some coffee for us. He looks strange and unnerved. 'Do you have your mobile with you?' What a peculiar question to ask me!

'No,' I reply, 'when do I ever have my mobile with me? That's a strange question.'

'Oh it's nothing, *rien*. Just something Marguerite said that's all.'

'Marguerite! When did you talk to Marguerite?'

'Just now, she rang when I was outside.'

My blood runs cold.

'We'll talk about it later,' says Philippe nodding his head in Ben's direction.

'Now I'm puzzled,' I say, looking at the floor, anywhere but at Philippe. Frightened, that's how he looks, frightened.

We drive home in silence. Ben, sensing the atmosphere, is for once subdued.

Marguerite and Yves are both there when we walk into the kitchen. Yves, standing with arms folded, greets his father but does not acknowledge me at all. He merely looks out of the window when I wish him bonjour, as if I have not addressed him at all.

I quickly turn to Ben, a mother's instinct, 'Run upstairs sweetheart, grownup talk,' I say and he disappears, released into the safety of his own room.

'*Putain,*' mutters Yves, looking directly at me now.

'That will do Yves, Marguerite please enlighten me as to what is going here exactly.' Philippe sits down in front of his two children, his face a mask of concern. 'Sit down cherie,' he motions to me to take the other chair.

'Don't call her that, you don't know who she is at all!' Yves raises his voice now.

Philippe ignores him. 'Please Marguerite, tell me everything that has happened because I'm more than a little confused as to what crime Elle is supposed to have committed, and I'm sure she is as well.'

'When I was here a couple of weeks ago,' Marguerite begins, purposeful now as she relates her testimony, 'I answered the phone, the landline in the kitchen, and it was a man who immediately mistook me for Elle.'

'What did he say?' Philippe asks.

'I don't really remember exactly what words he used but something like, "I need to speak to you," or similar, no, I know, he said he hadn't finished what he was saying, like he had been cut off before or something, anyway I thought it was weird, so I wrote the number down.'

'*Quand,* when did you say this was exactly, before Christmas? When I was away? When?'

'It must have been when you were away, yes, more like a few months ago than weeks.'

'Probably been going on for ages then,' Yves chips in.

Philippe ignores him, 'Carry on Marguerite. What else?'

'Then I overheard her a few times on the phone, sounded like she was talking to you, but she wasn't.'

'I wish you would all stop talking like I'm not here,' I interrupt fiercely. Patrick is a friend and work associate, that's all. Am I not allowed to have friends? Your father has friends that he works and drinks with, you don't monitor his phone calls nor do you ask who he meets up with in the Bar du Port.' I know I am becoming visibly distraught, and Philippe holds up his hand to silence me.

'Shhh Elle, let Marguerite finish what she has to say.'

'I kept the number and I called him today pretending I was Elle. I knew he would believe I was her. I asked him to come here, said I was in trouble. And he came, straight to the shop and walked in the front door. I took a photo of him on my phone.' Marguerite holds the picture up for her father and Yves to see.' Philippe barely glances at the image.

'What did he say?'

'Not much, he called out to Elle, thought she was here I suppose. I asked him his name and he said it was Patrick and then he just went back out, and slammed the door, behind him.'

'I am not sure that this escapade proves anything. Elle, where is your mobile phone?' Philippe looks at his wife and Marguerite can see the sadness etched on his handsome features. She was treading a tightrope between man and wife and she begins to wobble aware of the abyss below.

'On the shelf in the kitchen.'

'Fetch it please Marguerite.'

He scans through the numbers but there are none he does not

recognise and there are no stored messages or sent messages. 'Well this tells me nothing,' he says shaking his head. 'Absolutely nothing. It is unusual that he should come running over here when he believes you are in a spot of bother though. One would expect a wife to call her husband, not a work acquaintance if she were in trouble?'

'If we were having an affair he would have known that I was at the hospital with you and Ben today and not at home. Lovers know each others movements and friends do not. For goodness sake this is all ridiculous!'

'Let me see the picture again Marguerite.' He takes the phone. 'But I know this man, of course I do, you introduced me to him and his wife Béatrice at that party we went to in the summer.' He looks at me for confirmation.

'Like I said, but no-one seems to be listening to me, he is a friend, a supplier of cake boxes, someone who I see and talk to most weeks. This does not mean I am sleeping with him.' Close to tears now I leave the room to find sanctuary with my children.

'I'm not convinced that you are right at all Marguerite, although the truth will out in time, I'm sure.' Just leave me to think on everything now if you don't mind and I will talk to you both later.' The children leave the distraught, unhappy man who is their father, alone, and he pours himself a large pastis.

PART 2

Après

12

How could everything change so much after one single day?

I can't sleep at all tonight. Philippe lies as far away from me in the bed as he can, well that's how it appears to me. He must be almost falling out on the other side in his need to distance himself. I rise at four to go to the toilet, my stomach in turmoil from the days events; I think I might even be sick. Creeping downstairs, bent almost double clutching my tummy, I find my way, without turning on any lights, into the kitchen. I reach up into the box on the shelf, and thank goodness, my mobile is still there, apparently untouched, since I replaced it after Philippe's interrogation. Nervously I turn it on and the light from the small machine illuminates the whole corner of the room, filling me with the panic of discovery. My whole body shakes as I type three words. *"Don't txt me"*

I enter Patrick's number, I know it by heart, then press send, and lastly I open the 'sent messages file' and delete the copy. I check and double-check my phone for any sign of the text or Patrick's number. I will have to be meticulously careful not to incriminate myself still further. I turn the phone off and replace it. I hope Patrick will refrain from contacting me now, if only I'd successfully ended our liaison when I'd tried previously, we would not be in this mess. It's his fault, surely having mistaken Marguerite's voice for mine once before he should have been on his guard. And I had told him I would be at the hospital, typical man, he just simply hadn't listened.

I make a cup of tea and sit in the kitchen in the dark. There is a thin line of strength running through the turmoil of my mind, difficult to catch hold of, like a rope in a stormy sea. Sometimes I think I've found it, but then it slips out of my grasp and I plunge back into the sea-sickness of my stricken thoughts. Will Philippe leave me? Do I care if he leaves me? I hated the way they had spoken to me, all three of them, Marguerite, Yves and Philippe. Like I was a rebellious teenager, worse than that; a disgusting form of lowlife not worthy of a fair hearing or justice. Patrick will have no idea what I've been made to suffer. Béatrice is away on business so she will be completely ignorant of all the trouble. Will he even tell her? As far as I can see my life has been effectively smashed to smithereens in the last few hours and his hasn't changed one tiny scrap.

Bugger him and his insistent bloody phone calls ... I would never have phoned *his* house. He is pig headed and stupid. I kick the cupboard door that stands ajar where I'd taken out the tea bags and it slams shut with a bang. I don't care, I'm furious now, boiling over with an angry, frothing rage, like milk on the stove when I turn my back for a second, spilling out and soiling everything beneath.

'What on earth are you doing sitting down here in the dark?' Philippe has snuck into the kitchen and I'm so absorbed in my thoughts I haven't even noticed.

'No law against sitting in my own kitchen is there? And what are you doing creeping about? Trying to catch me doing something I shouldn't be perhaps?'

'Now there's no need for that.'

'How do you expect me to behave with you lot accusing me of all sorts of stuff I haven't done.'

'Why don't you come back to bed and we'll talk about it properly in the morning.'

'What's wrong with now? Patrick is my friend, Philippe, we talk sometimes, not everyday, he actually listens to me, which you never seem to anymore. He cares about me, as a friend would, which is why he jumped in his car to drive over here and see if I was all right when your daughter pretended to be me. How dare she play such a prank at my expense? You never put my feelings first, and you never, ever, put your daughter in her place when she is wrong.'

'You are being hysterical now, this isn't about Marguerite, it's about you and me and our marriage.'

'I'm not hysterical. I don't understand why I'm not allowed to have friends. Why do you lot have to make a friendship into something deceitful and sordid?' The lie comes easily to me. After all I'd tried to end the contact with Patrick before it went any further and we'd only been closer than friends on that one day which I whole heartedly regretted. And it's Philippe's fault, if he hadn't been so horrid to me on my birthday, it would never have happened. We would have remained friends, nothing more, and that's the truth I have decided to recognise and no other. If I was involved and in love with Patrick I'd have told Philippe, brought it all out into the open, but I'm not and that's that.

He covers his face with his hands as he sits at the kitchen table. He can hardly bear to look at me. 'So have you ever met him away from here? That's a fair question isn't it?'

'Not intentionally no.' Another lie.

'What do you mean, not intentionally?'

'I bumped into him one day when I was shopping and we sat down and had a coffee.'

'And where exactly did you "bump" into him?

'In Nice, I can't remember exactly when it was.'

'When I was away I suppose.'

'I expect so, yes.' I'm not enjoying this cross-examination.

'What did you talk about?'

'I don't remember. For God's sake Philippe it was ages ago.'

'I just wonder what you would find to talk about with a man like him.'

'What do you mean, "a man like him".'

'Oh come off it Elle, he's hardly your type.'

'And what is my type exactly? A man who swears at me when he's had too much to drink perhaps? A man who has struggled to support his wife and family and in fact still does not appear to have succeeded on that score.' I know this is below the belt but I can't help myself. After all I have had to put up with, feeding my own children and his as well, most of the time. This relentless questioning of my movements is so unfair, given the circumstances.

'So let me get this straight, you had a coffee with him and then he began to call you sometimes.'

'Yes, that's right. He has to call me one a week to take my order for the shop, so we would end up chatting. Nothing in particular, just about kids and work and stuff. He's interested in me, he doesn't have any other English friends.'

'Bully for him, I am so glad my wife has been selected for this service.'

'Now you are being flippant and silly.'

'This is not getting us anywhere Elle, I'm going back to bed.' He disappears, treading cautiously in his bare feet across the kitchen floor, but I sit there until the dawn breaks.

Nothing has been said for a few days, but Marguerite hangs around me, truanting from school and spying on me at every opportunity. Each time the phone rings she appears as if by magic and leans upon a door way, openly listening in to my conversation until I replace the receiver. I'm as nervous as a hunted animal in case Patrick should try and contact me. I try not to jump every time the phone or the shop bell rings, but my terror must be apparent. I float in limbo, it's difficult to work or concentrate on anything other than my own predicament and how it might eventually be resolved.

Philippe has brought the local paper home with him from work and pours over the property for rent section when he thinks I'm not looking, but I realise what he's doing. I've thought about what things would be like if he left me. I will be disgraced in the town. He will tell everyone that his wife has been sleeping around which simply isn't fair.

'I'm sure we can sort this out Philippe, if you can only trust me,' I say, but he won't answer me. He isn't ready, I can see that, he is still struggling to gather the facts and organise them to find the truth. Then, I guess, he will be ready to make his decision.

I read Ben's diary. It peeps invitingly at me from its hiding place amongst the rubbish under his bed. I've never looked at it before, but I have to now. The thought that I might be upsetting the children worries and distresses me more than anything else. I don't give a stuff about Philippe, it's the children that matter. I pull it out wiping the cover with my hand. So deliciously scruffy, sticky from busy fingers always covered in glue, paint or oil from his bike. I hug it to me and inhale the scent of his boyishness. Not many entries but there was one just yesterday. *"Marguerite told me that Mummy is in love with another man, not Philippe, she doesn't love him anymore. I wonder if he will leave us all alone. I don't want a new Daddy."*

That thoughtless cow of a girl hadn't needed to say anything until all is sorted out one way or another. How could she? I wipe one of my own tears from the cover before I carefully replace the little book under the bed.

Patrick rings the shop pretending to be a customer in a silly, badly disguised voice, in case he falls upon Marguerite again.

'I know it's you,' I say. 'I told you not to contact me.'

'For one, I had to be careful in case your stepdaughter was on phone duty, and secondly, you said don't text, nothing about not phoning you.'

'Don't you think you have caused enough trouble with your stupid, thoughtless calls, you have no idea what's been going on here. I've been made to feel like a wicked criminal. I'm not eating or sleeping.'

'That's why I called, I'm worried about you.'

'It's a bit late for that. You knew I wouldn't be here on that day, you fell in her trap like an imbecile and I have nothing to say to you.'

'Listen, I have to tell Béatrice before someone else does. She is coming back tomorrow. I don't know how she will behave, she might come and see you.'

'And what, exactly, do you intend to tell her?'

'That we are friends, the same as I presume you have told Philippe.'

'Well, that's certainly all we are except for one bad error of judgment, and now I doubt if we are even that. I certainly want no more to do with you.'

'Thanks, how cheerful of you.'

'I mean it, you have no idea what it's like for me here, and the children are already suffering because of your foolishness. Now leave me alone.' I throw down the handset, and sit on a stool in the kitchen with my head in my hands. I should try to repair things with Philippe. But then again, there is another door beside me that slides into my consciousness, a hazy, dream-like door. When I push it and peep through the widening crack I can see a path and feel my feet walking through alone. I can imagine the burden of my troubled marriage being totally lifted from my shoulders leaving me free to find my way on, with my children close behind me. Should I embrace this image that grows clearer by the hour?

I have dislodged some slates from the roof of our marriage for sure by befriending Patrick, but had not the rain already been leaking through I'd never have looked twice at him. Philippe belittles me and makes me feel so worthless. I'm desperately in need of establishing my own identity again. I have found myself, my own true voice sounding in my ears when I'm in Patrick's company.

Moreover, I'm horrified that Philippe's own misdemeanours within our marriage can be washed away by the incoming tide of my own, one small mistake. I'll be cordial with Philippe and wait. His children are merely venting the pent up anger they were unable (for obvious reasons) to release upon their own mother, when she had first betrayed their father. They are damaged kids. Yes, I will wait, things will calm and settle in time.

Béatrice comes, she rings the doorbell on a Sunday morning and Philippe answers, ushering her through to the kitchen, guiding the tall french woman by the arm, as if she were a patient convalescing from some terrible accident, and only he will know the right words to comfort her. My nerve weakens in the presence of this poised, self-assured person, standing, glaring at me from the other side of my kitchen island. My husband is no help either, glancing at Béatrice with the lowered eyes of one who has suffered a mortally wounding blow to the heart.

'We can talk about this in French or English which ever you prefer,' she says in perfect English, immediately revealing her control over the situation in one simple sentence. 'What exactly is the relationship between you and Patrick? Friends, lovers? I think we have a right to know as I am sure you will agree this detail affects all of our lives from this moment on. I have been away working and now I come back to this … this, what can I call it, revelation?' She is not aggressive, or even sad in her deliverance, only direct and forthright. A woman in search of the truth, in order that she might react accordingly, correctly.

I try to keep it simple. 'We are, or should I say, we were friends. We chatted about work and customers, it's a relief to have someone to have a good moan to once in a while, instead of always boring one's spouse with everything. I am sorry he came rushing over here. As I expect you know, I wasn't even here so I had nothing to do with the whole sorry thing. Blame Marguerite and her games. None of this would be happening if she hadn't started playacting.'

Philippe looks out of the window at the mention of his daughter's name.

I continue, 'I bumped into Patrick one day in Nice and we sat down for a coffee. Was that such a crime?'

'Patrick never mentioned anything about that, he said he had never seen you anywhere but here, perhaps he thought it unimportant, or maybe he thought it would imply a more serious relationship, who knows. Anyway we are going away for a few days together to talk it over and I would like you to stop buying from us, or having any communication with Patrick or the company.'

'That's a bit drastic isn't it? Losing my business over nothing?'

'It doesn't feel like nothing,' Béatrice replies and shaking Philippe's hand she takes her leave.

It appears to me to be an extraordinarily unlikely coincidence when Patrick jumps into the front seat of my car as I fill up with petrol one evening after work.

'How did you know I was here? Have you been following me? I don't want to see you or be seen with you either.' I am outraged.

'I have to talk to you, to know what's happening.'

'What do you mean, what's happening? My marriage is in tatters and my husband interrogates me from dawn 'til dusk, that's what's happening. And how about you?'

'We are going away to talk about it for a few days just Béatrice and I.'

'I know.'

'How do you know?'

'Béatrice came to see me.'

'She hasn't said anything about it, what did she say?'

'She wanted to know what we are or were to each other. And all that stuff you told me about your separate lives and how you are like brother and sister, if that were indeed true then she wouldn't care who you were friends with. Nothing adds up about your version of the situation, and you have successfully turned me into a home wrecker!'

Patrick skillfully avoids answering my accusations. 'Philippe would never make you happy anyway. Really, I believe I may have done you a huge favour.'

'Well thanks a lot, it doesn't exactly feel like that from where I'm sitting.'

Patrick rolls down the passenger window as we sit in the glare of the early evening sun. 'Things will settle down, you'll see.'

'Where are you going for your romantic healing weekend?'

'I don't know Béatrice has booked something. If I didn't know you better I might suppose you are jealous.'

'You are quite wrong; jealous is not the right word, disgusted maybe. Now please go and leave me alone, I need to be at home with my children.'

With a smirk, which irritates me past bearing he lunges across to try and kiss my cheek but I catch his intention and push him hard away from me. He climbs awkwardly out of my small car and walks away without a backward glance. I find myself trembling with anger and fear. I drive home dangerously, pre-occupied with all that Patrick has said. Philippe is watching out for me from the shop window and he comes out to meet me as I am parking the car.

'Where have you been?'

'To fill the car up at the supermarket, I've only been gone ten minutes!'

'Why is the window open on the passenger side, you have been with him haven't you? You picked him up and drove somewhere.'

'Don't be so utterly ridiculous, I haven't picked anyone up from anywhere, I was hot in the car that's all.' I thought later that if Philippe hadn't been so furiously angry and quick to jump to conclusions, I might have told him the truth, but his attitude sent me spinning away from revealing what had actually happened. 'If you don't trust me at all and are going to keep interrogating me day in and day out, you may as well go and rent somewhere to live with Marguerite as she could do with your full attention. Maybe we will try again later when both of you have gotten over your phobia of me running off with other men.'

'You really mean that don't you.'

'Yes Philippe, sadly I do.' I take my bag from the car, and go straight indoors. I have the impression that the residents of the whole street have listened in to our conversation and my ultimate dismissal of my husband.

14

"Never love anybody that treats you like you're ordinary."

Oscar Wilde

For a while I can think of nothing except how I long to go back to sea again. Of course I will never leave the children, but I long to sit alone staring at the movement of grey waves all around me, with only the horizon and the weather for company. I frequently drag Ben to the beach, wintery as it is, so that I can gaze out to sea. The need to escape is so great it brings tears to my eyes, the sea adsorbs all of the emotional storm inside me and tosses it free in the spray.

The time it takes for Philippe to grasp that I have actually asked him to leave turns into a painful eternity. The questioning continues, but with less ferocity now a decision has been reached. It really doesn't matter about the details anymore. Philippe is never going to be able to trust me again. Even if he does believe in me, he still has nagging doubts which are continually reinforced in his ear by his children, and anyway there's a list of reasons why I yearn to be on my own again. I can't wait for him to go.

I have talked to my three about the situation. We went for a walk along the beach one evening, wrapped up warmly against the chilly night air.

'It's cold,' grumbled Frannie, who was never inclined to walk.

'Be much colder if we were in England, probably snowing,'

said Ben, 'but we aren't,' he finished, with the ingenuous logic of a seven, nearly eight year old.

'Would you mind, you three, if it were just us again?'

'What do you mean?' asked Ben.

'I mean if Philippe were to go and live with Marguerite and Yves in another house for a while, maybe not forever, but to give us a break, some space, to be just us again.'

'Whatever makes you happy Mum,' said Flo and I loved her more than I thought possible in that moment, when she could have said any number of things which might have made me question the decision I'd already made. Flo was the more mature of the twins, still a child in many ways but with profound flashes of the woman she would become. The twins ran laughing down to the water and back, the wind blowing through their thick, brown hair, their father's hair and as they came back towards me, I saw him again in their smiles, and gaiety. I knew in that split second that with me alone they would have a happier foundation for the successful people they were destined to become, coupled with the ability to form normal relationships. They had never been cast adrift, unloved, like I'd been as a child. Why I persisted in trying to find a father for them, I'll never know. I thought I needed a man when of course I was perfectly self sufficient, always had been and always would be. I was capable of being everything to my children even though I acknowledged that at times, life would be hard.

'Will we still have a shop and do fun things?' said Ben.

'Of course we will, in fact I will have more time to think of fun things to do when I don't have to cook for everyone anymore, only us.'

'Of course it's fine Mum and I shall be the man of the house.' Ben puffed out his chest and Frannie, annoyed at his smug superiority in claiming this new role, ran at her brother and walloped him on the stomach with her fist.

'Ha, didn't hurt so there,' teased Ben.

'Shhh you two, none of that now. Let's go home and not a word to Philippe or the others, we must let things happen and settle without anymore cross words because there have been enough of those just lately.'

'We didn't hear any,' said Frannie.

'Well good,' I replied.

It's nearly May before Philippe finds a house to live in with his children. The search has been made more difficult by the pressure of his work, with his short absences to Monaco for the Grand Prix and then to Cannes for the film festival, and finally the deadline of his imminent departure for the summer season cruising. I overhear Amelie trying to reason with him, to persuade him to work at saving the marriage.

'*Si elle avait un copain* ... if she did have a boyfriend for a short while, does it really matter? Could you not put the whole business behind you and build on the strong parts of your marriage? I'm sure Claude was seeing someone years ago, but we managed to repair the hole and carry on, we are only human, these things happen and you were away so much last year.'

'You don't understand Amelie ... she wants me to move out, she doesn't want me to stay at all, so there is your answer. Maybe she will take me back when Marguerite makes a life of her own but that certainly won't be for some time yet. Elle wants to be on her own.'

'Are you sure she doesn't want to be with this other man?'

'Time will tell.'

I move away from behind the shutter from where I could hear every word of their conversation in the street outside. Anger wells from the depths of me again at his last insinuation that I might be hankering after Patrick or even worse, planning a life with him. Of course I'm not, he had it right the first time, I want to be as he had said to Amelie, "on my own".

The days are strained with little intimacy left between us. At last Philippe finds a property and on the May bank holiday, he moves out with his daughter. He leaves on a wonderful, sunny May Day when all the women who are loved receive Lily of the Valley from their spouses and partners. I have no contact with Patrick during this time. He tries to call me occasionally but as soon as I realise it's him I hang up. My anger towards him has mellowed because thanks to him I have my impending freedom from Philippe, looming in front of me like a far-reaching view with a solid blue sky.

I begin to pack Philippe's trinkets in cardboard boxes whilst he's at work and their disappearance is liberating, the house breaths again as though spring cleaned of all the tensions that have passed between us since our hasty marriage three years ago.

Amelie and Claude watch with sad eyes but refrain from passing further comment to either of us, not wishing to support one side against the other and I respect them for their stoicism.

Daniel comes to see me in the shop and I'm so relieved to see someone I can ask about what is happening in the other camp; behind the walls of *Le Carteaux Blanc*. I am desperate to know for secretly I want Patrick to suffer as I have done.

'Everything seemed normal,' he says, 'until one day last week when all hell broke loose.'

'What do you mean, what happened?' I'm impatient for details.

'Well, I saw Béatrice come out of the house with a cup of tea for Patrick, next thing I knew she had thrown it all over him and smashed up his office.'

'What on earth pushed her to behave like that when only a few weeks ago they were off staying in a hotel somewhere trying to sort themselves out.'

'I'm not sure, she must have found something to incriminate

138

him or heard some gossip, who knows. Anyway, they weren't getting along before but now they're not even speaking.'

'It can't be my fault, I have done everything I can to avoid any further contact with him.'

'Don't worry about it, I'm sure it will blow over in time. I heard your Philippe is moving out?'

'Yes but that situation isn't just because of my friendship with Patrick, it's about our own in-house problems too. It's difficult with second families. Neither of us realised that our marriage would not be exclusively about us. I'm sad but I'm happy to be on my own with my three, all the stress just vanishes when he's not here.' I feel relieved talking to Daniel about it all, somehow he seems to understand or maybe he's just a good listener. After all I've no one else to open up to, no one who is impartial or uninvolved. I wonder if Patrick speaks to anyone in a similar fashion. Somehow I doubt that he would, he is a complete loner. He has spoken to me about many things that he said he has not shared before. I know that for a fact.

The days are strange. Dislocated. The first Saturday night without Philippe beside me, I sleep fitfully, wrapped in crisp new linen. I have rearranged our bedroom, mine now, a man free zone, fresh and clean. When I look in the wardrobe I see only my own clothes. Philippe, who had said when he moved in that on no account must his shirts become muddled amongst my dresses, now has his wish. I imagine his things in another place, a room I've never seen. I stare intently for a moment or two at the photos I have of us on our wedding day and then placing them carefully face to face, I wrap an old T shirt around them and put them in the bottom of the wardrobe. Away out of sight.

I dream briefly between long periods spent longing for sleep to take me. A spider on a saucer, but when I look more closely it is a toad, and then a kitten, small and grey with playful paws. Philippe has always said no pets to my children who had cravings for anything small and furry. Now they can have whatever they want, I will indulge them in the fresh fabrication of our altered household. I creep around the house at dead of night just because I can, and I want to cry at the sight of my peaceful, sleeping children. Quietly, I smooth bedclothes and gather toys and discarded clothes as I go, lest I should wake them.

Marguerite and Yves are gone forever too, I never want to see either of them again. I will redecorate the rooms they've used as soon as I can, to erase all trace of them. The cloying, sweet smell of Marguerite's make up bag lingers, haunting me with unimaginable terrors both for myself and for the children. I know, without a doubt, that I have done the right thing.

Waiting for sleep I count the restrictions Philippe has placed on me. He has trodden upon my creative spirit; I want to paint and draw, to write a book, maybe even two, but he has always dismissed my ideas. "No time for all that", he'd said, crushing any creative urges I might choose to nurture. Our union has always been flawed; I can see that now. Our increasing misery has become like a dense fog in which we have lost each other and ourselves. That was probably why I reached out to someone like Patrick, I needed a friend for guidance to help me escape but I never wanted or intended to take a lover. "Out of the frying pan and into the fire," inadvertently, that was what had happened. I should have been wiser and not involved anyone else, I understand now. I will keep well away from Patrick and not involve him further in my new life.

On the Sunday morning of the first weekend of my freedom as a single parent, two things happen. Patrick sends me a text ... *"How are you, I hear nothing from you and you don't answer my texts, I miss you xxx"*

I decide to ignore this and delete it without a second thought. I am standing with the phone still in my hand when the second thing happens. Philippe walks in announcing that he has come back for breakfast because he has nothing else to do. He looks at me and raises his eyebrows. 'Were you about to call someone?' he says.

'No,' I say, flustered, and I know he has not missed the blush that rises in my cheeks.

It's hardly fair surely, this popping back to spy on me. Well, this is was what I suspect him of doing. He just doesn't trust me. I make coffee and we sit as we have always done at the kitchen table and it's as if we have entered a time warp sending us back to the beginning again. Perhaps all the pain we have experienced will have to be re-suffered, the wound reopened and cleansed afresh before we can move on separately.

Frannie appears, dazed with sleep and solemnly looks from one of us to the other.

'*Tu es toujours ici?*' she asks Philippe, claiming the chair next to him. 'I thought you lived somewhere else now.'

'*Bien sur,*' I say, 'he does, cherie, he does, he just came back for breakfast, that's all.'

Frannie accepts this explanation and disappears into the sitting room with a bowl brimming with cereal.

'You see,' says Philippe, 'you let them do exactly as they please. She's walking around with a plate of food when she should be sat up to the table.'

'Don't even start on the subject Philippe, it's not a good idea for you to keep coming back so early in our separation, not for the children, and most certainly not for me.'

'I shall be away cruising in a couple of weeks anyway, so then you will be able to do exactly as you please.'

I ignore this comment. 'Until we can talk sensibly about things without having a row, I think it best that you stay away and focus on setting up your home with Marguerite.'

'Perhaps you're right,' he says pushing back his chair with a harsh squeaking sound upon the wooden floor. 'I'll go then, see you sometime.' He leaves, his last comment having been delivered with a trace of the harsh bitterness I knew so well.

There are tears in my eyes as I clear the table of our cups. It's all about spaces really. You let someone into your space and then when things go badly you push them out and away from your precious inner sanctum. The separation was never going to be easy for either party. I'll miss having someone to bounce off, to discuss ideas with, or will I? Philippe never listens anyway, and if he does he always comes up with answers I don't really want to hear. I'd fallen ill on our three-day honeymoon in Italy, with chronic food poisoning, a bad omen right from the start. He had been so inconsiderate, stuffing himself with food and wine in front of me every day when I felt ready to die. And Ben had cried for the whole time having been left with Amelie and Claude. How could I have done that to my son, and all for nothing in the end? A waste of all those tears and all that emotion. If only I could erase everything, rub out the whole marriage, like chalk upon a board.

Kneeling in front of the cabinet in the living room, I search through my old CDs that I've not looked at since my marriage. Carefully selecting one, I place it in my old player, dusty and abandoned beneath the television. Turning the volume up loud, I return to the kitchen to plan my day off with the children.

The twins emerge from upstairs, driven from their room by their mother's invasive music.

'This is not like you usually are Mama,' said Flo, her eyes narrow with confusion.

'Yes but it is, my darling,' I say, 'this is me again, just as I always was before.'

'Before what?' says Frannie burrowing for a biscuit.

'Oh I'm not sure really, before Philippe was here, I suppose.'

'I like it just us.'

'Bless you both,' I say, as I bend to kiss my daughters' dark heads.

The music takes me back to finding my way lit by the moon, the path toward a rolling horizon, waves encircling and protecting my Sea Witch self, buried deep within my soul.

The spring is turning into summer but not without some unseasonal heavy rain in-between the blasts of welcome hot sun that May days in Provence bring. I notice that the gutter must be blocked on the back of the house as rain is flooding down the kitchen window and seeping in onto the sill. Annoying house, always presenting me with problems anew; fix one and another appears. There is nothing I can do but try and solve the problem myself as the window cleaner isn't due to come and clean the gutters for weeks. After I close in the afternoon, the rain has abated so I take the long ladder out of the shed and prop it against the wall. I thought later, after the events of the next few moments that my ability to pay normal care and attention to my own safety is probably impaired by my frame of mind. I have, after all, been through a lot in the last couple of months.

The end of the ladder slips out and backwards on the slightly damp slabs of the mossy patio and I fall heavily onto the ground, still clutching the ladder. I scramble to my feet, muttering to myself. 'I am all right, I am all right,' But of course I know I'm probably not, and I sit dazed and quiet now on one of my garden chairs.

Ben's head pops out around the back door. 'You ok mum? I heard a crash.'

'Yes, I sort of fell a bit, I'll be fine in a minute.'

He looks at me and then at the ladder lying on the patio as if adsorbing the possible sequence of events and then he comes over and puts his arms around me.

I begin to cry, shock and pent up emotion drowning me all at once. 'Oh Mum, don't cry, are you sure you're all right, nothing broken?' he says, the child becoming the carer in the face of his weeping mother.

'Yes, it's a bit of everything I think, shock perhaps,' I try to reassure both of us, 'my back hurts quite a lot though.'

'Maybe you should be checked out, I'll call Philippe on his mobile and he can take you to the hospital.'

'I'm not sure, you should ... well maybe yes then, it's an idea.' I think that actually the presence of my husband in this instance might be comforting and surely he wouldn't mind taking me.

Ben runs indoors and comes back a few minutes later during which time I try to move off the chair, crying out in pain as I move. The middle finger on my left hand is definitely broken, having somehow become trapped in the ladder, although I can't remember the falling bit however hard I try to reconstruct my descent.

'He says he's busy because Marguerite is cooking him supper and he has just poured a beer, and is it really urgent.'

'Bloody marvelous.' My well being has been tossed aside in favour of a beer and a plate of food. 'Well, could you tell him, politely of course, that I may have broken something and I need his help. Just this once to get to the hospital.'

Out he comes again. 'He says he will be there in a minute.'

I have begun to shiver uncontrollably. 'Fine, can you make help me a cup of tea with two sugars while we wait and don't say anything to alarm the girls.'

'Of course I can and of course I won't. I'm not a kid anymore you know. Why don't you come indoors and lie on the sofa?'

I half walk, half crawl to the old sofa in the kitchen. I am worried for the children, they will never comprehend that inevitably sometimes I can fall ill, or be injured in some way, rendering me incapable of performing my motherly tasks. Their routine destroyed, they will look at me with worried faces, mostly concerned for themselves, this is nature's way. I lie there to wait and find myself dropping in and out of sleep. I am second best again. I should have guessed the outcome of contacting Philippe and I wish now I hadn't made such a plainly obvious cry for help. His beer growing warm and uninviting, alongside not disappointing his wonderful daughter on her first culinary attempt has to be more important than his wife tumbling off a ladder, of course! I'm playing right into his hands by summoning him at the first hurdle. He had shouted at me the night before he left. *"Vous ne serez jamais gérer sans moi"*, (you will never manage without me) and now, oh horror of horrors I'd already proved him right. In the first few hours of starting afresh on my own. I can imagine his satisfaction. "I told her she wouldn't manage and it's obvious now that she can't". Only this once, for I swear I will never bother him again.

Philippe is distant and impatient to dump me at the hospital and leave me. I succeed in persuading him to wait, assuring him that being checked over will not take long. They strap my broken finger tightly to the next one, instructing me to keep it bound for protection and strength. There isn't much they can do for fingers apparently. My back, (which hurts like hell) they said is fine, but that I should see her doctor if I have any concerns. By now I'm shaking with misery and shock and wish I'd stayed at home on the sofa. The whole hospital idea had been a mistake.

'Will you be all right now, *je dois mon aller.*' Philippe is literally jumping from foot to foot in his urgency to return to his newfound domesticity with his daughter.

'Yes, off you go, don't worry about me.'

'Now don't get nasty and sarcastic.'

'I'm not, I'm serious, I want you to go. I'm sorry I bothered you.'

He studies me intently for a second and then he leaves. I

expect him to say something but he doesn't, he just goes out closing the door unusually quietly as if he doesn't want to draw attention to his departure. Guilt perhaps? I immediately lay my head back and drift into a healing doze, where the throbbing of my finger becomes a background noise, not unlike the ticking of the kitchen clock.

13

"Unrequited love is a ridiculous state, and it makes those in it behave ridiculously."

Cassandra Clare

I feel ill, downcast and pathetic. All of the fiercely optimistic spirit I'd had before the fall has disappeared in a cloud of vulnerability. It hurts to stand up, even more to sit down and my finger makes the baking almost intolerable. Somehow I have to pick myself up and ride this storm to a better place. Surely I've been through worse? Somehow I can't remember anything as bad as this mental and physical onslaught. Philippe's departure had seemed a good thing, and a positive step forward but since the ladder incident I've slipped back from the starting line of my new life.

My mobile phone lies abandoned in its plastic tray. Sometimes in the last few days I've examined the blank, black face, my finger almost pressing the power button. I was tempted and nearly succumbed but then I think about Patrick, triumphant at last as his message status changes from sent to received. He would know of course and resume bombarding me with texts just as he had done in the past. I certainly don't want that, I must be careful not to encourage him in any small way. Our friendship is over.

The bell gives a welcoming tinkle and I drag my aching limbs from the kitchen to the shop, summoning a smile as I walk.

Patrick stands there and the shock makes my legs weak.

'Why are you here? I don't want you to come into my shop,' I am furious that he should have the audacity to intrude uninvited, but I'm aware that I sound like a petulant child.

'I came to make sure you are okay after the tumble you took. *Je m'inquiete tu sais.*'

'Well you needn't worry, I'm fine. How did you know I fell anyway or is it common knowledge? Am I being laughed at because not only have I lost my husband, but also because I'm making such a poor job of managing without him? Gossip material on street corners I expect. You can go away, I don't need either of you.'

'Is Philippe gone?' (Does he not know? I can scarcely believe he is totally ignorant of my change in circumstance.) 'You don't look too good, in fact when did you last wash your hair properly?'

'I have one hand almost out of action and the rest of me is shaky but I will be better in a few days. Now please leave me in peace and go back to your perfect life. I hope, no I expect, you have managed to lie your way out of any problems with Béatrice, and I sincerely wish you the best of luck.' Angry now, I leave the shop for the sanctity of my kitchen and after a few tense moments, in which I do my best to compose myself, I hear him leave.

I decide to go to the hairdresser after work, a hasty decision but an idea that immediately improves my frame of mind. Having asked Amelie to pop round and sort Ben out after school, (she too agrees that it's an extremely good plan for me to treat myself) I make my way across the town to be pampered for an hour or so.

Is it my imagination or does the Madame on the desk, whom I have known for years, appear distant with me? My mind runs riot. Do they all know? Even down to the young girl who sweeps the floor and gathers the towels? I am overcome with shame and try not to meet their eyes for fear of seeing their perfectly justified condemnation. Perhaps Béatrice is a customer here and has told them that her husband has cheated on her with *L'Anglaise* at the English cake shop. I can hardly wait to be home, behind closed doors with the reassurance of my small, loyal family to comfort me.

About a week later, I find the first bunch of pinks, propped carefully in the crate alongside the milk on the step. Of course I know immediately that Patrick must have put them there and the first lot does not worry or annoy me at all, I simply carry them indoors and finding a vase set them on the table in the kitchen without a second thought. When the second bunch appears the next morning, it dawns on me that he is playing some sort of game. Trying to prompt a reaction perhaps, as I have still refrained from turning on my phone, for fear of his endless, pleading messages. Pinks, a cruel choice of flower. Had I told him that my mother used to grow and sell them in the days when my parents were still together? Their scent is a key for memories of precious, happy childhood days before my father left us.

If I hadn't approached the front door early that Friday morning to retrieve the milk, I probably would not have noticed the figure hovering on my doorstep. Even through the mottled glass I know it's him, distinguishable by his body mass and the turned up collar on his shirt. A split second decision is the wrong one. I'm torn in my mind by the proximity we've shared as friends, but as I open the door a crack and he jams it further open with his knee against it, I'm sharply reminded of his brutal, and clumsy penetration of my body, and I began to tremble with anger.

'Please go away, I don't want to see you and I don't want your flowers.'

'That's not like you, how different you are from the girl I used to know.'

'I'm not different at all. I am on my own now, and somehow

149

I see everything more clearly. I want to be left alone, in peace with my children, to move on from everything that has happened, so you can take your flowers and go away!' I shove the door hard, a desperate summoning of my strength that takes him by surprise and he sways back allowing me to retake control and slam the door with him on the outside. I lean on a stool in the kitchen, struggling to stop alternating tremors of fear and fury from overcoming me in waves.

Peeping out I can see he is still standing on the doorstep. I must wait for him to go. I have to see the van go on past up the road before it will be safe to venture into the shop or the hall. It is true of course, I can see things more clearly now, without Patrick in the equation, my marriage breakdown becomes completely the result of my unhappiness with Philippe and nothing to do with any infidelity with a third party, because in my mind there has been none. Well, almost none, certainly nothing serious enough to part us if we truly love each other. But I don't love Philippe, I know that for certain. I'd known before I married him, that was the silliest thing, I had just been carried along by a sequence of events and the desperation of having three children who I thought needed a father, which of course they didn't. I can cope perfectly well, and it's easier financially too.

How beastly it is to have to hide like this, for fear of him trying to force his way in again. How dare he behave as if he has the right to come into my house? If I continue to keep out of his way, and not to respond to his attention in any way, he will give up in the end, I'm sure of it.

The pinks carry on appearing day after day, their sweet smell, not unlike cloves, which used, touchingly to remind me of my mother, now makes me feel slightly sick and I begin to throw them away. Bunch after bunch.

I hadn't bargained on his taking advantage of the quiet hour or so when people were relaxing after lunch either. Many of the shops close for siesta between one and four but I keep fairly

British hours in my shop so I can finish work when the children return from school.

Patrick just walks in as pleased as punch with himself one Thursday afternoon, requesting in a stupidly affected, polite voice if he might order a filled baguette.

'I thought we had agreed you wouldn't come here,' I say, trying to sound confident and dismissive but now he is in front of me, it's far from easy.'

'I am just a customer like any other,' he says, 'or is that not allowed. Do you not want custom anymore.'

'Now you are being ridiculous. *Bete en fait,* stupid in fact!' Can you not see the sensible thing is to leave me alone, after all the trouble our friendship has caused.'

'I don't see why we can't carry on being friends like we were before. Or am I too inferior to be the friend of the high and mighty English woman, perhaps that's the answer?'

'I would just like you to go away, you know I am on my own here in the afternoon, you are just taking advantage of the situation and that's not fair.'

'It's not fair that you should have changed into a horrible person. What happened to the girl I met first of all? I keep hoping she might come back.'

'I haven't changed at all.' I'm quickly beginning to understand that our talking is a waste of time and energy. A completely non-productive argument that will achieve absolutely nothing.

'If you don't leave now I shall go outside and stand in the road until you do, because I don't want to stay in here in your company for one moment longer.'

'Now who is being stupid?' He takes a large step towards me and I take a step firmly back. I suspect for one awful moment, that he will attempt to touch me.

'I'm the only sensible one here, now go … before the children come home. They don't need any more heart break than they have suffered already.'

151

Patrick stands his ground, leaning on my counter, which serves to infuriate me even more. When he had attempted to force his way in early in the morning, while the streets were deathly quiet, I had felt frightened of him, but now in this scenario, although there were not many people around during the early afternoon, I'm braver. I'm frustrated and cross that this man encroaches on my personal space and can be so stubborn as to refuse to leave when I ask.

I push past him and go out of the door, leaving it ajar to facilitate his departure, and I stand there leaning on the frontage of my shop. Should anyone question my motive for such bizarre behaviour I'm quite ready to say, "there is a man in my shop who refuses to leave". I don't have to wait long for a customer and Patrick comes out as he enters. After giving me a grimace, he turns to go. 'If you do this again I will call the gendarme,' I tell him to his retreating back.

'You just you try it,' he says.

The flowers continue to appear, almost everyday. Sometimes he misses a day and I hope he has abandoned the idea. Surely he must have work to do? His early morning habit of frequenting my doorstep must eventually become wearisome and pointless. But no, with only the occasional respite he carries on. I have learnt to lie low at the predicted hour of the morning when he might appear, switching off lights in the shop and hallway so that if he tries to peer in he cannot see me. I know I shouldn't have to live with this constant early morning fear. And then there are the afternoons when I pray for the shop to be busy to discourage him from entering my door, where he will surely make a fool of himself when I ignore or dismiss him abruptly in front of my customers.

I attempt to discuss the situation with close friends but they are disinclined to believe me, with responses that are both bewildering and unsupportive.

"You are imagining things ... exaggerating surely ... flowers everyday? You should be so lucky," or, "I know of him and his wife ... he's a family man who works hard to look after his own, he would never behave like that." Such are their attitudes that I begin to wonder if I am indeed seeing things out of all proportion. And then he breaks in through my back gate.

Admittedly the gate was a trifle rickety and not hard to force but he has broken the lock completely, probably I imagine, by placing his shoulder in a sideways charge, like the bull that he resembles.

I stand, silent in open-mouthed stupefaction, when I first behold the hanging basket of enormous proportions that he has placed upon my dustbin. He has removed the domed lid so that the round array of plants can sit squarely wedged in the top of the bin, with ivy and other trailing plant species dangling most decoratively down the sides. It is, without a doubt, the most luscious and cleverly planted basket that I've ever seen. It is also incredibly heavy and I have not the faintest idea what I should do for the best, as it would certainly be a shame to destroy such a magnificently contained garden. There is nowhere really to place it around the back of the house and by hanging it over the front of the shop, will I not be rewarding him with enormous satisfaction? I consider the problem for a while. I heave the basket around to the front and by standing on a chair, I manage to hang the chains firmly on the hook above the shop door. If anyone asks about it, (as they surely will) I will say I bought it from a garden centre near Nice. Well, I could have done exactly that, my story is entirely plausible and needs no further discussion. Watering it is a bit of a trial, but the flowers look wonderful. Yet there's no denying that the arrangement is rather oversized for the purpose of adornment over my shop door.

Amelie is the first to comment and it's obvious to me that my explanations about the origins of the basket are not well received, nor entirely believed either. The atmosphere between us has been strained since Philippe left, not cold exactly but it is almost as if neither of us dare to mention his name. Amelie is, standing on the fence between her two dear friends, but she has known Philippe a good while longer and I am English, a foreigner after all is said and done. I should have liked to have consulted her about the problem with Patrick but I know every word of any discussion we might have would eventually be laid before my estranged husband.

'*Mais c'est magnifique ton panier,*' the Belgian woman remarks, with her eyebrows almost touching her hairline.

'Yes, but difficult to water every day, I didn't really think of that when I bought it.'

And so there it was, the lie so easily spoken, and one that I am to repeat so many times I begin to believe it to be true. Surely this is what happens in the end to the teller of small untruths? Claude appears to be his normal self but when I catch his eye he looks away. This unspoken avoidance tells me more than any words can possibly say. He doubts me and this makes me sad.

I arrange to have the gate repaired and fitted with a new handle and lock. I am terrified that Patrick might gain access to the garden or even worse to the house whilst we are sleeping. How dare he frighten me like this? I'm sure all he wants is for me to respond and so I keep my phone turned off and let the answer machine monitor all the calls to the house phone. I don't want to speak to him, there is no point, he's incapable of listening anyway. All the time I spent trying to talk to him on the afternoon of his visit to my shop, had been a waste of my breath.

The next thing to arrive besides more flowers, is a box through the post. I know Patrick sent it, I know his handwriting as he writes all the invoices from *Le Carteaux Blanc*. It is unmistakable like the sound of his voice. I sniff the package wondering if it holds another plant species, something exotic perhaps growing in a pot, although the parcel is not heavy enough to contain soil.

'Why are you smelling that box Mama?' demands Frannie.

'No reason, just interested to see what it smells of I suppose, it's not for me,' I say, placing my hand over the label, 'so I will send it back straight away.'

'How do you know where to send it?' Why were children always so painfully inquisitive?

'I shall just return it to the Bureau de Poste. That's the correct thing to do.'

I wait until Frannie has completely lost interest and stick a new label over the one addressed to me. I write the name and address of Patrick's office carefully. What if Béatrice should be standing next to him when it arrives with the courier. That will surely teach him a lesson. Fairly difficult explaining that one away, although I'm sure he will have something up his sleeve. I did wonder what was inside but in the end decided it was for the best not to look. It's better to prove to him just how disinterested I am. I'm flinging the ball back at him with grand style and I'm quite pleased with myself, only wishing I could have done the same with the hanging basket.

Daniel, Patrick's driver comes to visit me, passing on his delivery round to the bakeries nearby. I'm so happy to see his friendly face and full of questions concerning his employer. I know I shouldn't ask but I can't stop myself. I'm desperate for someone to understand and sympathise with my plight and also to confirm my dark conclusion that Patrick's behaviour is becoming that of a stalker replacing the friend that I'd unwittingly allowed into my life. He is the Jekyll and Hyde in the end, not me.

'Daniel, *tu m'excuse mais il faut que je te demande*, I have to ask you,' I begin, 'what time do you start work? Do you ever see Patrick with bunches of flowers or hanging baskets, parcels or anything like that?'

'We have all seen him early in the morning or at the end of the afternoon with flowers, hiding them in the van, under or in empty boxes, it's become quite a joke amongst us now, because he thinks we don't notice.'

'I don't suppose you know what he does with those bunches,' I say, overjoyed now to have a witness, 'he puts them on my doorstep every single day, surely that's not a normal way to behave especially as we are no longer even friends as far as I am concerned? The flowers have become a menace to me, a threat, a blight on my personal life, do you understand what I'm saying? I'm scared of him now, and although the term may sound harsh or far-fetched I think he's stalking me. I daren't even turn on my mobile phone because I know there will be messages, probably masses by now and if I do turn it on he'll know I've seen them.' I speak quickly as if I cannot tell him fast enough, lest someone or something should intervene and stop me. I begin to shake again, either with the relief of having a listening ear at last or with the renewed fear that engulfs me as soon as I voice my thoughts out loud.

'We guessed he was up to something peculiar, he seems to have lost concentration at work as well, he usually has his finger so firmly on the pulse, as it were. Did you say something about a parcel?'

'Yes, he sent me something in a box, I don't know what it was nor do I want to, I readdressed it and sent it straight back. Did you see it?'

'It arrived when we were all sitting in his office for a meeting, he looked at it, seemed rather embarrassed then kicked it under his desk. I wonder what it was.'

'We shall never know. What on earth is he playing at? Do you ever see Béatrice?'

'She's around cooking and looking after the boys as she normally does, but they barely speak to each other. That's noticeable for sure.'

'She must know what he does from day to day, do you think she chooses to ignore his strange comings and goings? I can't understand his motives at all,' I slowly shake my head. 'He is just making everything so much worse for everyone, when if he had left me alone the rest could possibly have been forgotten in time.'

'He's making a complete fool of himself, *ne s'inquite pas,*' he says as he leaves, and having someone on my side comforts me.

14

"For incensed love breathes quick and dies,
When famished love a lingering lies"

Thomas Hardy, Two Men

Zanne (six weeks after)

'Ma pauvre.' Zanne's dearest friend reached across their lunch
table strewn with scatterings of bread and the remnants of their
meal, to take her hand as it lay upon the table. She has listened
to the details of the tale of her son's failed marriage to the
English girl so many times. Such a common problem amongst
the elderly; their biggest worry and upset monopolises all
thought and conversation to the exclusion of almost anything of
interest, which can be hard upon the listener. So it was with
Zanne. She had talked and thought of little else for some weeks,
since her son had moved to a house with his children leaving his
wife on her own with hers.

'And how am I supposed to feel about all that has happened.
Philippe won't discuss the situation with me at all and I know he
loves her still. He has forbidden me to go and see her, to try and
find out the real sequence of events for his peace of mind. I miss
her three children so, they have become almost as dear to me as
my own grandchildren. Marguerite won't listen to me at all; a
hot headed teenager that one, and Yves just falls into line behind
her with no mind of his own. I have questioned Amelie, she
would not hide anything from me, she says she saw that other

man putting flowers on Elle's doorstep but she has a feeling they were not well received. The trouble is we are all creeping around not daring to speak about the mess they are in, my son and his wife, as if the problem is not ours to meddle with. But of course it is, it affects all of us, we are all suffering one way or another.

I was to discover that the sounds and smells of late springtime would haunt me forever, reminding me of the day that Marguerite had executed her plan, revealing my dalliance, or whatever one could choose to call the friendship which has caused such misery. I know my marriage would have collapsed anyway, but such a dramatic episode could have been avoided. The chatter of the small gulls flying inland to nest, and the cry of their young like sharp whistle blasts dying away with the weakening breath of an unseen blower. The burst of the jet wash around the harbour cleaning the yachts before relaunch, the aroma of freesias and warm, freshly picked tomatoes. Inside the sweetness of these things lies the provocation for my sorrow; a terrible curse on the joy of my favourite time of year with the memory of the bite of disgusting words like "*Putain!*" and "*Menteuse!*" from the lips of Philippe's children.

I'm conscious now that there may only be two people at the centre of a relationship but if one was to imagine a series of radiating circles around them, like a pebble thrown onto the surface of a lake, the reach of the destruction of their uncoupling is like a small earthquake, with the effect gradually diminishing as the tremor reaches the outer circles. Immediate family are close to the middle, with friends ebbing away to the outer edges, but none escape entirely.

Frannie repeatedly asks when Zanne will be back to stay, and Ben is not yet ready for his promotion to his new role as man of the house. I can see his shoulders find this burden a heavy one that weighs him down, almost to the soles of his small, school shoes.

Amelie and Claude appear to be less like family than they were to us, a little colder and more distant, but then perhaps I'm imagining a situation that doesn't exist. I have no doubt about their fondness for my children and me. I feel guilty and responsible that their lives are so changed, but I know it's my only way forward, a better thing for all of us, and as time begins to heal, the children will forget, they are young after all. I hope Amelie and Claude will come to accept why I can't be with Philippe anymore.

The summer is hot and the flowers are dead before they even arrive upon my step with their unceasing regularity. I just throw them away, without further ado, from step to *poubelle*, this is their fate. I love the French word for dustbin, so much more enchanting than the English. My brain flicks from one language to the other these days; the children have reverted to English at home now Philippe is no longer with us.

Patrick has started to put cards through the door occasionally, pictures he knows I'll like, and messages written in pencil that he hopes I will read. I still never turn on my phone, I'm too frightened to read his texts. The trouble is he knows too much about my life. My habits, my likes and dislikes, I had told him far too much when we had shared those endlessly long conversations over coffee, or sitting in the grass at Peillon. What had possessed me to take him to my most favourite place in the entire world? So many regrets, I could fill my straw shopping basket with them. The cards sometimes reveal his thoughts, mostly dismay and anger at my coldness toward him but at other times he writes to me of things he has been doing. They are written in a friendly vein as if I might be interested in his days, and need him to recount the details of his daily life; like a diary. I begin to fear for his rationale, and for my own safety. The greetings cards he chooses are carefully selected, always depicting scenes he knows will please me. Peaceful wooden boats at anchor, or valleys full of flowers and bubbling streams. I imagine him wandering around the stationers choosing such cards, writing in them in his studied, pencil hand and perhaps concealing them for a few days before he sneaks them through my door. Sometimes they are posted to my address. It is beginning to annoy me not having a mobile phone. Perhaps I should arrange another one, a new number that he will never know, a fresh start. The more I think about this plan, the more it seems a good solution to the text problem. Would the children ask? I can just say the other one was broken, end of story.

I have no intention of attempting to look for another relationship, I'm wounded and I need to drive myself to work. My personal upheaval has restricted my enthusiasm and my normally creative spirit. The added encumbrance of the wretched man, who appears to have developed an obsession for me since I ended our friendship, makes every day complicated and distressing. But people with whom I sense certain chemistry have a habit of appearing in my life when I'm not expecting or wanting the attention. At this time nothing could be further from my mind.

I've noticed the regularity of this tall, gingery haired stranger who passes by for coffee and sundry small items at least twice a week. I admire his stature and the familiarity in his blue eyes. I find it easy to feel drawn to him, but tell myself he is probably taking cakes back to his wife or girlfriend somewhere and I would be wise to think no more of him than any other customer who comes through my door.

'Jean-Paul,' he had introduced himself on his last visit, firmly shaking my hand.

'Elle,' I said.

'Enchanté,' he bowed low, as Frenchmen tend to do, part of their showy nature that makes me ill at ease. I felt inadequate and nervous at his gesture, which was not a good sign, and I stood as if spot lit by his scrutiny upon a stage behind my counter.

His visits become more frequent and I wonder if he has recently moved into the area, or if I've just simply never noticed him before. Sometimes he chats to me amiably on a variety of subjects frequently grinning and making teasing jokes about the variety amongst my clientele, for example the ratio of men to women who come in my door. He appears to enjoy laughing at his own humour. But there are other days when he sits engrossed in a paper or book, as if he is in a glass case, alone in his own world, and on these occasions he barely acknowledges me at all.

I notice small details about him, how he bites his nails to the quick, and after he has left his table, there's a warming trace of Chanel with some other aroma incorporated as well. I breathe in deeply as I clear his cup, it's lavender, finally I identify the smell, combined with a whiff of wood smoke. His scent lingers, an invisible cloud, as the taste of wine rests upon the palate. These fancies are dangerous, I have enough troubles with men to last my lifetime, without looking for more. But he is a distraction and occupying my mind with something different helps to diminish my concerns about Patrick and his crazy behaviour. There is more to life than worrying about him, I'm moving on.

So much to do. Rushing to the market early in the day, I gather the glorious, seasonal produce as fresh as possible, giving me inspiration for my daily bake. Cherries for clafoutis, bleeding through the inadequate, brown paper bag. Asparagus for quiche, and apricots, bought from a cascading mountain of fruit on a trolley, for my jam. I stop at the market bakery, open from six am, the large Madame within grins when she sees me, beckoning me through her irresistible doorway. 'Beignets pour tes enfants adorable? Je sais qu' ils les aiment.' I buy three apple doughnuts, their favourite, oozing with tangy filling and perch the bag on the top of my basket. I've left the children sleeping. I know there's a tiny element of risk in doing so but they know I'm in the market, almost within shouting distance of the front door so they can come to no harm. I happen to glance out through the bakery window as I wait for my change, and, just at that second, I see the person I dread most to meet. Patrick is walking fast behind the stalls on the opposite side of the market, looking around to left and right, either he's searching for me, or hiding from me, instinctively I know it's one or the other, and in a blind moment of panic, I'm desperate to run home.

This particular morning I had begun my day feeling positive and bright, not exactly happy but as near to it as I've been for some time, probably since the whole drama occurred. There is a new man in the far corner of my mind whose attentions (although only vague) have lifted my spirits. I am desired and because of this I'm optimistic, ready to embrace my single life. The moment I saw Patrick from inside the bakery it was a though I was plunged back into darkness, once more pre-occupied with worries afresh and oblivious to everything, my legs weakening.

'Madame.' I am deaf to the shopkeeper who still holds out my change, I'm frozen in time watching him. He hasn't seen me yet, but he is keen eyed and hunting, and the thought of a confrontation alarms me.

I slip out in the wake of a large man with his arms full of baguettes and run, as best as I can with my heavy shopping basket, back to my porch, kicking aside the packet of lilies that lie there, with a grunt of annoyance. He must have come here first to leave his wretched calling card. How can I have such hatred for these poor innocent flowers?

Once inside I feel safe and taking a deep breath I walk calmly back to the kitchen to unpack my purchases. Nevertheless I'm beginning to be as jumpy as a cat. I'm trapped in my own home.

I shoot off to the supermarket as early as I can on Monday morning to avoid the heat and the traffic when another incident occurs, worse this time. About three cars back in the queue at the traffic lights I can see what I reckon looks suspiciously like one of his company vans. 'You're getting silly about it now ...' I say aloud, fully realising that talking to myself could possibly be the first sign of insanity. With frequent perusal of my rear view mirror but trying not to drive too dangerously, I hop from lane to lane at each set of lights, and am finally satisfied that the van doesn't appear to be following me. It could of course, be driven by any one his drivers and not necessarily him at all. It's on my way home that the trouble really starts. He appears behind me on the final, open stretch of road before the lights at the entrance to the town. He is so close upon my bumper that I can plainly see his face hunched over the wheel, his expression is determined and humourless. I certainly don't deserve this, why can he not leave me alone?

I feel a nudge on the car accompanied by a noise of metal touching metal and realise to my horror that he is actually trying to force me off the road. Seized by fear and anger, I see a side road looming, and at the last moment I pull sharply off the road without indicating. Much to my relief he has no alternative but to carry on past the turning for he has a stream of traffic behind him.

I make my way tentatively home, winding my way through the back ways into the town. I stop momentarily at each junction, to consider the best route to further confuse him, if he is indeed still behind me. All this brings back to me the terror of

Antoine, the security guard, who had stalked me from port to port all those years ago when I was living on my boat *Galuette*. How can I possibly find myself in this predicament yet again, twice in one lifetime?

As I drive home I start to seriously consider going to the gendarme. Being nearly driven off the road has seriously frightened me. He has gone too far this time, I have the children to worry about after all. What if he tries the same trick when I have them in the car? This develops quickly in my mind into a terrifying scenario and I know I have to do something to stop him.

No time like the present, I have the opportunity and I take it, driving past the turning to the street where I park my car, I carry on around the town and park outside the Gendarmerie. I intend to talk to someone and hopefully receive some advice.

If he's still following me he will surely be surprised on discovering my destination. Maybe just that will suffice to deter him, but I doubt my problem can be solved that easily. As soon as I walk in the door, I'm tempted to walk straight back out again; I'm intimidated and unsure of how to present my story. How can I explain that I'm partly to blame for this man's behaviour. Would they be sympathetic and listen to my fears, or will I be dismissed as a time waster? With a nervous sigh, I walk up to the desk.

'*Je voudrais parler avec quelqu'un,* I would like to speak to someone.'

'*Oui Madame deux minutes, s'ils vous plait.*'

I sit to one side on a rather hard chair, going over and over in my mind, choosing the best words to use. I'm feverishly hot in the airless hall, and I'm eager to know if there's a toilet I can use.

A female gendarme appears, a motherly sort of person, her uniform tight against her ample figure. '*Suivez moi,* follow me,' she says.

The woman leads me through to a private office, equally

165

stuffy with no window and the door firmly springs shut behind us. There is at least a fan, but I am in an interrogation room, and I have to remind myself that I'm here as a victim and not an offender.

'What would you like to tell me? Are you in some kind of trouble? Vous avez l'air très nerveux.'

I'm more than nervous, I'm petrified and there is a hysterical laugh brewing somewhere inside me. I swallow hard. 'I was seeing this man, well, not really seeing, we were friends who met for coffee, both of us were married, my husband has gone now, not really because of this, there were other reasons.'

'Doucement, go slowly and let me understand,' the woman says, more kindly now. (Is my French really that bad?)

'After my husband found out about our friendship, I told him, this other man I mean, that I didn't ever want to see him again, explaining how our relationship was damaging for his children and wife, and for my children as well. I just wanted to be left in peace. He wouldn't accept my decision, and now he follows me, places bunches of flowers on my doorstep nearly every day, and sends me cards through the post, and messages to my mobile. I daren't even turn it on anymore. Today he tried to drive me off the road by pushing the bumper of his van against the back of my car. He's broken into the back of my property on at least one occasion to leave flowers, and I am scared he could enter the house.'

The gendarme is scribbling furiously on the pad in front of her, and I wonder if I've made any sense at all with my short speech. 'He sounds like a bit of a brute to me, it's a shame you got mixed up with him in the first place. I know the type, a bully of a man.'

I hadn't expected such an understanding ear and I begin to feel less anxious. 'What we need is do is to prove what you have been going through, otherwise it's just his word against yours and he will obviously deny the behaviour of which you are accusing him. There are no specific laws in place in France at this time to protect women from stalking but if there are elements within his behaviour that are prosecutable under other legislation we may be able to do something to help you. For example, trespass, damage to your property or sexual harassment.

'So what must I do? Take pictures or something?' I'm at a loss to understand how I can supply the proof she needs.

'Not necessarily no, but you should take a small notebook and record everything from now on, dates, times, places and the registration number of any vehicle he is driving whilst he is delivering these flowers or following you. You should also write down, word for word the text messages and keep the cards too, for us to look at. Later we might borrow your phone but for now we need to catch him in the act, so turn it on and don't delete the messages. Don't what ever you do reply, as that could be seen as encouragement.' She rises from her chair. 'After a few weeks, if he carries on, as I am sure he will, come and see us again with the information you have managed to collect. We will analyse all that you give us and look for these other crimes that I have mentioned within his actions towards yourself, and if we are satisfied that he breaks the law in any single instance, we will pay him a visit.'

'Merci Madame,' I say, 'you have been most helpful and I shall do all that you have suggested.' We shake hands and I'm more hopeful of a result with the information I've received. I drive home without fear, almost willing him to appear so I can record his next misdemeanour in my notebook as soon as I can.

15

"Forgiveness is the fragrance that the violet sheds on the heel that has crushed it."

Mark Twain

Patrick walks into the shop one quiet afternoon the following week. I'm not sure whether telling him that I've been to see the gendarme is a good idea. On the one hand this disclosure might stop him bothering from me but on the other, it could make him really angry, aggressive even and that's not an option I care to contemplate, so I keep my silence. In fact I decide not to speak to him at all. Conversation is pointless, as nothing I can say can change the way he is, nor his behaviour. He craves a reaction more than anything. His confidence is fed in some strange way, by seeing me and managing to provoke some kind of comeback from me. He is far from normal, but then what man can one describe as being completely normal? They all have disagreeable traits that after time will come to light. Relationships are a question of levels of tolerance.

'So which Elle are we today, the pleasant one or the horrible one?' he says standing, grinning in front of me. I turn my head sideways and look out of the window praying for a customer to come in for then I hope he might go away.

'*Toujours la fille que je ne connais plus,* still the girl I don't know anymore, by the looks of things.'

I find his tone patronising and disagreeable, he's the one who has changed, causing an inevitable about turn in my attitude

168

toward him, but I say nothing. A customer comes in, and I wrap her purchases slowly and carefully making pleasant conversation about the weather. Patrick walks as if to the door and then turns and sits down at one of the tables. I can't believe it, how dare he? I can feel my temper rising and I know I can't stay calm for much longer. I'm pressing my nails into the palms of my clenched hands until I can feel the pain. The customer pays and departs and when I walk over to him, all my control has gone, my private vow of silence is about to be shattered in the quiet of my shop.

'GET OUT!' I scream at him in English, I don't care who hears me now, he has stepped over the line, imposing himself on *my* life and *my* privacy, never mind interrupting my work. I stand there and continue to shout at him, something has broken inside me and I've lost all control, whilst I screech and point at the door. Finally I open it wide, so my ferocious outpouring can be heard far down the street. Amelie is peeping from her shop looking worried but she stays inside, not wishing to be involved in what is fast becoming a public display of a passionate nature.

'LEAVE ME ALONE!' He's standing up now starting to look a little taken aback but still wearing his horrible, sardonic grin. I'm visibly shaking and fear I might cry, when suddenly with no preamble he walks straight past me and out of the door. I close it firmly, and lean upon the frame for a moment, needing some support for my weak legs. I lock the door and slide through to the hall feeling overcome with strain and exhaustion.

There is a silence, like the empty vacuous quiet that falls after some tragic accident, the harsh sound of my voice still hangs in the air like falling leaves on a windy autumn day. I inhale a sweet, almost sickly, and yet familiar perfume as I walk towards the kitchen and there, motionless before me, is Marguerite.

The last person in the world I expect to see. 'Marguerite.' I just say her name, nothing more. My step daughter comes towards me and I've no idea how she will react to the scene she has obviously witnessed. She puts her arms tightly around me, and through her tears she tells me she is sorry. I'm not quite sure what she is apologising for, but hope it is for the final destructive blow she had inflicted on my marriage to Philippe. *'Papa il t'aime toujours tu sais,'* she says.

'*C'est trop tard, Marguerite*, it's too late for him to love me.'

I write everything down, diligently, in the small note book that I'd purchased for the task of recording every detail of his behaviour. I write the time, all that was said, as best as I can remember, and the number of the van he was driving as he roared back past my shop after our altercation. The next day there are flowers of course so I simply wrote, "*freesias, 6.30am, 16 Juillet*" and left it at that. I didn't see the vehicle and I'm not exactly sure of the time but I know it was while I was baking at the back between six and seven. With the big oven roaring I would not have heard either the van, or the rustle of tissue as he placed the flowers on the step. I want the book to fill quickly so that I can present it at the Gendarmerie and end my nightmare once and for all.

I receive a surprise phone call from Philippe, he's on leave for a few days and has invited me and the children for Sunday lunch at his new home. I'm in two minds as to whether to accept, but I have to make a quick decision over the telephone, so I say yes. I think that it might be a good idea for the children to see that there is no longer any animosity between us and that we can all remain friends. I know that his invitation will have been prompted by his knowledge of my fierce dismissal of Patrick. Marguerite must have told him at the first available opportunity, but I hadn't expected such an immediate response from Philippe.

Ben is happy and excited on Sunday morning but the twins are content with the way things have turned out and have no wish to see their mother back with Philippe, nor do they want the fearsome Marguerite in their midst again.

'No, my darlings,' I say, quick to reassure, 'I like things the way they are now so there is no need to fret. Philippe is not coming back to live with us again and that is that.'

He made pizza and lemonade for us, not quite what we expected for Sunday lunch, but a safe bet for the children, and there is absolutely no sign of Marguerite, nor has she been mentioned yet.

I wander through the modern bungalow to find the toilet. I can't help but notice all the gifts I have ever given Philippe during our time together are on proud display, the model wooden boat, the glass dog with a curious bent tail, and the picture I'd painted of Amelie and Claude in their boat hangs above the mantel piece. I go into his bedroom as he had instructed, to find the ensuite beyond. Yachting magazines lie in piles around the bed with more pushed underneath, typical Philippe, no one to nag him now, to tidy up, or to run around behind him.

His bedroom proves to be a shock as I look about me. His chest of drawers is littered with photographs of me, and our wedding. They have all been carefully framed, which they had certainly not been before. On the wall there are more and I felt I had entered a shrine in memory of our time together, whereas I was guilty of tucking away anything that reminded me of him. I move quickly through to the bathroom lest he should come and catch me looking and see my surprise. Marguerite was right in what she said then, he does still love me. It's sad for it is indeed all too late, my love for him has died, and in my memory, the feelings I previously had for him, have slipped into a blurry past. I'm hollow, there's nothing left for him to build on, no possible chance of reconciliation. The strange thing is that our ultimate separation had nothing to do with Patrick. There must always

171

be something wrong in a marriage for either partner to turn their eyes elsewhere, of this I'm sure. I had not come between Patrick and his partner either, their relationship must have been wavering on stony ground long before I stepped into the picture, although of course, I admit, I hadn't helped.

There's a message on my answer phone when we finally return at the end of the afternoon, somewhat delayed by the children's urgent need to stop and eat ice creams at a glacier we passed on the way. It is the woman from the Gendarmerie enquiring if I'm safe and hoping I'm enjoying a pleasant, worry free weekend. How kind! A caring touch from the lady who had listened to my problems so sympathetically. I will turn on my phone as soon as I have a quiet moment and try to copy down all the messages I know will be there, in order to take them to the station, to lend some credibility to my complaint against Patrick. I'm frightened at the prospect of perhaps reopening the line of communication between us, but I have to be strong. As long as I don't reply, he might tire of trying after a while.

The twins are off out to a prearranged cinema date almost as soon as we arrive home. Ben seems content to relax in front of some nonsense or other on the television so really I've no excuse not to tackle the task that weighs so heavily on my mind, straight away.

I take my phone, turn it on and with my note pad in front of me I wait in dread as the screen lights up in my hand and the instrument begins to vibrate as the messages arrive. There are so many! For goodness sake, this is going to take me forever.

I toy with the card I'd stapled into the note pad yesterday. It's a picture of a bistro in a place called Montparnasse, where I've never been. I've never even heard of it before, but I suppose he'd chosen it because it was colourful and there were vases of flowers on the tables. Inside he'd written "There will always be flowers for you." He's definitely not joking on that score. Wretched flowers!

Reading the messages is more upsetting than I'd anticipated and sends me running for the toilet; the stress of finding out exactly how his obsession has grown attacks my body both mentally and physically.

"Elle. J'espère que tout va bien. It doesn't matter how horrible you are to me. I will never give up on you. M C A E xxx" I guess that the abbreviations stand for "Ma Cherie Amour Elle". At a glance he seems to have added those letters to almost every text.

"Bonjour Elle I am on my way to Nice, I would love to see you, let alone talk with you. I wonder what you are doing this weekend. M C A E xxx"

"Elle. ca va ce Mardi matin? What a lucky glance that gave me a glimpse of you yesterday when I drove past. Moments like that tell me we are on the same wavelength. Have a good day M C A E xxxxx"

"Elle. Mercredi matin. Oh dear Elle, what have I done that is so bad?? You used to be so pleased when I came into your shop and now you are so hostile and horrible. Why? This is not the girl I used to know. I don't like this girl at all. Please turn the clock back to the REAL you. please M C A E"

"Elle. hope to see you maybe later. Have a good day. E A"

"Elle. A little cold this morning and I have thoughts of you alone in your bed. I had better stop there before my mind plays tricks on me. Have a good day. M C A E xxx"

"Elle. I don't know if you get all these txts but I hope so. Take care see you soon M C A E xxx"

I'm glad that I hadn't read these texts every day as they arrived, for they would made me worry for myself and the children on a daily basis. He is surely mad. I read on …

"Elle. A dreary wet day. I caught a glimpse of you this morning when I drove by. Have you had your hair cut? I wanted to come in but I was late xx"

"Elle. J'ai vu Philippe hier. He walked right past me. He looked well in spite of losing you."

"Elle. Ça va? Ages since I saw you. I will change that soon xxx"

I feel more threatened every time he writes that he will see me soon. And where could he possibly have seen Philippe? When was that? I tried to work out if Philippe had been back in town on the date of the text but I don't think he could possibly have been home. Was Patrick making things up? I don't trust him at all, he is a liar and a fantasist. *Un fou,* I know that now.

"Bonjour Elle. I hope to see you this weekend. I still miss you I always will."

A chill blows over me through the open door from my backyard. I've been staring at my phone for ages, the horror slowly dawning, the detail of my stalker's mind revealed. I have to read the all the rest of the messages before I write them down, or maybe I could just hand over my phone. Yes, that's the best idea. There will be no doubt then as to the origin of the texts, and no possible denials from the sender. I set the miserable thing aside. It has become an instrument of terror for me. It's more than just a phone, it's the route he's using to continue tugging away at me, like a string he's attached to me in some mysterious way. Soon the gendarme will have all the information in front of them. I'm not sure why I haven't thought of handing it in before. Had she in fact suggested I should? Probably because I had not even begun to guess how many messages would be hiding in there, nor the content, and maybe I have a peculiar reluctance to share them borne of how close we once were. I go wearily upstairs to run a bath for Ben, hoping my twins will be home soon. Strength lies in family.

18

"The beloved – frequently distant, uninterested, unavailable, or unapproachable – can remain an object of indefinite idealisation."

Leon F. Seltzer Ph.D., *Educating the Self*

"Elle. I was home alone last night watching a film called "Chocolat" xxx"

"Elle. What I would give for an hour in your kitchen."

"Elle. ????"

"Elle. I am kicking boxes xxx"

"Elle. I don't think you get all these txts. I wonder who is supplying you with boxes for your cakes. I might see you today."

"Elle. Don't work too hard – we have limitations don't we? I know that lately."

"Elle, bonjour. Dimanche matin. I am thinking about you."

"Ma cherie. Ages now since I have seen you and I still don't know if you get these txts. I miss your sparkling eyes and that enigmatic, wry smile. I used to see it often when I delivered your order. I am sure I will see you very soon, you are always in my thoughts."

The phone buzzes and vibrates in my hand, shocking me so I almost let it fall. Of course he would know I've turned the wretched thing on by now. I don't look at the new, incoming message; I just carry on reading the old. Day after day he had sent them, hardly missing a day like the flowers.

"Bonjour Elle. How are you? Sometimes I call your phone just to hear your voice on the answer machine. How sad is that?"

"I sit and wonder about you and rarely see you and when I do you are always hostile towards me. I wish we could chat like we used to or go for a walk. So much to catch up. M C E A"

"Elle – I am here alone but I have the children with me, and I guess you have yours too. Take care, mon ange. xxx"

"Very busy, thinking of you and the hot cross buns that you introduced me to. M C E A"

"I want to see you, Elle ma belle. xx"

Some of the texts make me so angry and afraid I want to delete them but I know that's out of the question. I can't quite believe how many there are; I keep on reading them now in the safety of my bed, ready to stuff the phone under the duvet if one of the children comes into my bedroom.

"Comment tu va? Manic morning and I wish I could deliver to you. I expect you are busy too. M C E A xxx"

"Do you know what day it is for me today? A special one for me and I just have to see you somehow this weekend xxx"

I realise that he must have written that text on his birthday. As if I would care about that! He's so desperate for my attention he's becoming a pathetic creature in my eyes. Not at all the man I believed him to be at the outset of our friendship.

"Are you open for biscuits this morning, I am out delivering and I would love one of your biscuits, the perfect start to the day for me as well as seeing you of course. xx"

The cheek of the man. I would have been constantly wretched and on my guard if I had read these texts daily.

"Bonjour Elle it's me with your regular morning txt. Do you still go shopping on Mondays? I remember how we used to meet So many things to ask you about. I miss you like a crazy man xxxx"

"Samedi matin. I just wish you would tell me how you are? Jolie dame xxx"

"I have been outside your gate and could feel your presence. Your gate was open so I shut it and I wished I had not forgotten to bring your flowers. Bonne journeé."

My blood runs cold at that one, I know I'm never careless enough to leave the back gate ajar, maybe one of the children had forgotten to lock it behind them. I must talk to them, without causing alarm, about the idea of a possible intruder. If I was still a smoker, (I dabbled years ago) I'd go now in search of a cigarette and sit boldly in my open window above the street, defying Patrick to come and spoil my life still further if he dares. But having no such reassuring habit to fall back on, I creep downstairs, being frugal with light lest he's out there watching, and make myself a cup of tea, padding silently back to my bed.

"Bonjour, ages now since I've seen you and I hope you won't be as cross as the last time when I do finally catch up with you. I miss you every day and I know I will have to come and see you soon. xxx"

"I need someone to look after me. Have a good day. M C E A"

"I thought I might get a birthday message from you but obviously it was not to be. I have to see you soon. I have to stop myself from driving past your house several times a day. xxx"

I lean back against my pillows letting the phone drop for a moment onto my duvet. I try to remember what it was like with Antoine, who had pursued me when I'd ended the relationship. He had frightened me too, but nothing as bad as this. Patrick is beginning to display an unbalanced mind with his endless text messages and flowers. Perhaps he's having a kind of breakdown. Surely this will constitute as sexual harassment. Just a couple of times, reading between the lines, he has hinted that he knows his behaviour is wrong.

"Coucou! The birds are singing … wonderful. I wanted to come for croissants but it's late, maybe later. I am going fishing for lobster would you like one?"

"Bonjour, comment allez-vous? I dreamt of you as I fell asleep. Funny how little things manifest themselves in my head for no reason."

"Elle mon amour, what can I say after seeing you yesterday except why??? I wish I could understand why you are so unfriendly and cold but I can't. I have feelings for you of admiration and want only to offer you warmth and comfort. We are perfect soulmates. I could never dislike you or have bad intentions towards you. It was nice to see you. xxx"

'If you really cared about me, you would leave me alone,' I whisper falling back again against my pillows in utter desperation. He must have sent this text the day after he had come in to see me and I'd stood outside in the rain to try and make him go. I can't remember exactly what happened or when; he's made several visits culminating in the awful day when Marguerite had actually seen how terrified and upset I was by his visit. I certainly wasn't putting on an act for her benefit, he had genuinely frightened me on that day, and I know he had exposed my vulnerability.

And with the next text, so arrogant with a hint of sarcasm … I begin to hate him.

"Nearly forgot my daily txt. How are you? As lovely as on Tuesday I expect."

"Off fishing again and a croissant would be perfect. I guess you are closed because it's Monday. Do you remember our Mondays? I still miss you every single day xxx"

"Another weekend has gone and I didn't see you. It's been too long since we spoke. Maybe we could have lunch or something? I am still here missing you, Elle mon ange. xxx"

What part of me not wanting to see him does he not understand? I've made my position perfectly clear. I want him to go away and leave me alone; there can be nothing between us. I made the biggest mistake of my life in befriending him.

"Elle, there is so much that I could talk to you about and I know you would be interested. Mon dieu … what can I do about you? xxx"

"I have seen you, but I don't think you've seen me. It's a long time now since I first met you and your appeal will never die. xxx"

"A glimpse of you in your shop. You look fantastic, beautiful morning, beautiful you. xxx"

"The weirdest thing happened to me yesterday and it involved YOU. They say the past does catch up with you but this was unreal. Take care as you are very special xxx"

I know what that last text is all about, he's trying to intrigue me, to draw me into his nonsense, to tempt me to reply, and question him to find out what he's referring to that involves me. No chance, I'm not that stupid, it's probably nothing at all, a made up ploy to entrap me into responding at last.

"Under pressure with many problems so only a short txt. xxx"

More of the same, designed to tug me back towards him, but he's only achieving the reverse. Sighing I carry on, I'm nearing the end now, only a few more to go, of the old batch. He has started afresh, but I won't read those now. I knew he wouldn't be able to stop himself, once he knew my phone had been turned on. The texting is a manifestation of his sickness and tomorrow I'll give all these messages as evidence to the officer at the Gendarmerie.

"Elle ma belle, a moonlit night, thoughts of you and me under an olive tree … I hope you read these txts. xxx"

"I came to see you yesterday and men were filling holes in the road outside your shop. I couldn't see you and didn't know if you were there. I am completely CRAZY, I have to see you. Please phone or txt me xxx"

"I came to your shop about 12.30 and I couldn't find your car in any of the places where you usually park. Did you go out to lunch or something? I can't bear it. xxx"

"Pinks on the doorstep with your milk. Bonne journeé. xxx"

"Mon amour Elle, I passed your house twice yesterday. I guessed you were busy in your kitchen, and wished I was there with you. I want to see you this week and hope you won't be horrible like last time. I just want to be friends and chat like we used to. Please don't be cross with me xxx"

"A bad morning for me, I just left you more pinks and I could feel your presence. I hope you find them, they are divine just like you, divine. I have so many problems and a friendly chat with you would help to solve them all. I want to hold you close to me, ma cherie, that feeling never dies xxx"

"Just one word HEAVEN, seeing you yesterday made me smile all day."

"So long since I actually spoke to you. I wonder if your girls are growing up to be as beautiful as you. Please consider lunch with me or a walk sometime maybe."

I notice to my horror that these last two messages have been sent since I turned the phone on, so he must have seen me somewhere. How on earth? I haven't been out of the house, so he must be using more trickery to try to trigger a response from me. Well he isn't going to get one. My stress rises in a staggered breath and I turn the phone off. Maybe I'll take out the sim card and silence him forever. It's as though his eyes are on me all the time and I have to run for the bathroom. Patrick has driven me to this.

19

"Let truth be told – women do as a rule live through such humiliations and regain their spirits, and again look about them with an interested eye."

Thomas Hardy, *Tess of the Durbevilles*

Monday morning with the children safely off to school, I take my phone, neatly wrapped in a plastic bag with my name and the number they gave me, duly attached with a brown parcel label. It occurs to me in my whimsical imagination that it resembles evidence in a murder trial or some other case far more serious than my own. In fact I feel a tiny bit of a fraud sometimes making such a fuss over what some would see as a trivial problem concerning a past relationship. But when I think about the hundreds of flowers, and Patrick following me to force me dangerously off the road, I know I've made the right decision in seeking help from an authority. I can't see anyone I recognise at the front desk, so I leave the package with an efficient young man who promises it will reach the female officer who is handling my complaint.

I make my way down to the small beach below the old town wall. It's too early in the day for tourists and sun worshippers, the staff from the *café-bar* who own the plot are only just arranging the loungers, cushions and umbrellas and take no notice of me walking down to the water's edge. I used to come here when I was working on *Sea Princess*, for a day off, a cocktail perhaps and a swim, to be waited upon for a change and to rest. A smile creeps to my lips as I remember Tom, (the Pole I almost married but for his affection for vodka). He was washed out to sea on his windsurfer here. He had become a tiny dot in the distance before I had realised that if I strained my eyes towards the horizon, he was waving his arms, above his head and not contentedly windsurfing as usual. He was eventually towed back to the safety of the bay by a lifeguard in a rib. It had taken a lot of beer to wash away the humiliation, and a good deal more to invent a story to cover his shame.

I have a million things I should be doing this morning but I need half an hour or so, on my own, looking out to sea. Will today be a day when the wind teases the sea to a mounting fury, flinging jetsam upon the beach? Pieces of my previous life are caught under my skin like splinters, which ever way I turn I feel them pricking, sometimes it's a tingle, and at other times, a fierce, roaring pain begins that threatens to make me weep without reason. Water, it's always water to save me from myself. The sea, or else a river or a stream, and even in the local pool as I swim; if I close my eyes I can touch the bubbles and see the cut of *Sea Witch's* bow through the oily calm.

My mind takes me back without warning to find myself sitting on the wall in Tarifa looking at a rough sea between Spain and Morocco. We had been storm bound for days trying to leave the Mediterranean behind us and set out for the Canaries and beyond. Until I told my partner of my pregnancy and he had been cruel and silent for almost a week before we decided to leave. We turned about to run with the wind, setting our course to return to France, abandoning long standing plans owing to my condition. Never had I felt so desolate as when I'd sat upon that Spanish wall, miles from family and friends with a man who looked away from me whenever I spoke, in his harsh refusal to accept our situation.

Once we'd returned to France and secured a berth, I had found a job working for a French company and at last established some routine in my life. When the pregnancy began to show I had to lie and say I'd been ignorant of my pregnancy when I'd accepted the job. They believed me, of course, why would they not? There was great comfort in knowing I would have maternity leave and a chance to return to work after the baby was born. When it came to light I was carrying twins, my partner became even more disagreeable towards me, envisaging how his life was inevitably on the brink of an even bigger change than he'd previously imagined.

He was a lazy man disinclined to work and often on my return I'd find he hadn't even bothered to do simple things, like shopping for food, or cleaning the boat. Whatever had I seen in such a man? I asked myself this question repeatedly. A kindred spirit when we were happy on the ocean for sure, but life cannot be an endless fairytale of billowing sails and sandy beaches. In reality we had to somehow earn a living. How would he ever have coped with supporting the small family he was about to have and when the twins were born, of course, he couldn't. The last few months of my pregnancy had been such a peaceful time. I'd started my leave towards the end of the summer, when the coast was crowded and hot, so we'd anchored for weeks at a time between the small islands near Cannes. I was able to float around the boat, my swollen belly weightless in the cool blue water, watching small fish as they fed on the weed that attached itself to the waterline, the noise of their nibbling and the lap of small waves as they hit the hull, lulling me into a trance. I wiled away the uncomfortably tropical afternoons in the cockpit, wiggling a makeshift aerial so that I could watch Wimbledon. Then, as dusk fell I would swim ashore in the sultry sunset to clamber awkwardly onto grey rocks to watch *Sea Witch* swing lightly on her anchor to face the evening breeze. The heat of the day awakened the quiet scent of the fir trees on the island and the sun dipped into a smooth, metal sea, shot with pink. I am sure those heavenly days of tranquility are reflected in the sweet natures of my beautiful girls.

We battled on for a few more years until Ben was born, he was a rather sickly baby and I began to realise that our life style was unsuitable for our third child. Should he be taken ill when we were sailing or even at anchor, I might be endangering his life. My decision was made, *Sea Witch* must be sold and we'd move ashore. And then my partner left me. The funny thing was I didn't really care, we'd been unhappy for so long, I could have a new start on the land with my children. I worried a great deal at first about the children's lack of contact with their father but as he had never been keen on the idea of fatherhood from the start, after the initial fear of abandonment passed, I grasped in the end, that his departure would work out for the best.

Maybe I should go and talk to Charles and Casja, my dearest, old friends, about the problem I have with this man who stalks me. They understand me, more like the parents I'd always wanted, than employers. They had always stood by me too, well until the 'Tom thing' anyway, but that was old history. I left him because he was a drunk and they had stood by him because they were fond of him and that had been the end of it. It all seems so long ago, my other life, living with them all in the close confines of *Sea Princess*, exploring the Caribbean Islands and crossing the stormy Atlantic. Charles, forever the captain of my dreams, was always so incredibly intuitive and sensible. My children and my shop impress them, and I know they would have the right advice for me. On the other hand I want them to believe my life to be almost perfect since I left the yachting life behind, with no messy edges. I hate to have to admit to the vortex in which I'm spinning, sucking me fast towards a deep hole, like a crumb in my kitchen sink.

I've done well and accomplished much. I know I'm justified in my pride in the children and the business, why then can I never make the rest of my life right? The personal side is always in a muddle, like the waves and currents in the sea pulling me this way and that, choking and drowning me. Does this mad French man truly love me? Or his passion for me a lie, born of his own misery and need? Is he a drowning man clutching at me as he flounders in the deep waters of his own personal turmoil? I stare far out to sea, before closing my eyes to try to recapture in my imagination the warm waves of the Caribbean sea enveloping me like a familiar blanket, soothing and calming my all troubles.

A voice and a light touch on my shoulder pull me back abruptly from my reverie.

Jean-Paul stands beside me and shielding his eyes from the bright glare of the early sun, he says, 'What do you see out there, a boat perhaps?'

'Oh no,' I say, fidgeting in the sand with embarrassed toes, 'I was just dreaming really, what are you doing here?' As I say this I realise I sound a trifle aggressive as if I have the sole right to this private oasis.

He has a joke ready in his answer of course, 'The little patisserie I know in town where I usually go is closed on Mondays, so I sometimes come here for an early coffee before too many are about. Maybe I could buy you one for a change and you could sit and drink with me.'

This was so prettily suggested, how could I refuse? I find myself sitting opposite this man I have only just come to know, drinking hot chocolate, and my mood lifts. He obviously likes me for there is a smile in his eyes, and as we talk of this and that I begin to feel strong again, the wretchedness of failed relationships ebbs away and there's hope for the future.

'What does your husband do?' the question comes at me like a bolt.

'He's an engineer on a large, private yacht but we are not together now,' I fumble for the right word.

'*Separé alors,*' he comes to my aid.

'*Oui cette exact,*' I sit back in my chair less nervous now we've established my marital situation.

'Maybe you would like to have dinner with me at some point in the near future?'

"Perhaps, that would be a both a pleasure and a treat.' As soon as I say this I think of a million reasons why I should have politely declined. I'm still married after all and I've three children to think about and the shop as well, never mind Patrick's antics; I don't have room in my life to even toy with the idea of a new relationship, so it is pure madness to accept his invitation. Maybe he would forget between our early morning chance meeting and the next time he sees me. I can but hope.

'I have to go,' I say glancing at my watch, 'I have a lot to do between now and the children coming home, if you will excuse me.'

Jean-Paul smiles and stands, circumnavigating the table quickly to kiss me on both cheeks. '*A bientôt.*'

'*Oui,*' I reply and I hasten back towards the road without a backward glance but aware that his eyes are following me. Lavender, it's most definitely lavender that I can smell about his person. Perhaps he lives amongst lavender fields somewhere, with a big garden and some acreage. I can visualise him in such a place.

I shop with the speed of one with a steady routine, drinks and snack foods for the children, some meats and cheese, everything else I can buy from the market or have delivered to the shop. No time to wander and gaze at things for which I've no need, nor can I afford. Each week is a scramble to meet the costs of providing for the children, they grow so quickly, casting aside shoes and clothes almost as soon as I buy them, or so it seems. I'll never let them go without, it is my top priority, and we will have a holiday again soon, just the four of us, to cement our unit without Philippe.

As soon as I'm home in my kitchen, laden with my shopping, I look at the answer machine. I always do, as there's often a cake order, or something else that needs my immediate attention. The light is winking red. It's the lady from the Gendarmerie asking me to call back as soon as possible.

My stomach growls in anguish. What can she want so quickly? It's only just over a couple of hours since I'd handed in my mobile at the station. I make a cup of tea and dial the number. I wait to be put through to the right person having to explain who I am, time and time again, until I finally reach her. '*Oui,*' the officer begins, 'these messages were just what we needed and because there are no replies from yourself, it proves that his attentions are unwanted. We have also noted the van registration that you gave us and it does belong to the man in question. I have met this type of man before and he may turn nasty, so we're going to bring him in and have a chat to him right away. I wanted to warn you, in case after our talk with him, he approaches you later today.'

'Now, this minute, you're going straight to his house?' I never anticipated any action being taken so quickly.

'Yes we are going shortly.'

'*Merci,*' I say, 'for letting me know, I mean.' I feel sick. Too late I can't stop the wheels from turning now, I'll lose all credibility. It has to happen, I've done the right thing, he's a danger to me and my family and I'll keep reminding myself of this, hard as it is to acquaint such behaviour to someone I believe held a genuine affection for me, a few months ago, at the outset.

I can't concentrate on anything during the afternoon, I wander around, drinking tea and wondering what is happening at *Le Carteau Blanc*. The call I'm expecting comes whilst I'm preparing supper for the children which makes the situation difficult as the twins are sharp girls who pick up on my anxiety. I take the handset into the kitchen out of earshot of my family and try to listen calmly to all the woman has to tell me without butting in with stupid questions. All will become clear to me in the end, I'm sure.

'*Bonne soir Madame.*'

'*Oui, bonne soir.*' I sit down with a bump at one of the shop tables, biting the nails of my left hand as I cradle the phone to my ear. There's a couple looking in my shop window, peering under the half closed blinds. I turn my back to them, in case they should try to catch my attention. I need to concentrate.

'*Nous avons pris ce monsieur chez lui, et l'emmené à la Gendarmerie.*' So they had picked him up from his house, or from his office, as far as I know he works adjacent to his home, and taken him in. Who might have been watching? His staff, his children maybe even his partner? I feared a more dramatic situation than I'd ever intended, but he had brought this all on himself after all.

'*Il a tout accepté.*' He has accepted everything. What does that mean, that he has not tried to defend himself at all or denied anything? Just accepted his guilt like a naughty school boy and maybe even laughed about it, I can imagine him doing just that. It would be so typical of him. He will have belittled his actions, saying that it was all a joke and he'd never meant to cause me any distress. I can almost hear him saying it.

'Mum,' Ben now, his head peeps round the door.

'What is it, I'm on the telephone,' I whisper, my hand over the mouthpiece, my face flustered and irritated.

'I need help with my homework,' he pleads.

'Ask one of your sisters and I shall be there shortly.' I feel sorry, I shouldn't take my worries out on my little boy, nothing is his fault.

'*Desolé,*' I say into the phone. '*Mon fils,* … and what happens now?'

'*Nous lui avons donné un caution.*' They've given him a caution? And what exactly did that entail? Most importantly, will it mean he will leave me alone and that the flowers and messages will finally stop?

'*Si il continue le situation peu devenir très grave pour lui.*'

'*Je comprends, merci Madame. Au revoir.*' This is all I answer although I would really like to ask what the grave thing is that will happen to him if he carries on. Hopefully he will have been sufficiently humiliated and he will now stop.

The next morning there are freesias on the doorstep. It feels as though everything I've done has been in vain. He simply doesn't care who tells him not to, he's still going to keep on persecuting me.

20

"Normality is a paved road:
It's comfortable to walk, but no flowers grow on it."

Vincent Van Gogh

I decide to ignore Patrick's renewed vigour concerning the flowers; they continue to materialise on my step as if by magic, for I rarely catch sight of his van. I suppose he's now taking extreme care not to be seen. My mobile has not yet been returned to me so I don't know if he is messaging but presumably he's guessed that the phone must be in the possession of the authorities by now.

I've told the children that there's a man who keeps putting flowers on the step. I don't want them to feel that I'm keeping something from them should they happen to notice, as there really are a tremendous amount of flowers about the house considerably more than I'd ever buy. I have help now every Saturday morning. It's wonderful to have another pair of hands to serve customers should I need to be in the kitchen. Stephanie used to have a stall in the market so she's familiar with many of the faces who come into the shop, and keeps up a surprisingly comforting stream of banter about our mutual customers and acquaintances. Seeing her cheery face at the end of the week when I'm flagging gives me a new sense of security, and purpose, although I can't exactly explain why. Amelie and Claude fall into an easy friendship with my new employee; she is one of the team who, with her friendly nature, peculiarly strengthens my position in the life of the commerce in my street.

I've told Stephanie everything, well nearly all, about Patrick and his unceasing attentions toward me, and she's more than happy to take flowers home with her on a regular basis, thereby saving them from *la poubelle*. " 'Tis not the fault of the flowers themselves so why should they suffer," she'd said happily, tucking yet another bunch into her basket before she went home. I can't remove the hanging basket because of the story I've told everyone about purchasing the wretched thing. However I long to destroy this mocking obscenity that taunts me daily at the centre of my world.

The summer heat becomes oppressive, wonderful if you are by chance on holiday, but working conditions in my small kitchen are tough with no sea breezes through open portholes to cool the air. Nor can I plunge into the sea throughout the day as I used to when I was cooking anchored in idyllic surroundings in Greece, Turkey or the Caribbean. Nevertheless a walk to the beach in the evening with the children for a late swim is always something to look forward to at the end of a busy day. I'm tired all the time for I sleep badly, with both the heat and the pressure of orders for the morning to follow, keeping me awake, as well as the shouts of the late night drinkers, making their way home from the English bar up the street. I have a reoccurring dream of oversleeping, forgetting orders and mixing them up, or worse still forgetting the oven and burning them. On one such humid night I wake suddenly and have no idea what day it is … maybe it's Sunday my day off? No, I don't think that's right. How awful to be so disorientated. Is this the result of the accumulation of worries and concerns in general? I blame Patrick wholeheartedly. What if I'm on the verge of some sort of breakdown! I manage to sort out my thoughts and realise it's Wednesday, but not time to turn the ovens on yet, still time to be asleep, for it's only three am. Mulling over making a cup of hot chocolate and craving the milky, sleep inducing taste on my lips, I go downstairs.

On the wooden table in the kitchen lies a single rose. Totally unnerved, I jump to the only obvious conclusion. Patrick must have put it there. I press my face against the window and peer into the dark courtyard, before taking the flower and pulling it to pieces. Thorns tear into my fingers. Such is my fury, I feel no pain, only see the blood on the stem with no comprehension of the injury. I dispose of the hapless bloom outside, as far away from me as possible. Sitting back down in the kitchen, I try to reason how Patrick could possibly have gained entry to my house, my haven of safety from the outside world. The back entrance is all securely locked and so is the shop; a complete mystery. I plod back up the stairs aware of nothing but my own fear, and lie down, fitfully dozing until the light and the noise of the sea birds tell me it's time for me to dress.

Ben comes down first for breakfast. Wriggling onto a kitchen chair still in his pyjamas, he says,

'Where's the rose I brought you Mum?'

I spin around from the sink where I'm busy washing up, 'You brought me a rose?'

'Yes, it was my teacher's birthday yesterday and she had so many flowers she gave me one for you, because I said you love flowers. I put it in my bag and forgot, so I came back down last night and put it here, on the table. Did you put it in some water?'

'I think I must have put it with the other flowers in the shop, early this morning, I will look later but thank you cherie.' I kiss him quickly on the side of his head and carry on making him some toast, successfully drawing his attention away from the unfortunate flower. How can I have been so paranoid when there had to be a logical explanation, for Patrick couldn't possibly have come into the house, unless he had come down the chimney, like Father Christmas.

I continue to write in my notebook never missing an entry. The date and the time he leaves flowers and the same when I catch sight of his car or one of his vans. I know the registrations by heart. He's taken absolutely no notice of the warning from the gendarme, so I must carry on until I've listed enough sightings to return to them again. I'll take the children away at the end of the summer; I'm nurturing the idea of flying the four of us to the Caribbean. If I work hard and save throughout the busy time, my plan is achievable. The feel of the warm wind and waters of the Windward Islands need not just exist in the past. I have the power to make them a part of my life again and show my children how their grandfather lived during his long exile on the island of St Lucia. The day Casja and I had found him in his impoverished situation still stood out as one of the most emotional and important days of my life. How insignificant my daily toils and troubles seem compared to such a dramatic moment in my own history. I'm determined to calculate the cost of the trip in October, at the end of both the hurricane season in the islands and the tourist season in France.

Jean-Paul always rattles my composure whenever he walks into the shop unannounced. No one else, (as far as I can remember) has ever had such a devastating effect on my state of well being. My knees begin to tremble and I lose the sense in everything, especially the words coming out of my mouth. Have you never been in the company of someone you would like to impress with your intellect and found yourself gabbling like an unenlightened duck? His presence never fails to disturb my composure in this way. He appears on a hot summer's day, and his eyes lift to span the tables taken with chattering visitors. I can detect his displeasure at the lack of seating space, and quite possibly, the likely limitations in my attention to his needs.

'*Un café noir,*' he says. 'When you have a minute.'

He doesn't greet me formally as he normally would but a

mutual understanding passes silently between us. I've already perceived that he doesn't like to be one of a crowd and I understand his discomfort. He sits in one corner with his newspaper and although the babble and chitchat carries on about him he is unaware, having only eyes for the written word and occasionally for me. I make an attempt to behave like my normal self, but his presence inhibits me and I'm not behaving anything like the usual me. I'm normally so in control in my own surroundings; the queen bee in her hive has transformed into a fly with a broken wing. I fear he might leave before I'm able to show him any further consideration, and finding a moment of freedom from the demand for coffee, I go to his table to clear his plate and share a moment with him.

'There is a concert on Sunday afternoon, I have tickets will you go with me?' he says without preamble.

'I have the children to think of,' I say, immediately regretting my reply because surely I can find some solution for one Sunday afternoon. I should be able to organise a small patch of freedom, without needing to disclose the problem.

'I have no children and so sadly I cannot understand,' he says leaving me totally perplexed at such an open, bare statement of fact.

'I'll try,' I say.

'Let me know,' he replies and he leaves before I've had a chance to ask how I would be able to let him know as I've no contact details for him at all. So be it, I'm sure he will telephone me in the few days preceding the concert. He knows where I am after all. I must go and set up a new mobile phone contract with a new number, a fresh inbox for my private life, and then I can give it to him.

I ask the children at supper, nothing quite like taking the bull by the horns.

'I have been asked to a concert on Sunday afternoon, and I was wondering if I might be able to go?'

'Of course, we will look after Ben,' says Florence.

'I don't need looking after,' says Ben.

We'll be fine Mum, just go,' says Frannie.

'I might ask Stephanie to look in on you during the afternoon, if that's all right?' I feel guilty already, I'd never put myself first in this way, well, not since I'd had Philippe and what a disaster that turned out to be in the end.

'We are thirteen years old now and quite responsible you know,' says Florence.

'Yes, I know but things happen and I would rather you stayed at home and didn't go to the beach unless you can persuade Stephanie to go along with you.'

The twins roll their eyes simultaneously and it strikes me how alike they are in mannerisms although they're not identical in features or stature. 'I'll take that as a "yes" then, I will be back for tea, it's just an afternoon thing.'

Jean-Paul rings me on Friday, only to tell me he will pick me up at two, there was obviously no doubt in his mind, I had already accepted.

After lunch on Sunday the children are busy half watching something downstairs, whilst setting up a board game for Ben's amusement. Luckily they don't see my various changes of clothes which might lead them to credit more significance to their mother's *première rendezvous*, than the occasion merits. Finally I settle on a blue summer skirt and a simple white blouse, demure and suitable for a concert of cellist and violin in a chapel. During a significant bout of unnecessary fussing over Ben, I look out and see Jean Paul sitting in his car just outside. Under a cloud of nervous distress, I go out to meet him wondering why I had accepted his invitation, an afternoon of easy relaxation at home suddenly appeals as the most desirable option. As if I don't have enough to worry about without placing myself in another vulnerable situation with a man I barely know.

As soon as I climb into his car he presents me with a posy of summer flowers, gathered, he hastens to tell me, from his own garden. Flowers are not exactly my favourite gift, anything else, chocolates, perfume, even nothing would be infinitely preferable, but when I examine the selection and bury my nose in the scent I have to admit that these are far superior to anything I have discovered on my doorstep. The stark orange of marigold and dahlia, is encircled by the subtle blues of lavender, love-in-the-mist, and catmint, with sprigs of rosemary for green and their heady aroma; the whole reminds me of an English country garden and roast lamb for lunch. I'm suddenly beset by homesickness, which for me is most unusual.

This sentiment must be plain upon my face for he says, '*Qu'est-ce qu'il y a?*' Is there something upsetting about the flowers?'

'*Rien*, they are beautiful, they remind me of home in England, that's all, I suppose sometimes I do miss the summers there, it's so insufferably hot here, and with so many people on the coast in high season.'

'I know what you mean, about the people,' he agrees, as we sit in a long traffic queue before reaching the turning we need to rise up into the hills to the villages behind the coast, to take us away from the steady stream of cars bound towards Nice and beyond. I gaze out of the window at the sea and we have no need for conversation.

21

"We all know him to be a proud, unpleasant sort of man; but this would be nothing if you really liked him."

Jane Austin, *Pride and Prejudice*

Outside the chapel people stand in small groups on the grass chatting, fanning themselves with their programmes in the sultry heat of the afternoon. They are mostly French but I recognise a few of the more well educated expatriates as customers who occasionally visit my shop, craving a taste of their homeland. The same ones who come in their flannel trousers and immaculately pressed casual shirts in search of Christmas pudding and fruit cake, at the end of the year. One or two nod to me in recognition and two or three more openly stare, and confer in whispers, knowing my face but unable to place me away from the counter of my shop.

'Does everyone know you?' Jean Paul bends to re-lace his shoe.

'No, not everyone at all,' I feel the need to defend my notoriety, 'just a few, they know me but I don't have a clue who they are. I see a lot of faces, in my shop, some I remember and some I don't.'

'*Tu me souviens,* I'm glad you remember me at least.'

I look at him but decide not to reply as I've no idea what to say.

'Shall we go in and find a seat where we can see and hear, before the rush.'

'*Bonne ideé,*' I say, smiling at him.

The atmosphere in the tiny chapel is solemn. As we enter I'm struck by the cool air trapped amongst such ancient stone walls. We take our place on hard wooden seats which remind me of Sunday services when I was ten or eleven years old with my father. Upon kneeling, I used to burn my knees on the central heating pipes in the church in the village. My father was a man of strong Christian faith and I rather envied him, for I had never found the same support from God, although I looked long and hard for Him during my Church of England upbringing and schooling. This was not to say that listening to music, choral or instrumental, in a place of worship did not fill me with uncontrollable emotion, sometimes even moving me to tears. But I was no nearer, to discovering my maker, and no closer to basking in the solace that He might bring me, or to receiving the peace that my father secured with the breaking of the bread.

All these thoughts spun through my mind as we sat quietly watching the cellist and violinist arranging the furniture to accommodate them. They begin to tune their instruments, followed shortly by the first few notes. I am lifted, until my heart lies somewhere between the tiled stone floor and the vaulted ceiling, wrapped in the beauty of the sound, and serenity settles over me. I glance quickly at Jean Paul and his eyes are closed, he too, appears transported to some private place.

The interval comes and we turn from the musicians to find each other's company again.

'I have a sister,' he says.

'And I a brother,' I reply.

He takes my face in his hands and kisses me slowly without warning, as if we are alone, and I'm acutely aware of my own mounting physical desire for this man, certainly inappropriate in such a holy place. He releases me and we sit silently again, straightening in our seats, waiting for the players to resume. I tremble and fidget trying to calm myself, longing to be immersed in the music once more.

Afterwards, in spite of my protestations about children and the time, which he appears to completely ignore, he informs me that I shall accompany him to his house for a short while to take tea. I wonder if he is proposing tea to satisfy my English habit as French men aren't normally partial to the drink in the afternoon, usually preferring coffee or even a small brandy or pastis. Claude and Amelie often attempt to lure me to the bar on the corner after work for *"un petit porto,"* when all I crave at teatime is a pot of Earl Grey at home. I am powerless to refuse him as I'm dependant on him to transport me back. I have no choice but to follow his wishes or to feel churlish and awkward by making further excuses.

His house is exactly as I anticipated it would be. All the answers are revealed to the clues that he wears about his person; the smell of lavender is from the blue fields that stretch widely around his house which is tucked in a valley below the town of Grasse. The hint of wood smoke must come from open fires as there are logs neatly stacked in piles under the porch.

The ground below the long drive falls away steeply with terraces and olive trees, a small cottage lies to the right of the private entrance gate. 'For the housekeeper that I don't have,' he explains, 'so it lies empty, and full of cobwebs I expect. I must tidy up in there sometime.'

He jumps athletically from the car and swings open the heavy wooden gate, like a child eager to show his toys, or in this case his beautiful home and grounds. To live in such isolation in the country must surely be a joy, almost as perfect as being at sea. The house is a typical French country, stone building with neat shutters and deep gravel that scrunches under our feet, like thick quality carpet between the toes.

'On rentre vers le jardin,' and so saying he leads me through an arch of unkempt roses and round towards the back porch. Old stone statues stand at each corner of a tiled swimming pool full of green water. The whole garden is evidently in need of

some serious work and attention, but the charm and the tranquility of the surroundings seduce me in one breathtaking second. I blink in the sunlight and then turn to follow him into the dark of the kitchen. The inside, in dramatic contrast to the garden, is neat and well cared for, with tidy piles of brochures on the kitchen table alongside a plentiful bowl of fruit. Jean Paul is already plugging in the kettle, swearing softly as he wipes some intruding ants from the surface near the sink. 'The problem with living in the country,' he says, 'is that I have to share the house with all kinds of unwanted guests.' He turns his beguiling smile on me and fills a teapot, slipping in two bags of Earl Grey from a packet on the shelf. 'You don't take sugar do you, because I don't have any.'

I shake my head not quite sure how to reply. How can a house be without any sugar at all? Just so out of the ordinary. I notice the range in the corner is cold, obviously extinguished for the summer and I wonder how he cooks in the mean time. He must be a mind reader for he says, 'I have a small electric hob in the pantry and a fridge, but I think they spoil the look of the kitchen so I keep them out of sight.' He disappears in search of milk and intrigued, I follow him. The hob, fridge, and washing machine and a sink, are all crammed into a small utility, with shelves of sparse dried goods above, but no sugar. Rice, pasta and several types of tea, a rack with red wine, a few bottles of champagne and one bottle of malt whisky with a sole glass upon the side. A hermit bachelor existence, I look and I understand. A childless man who has probably never known disorder in his life.

'*Et les voisins?*' I ask, 'Do you have neighbours? I need to say something to break the hush around us.

'A shepherd only, further up the track. Sometimes he grazes the sheep on my land to keep the grass down. But I like the grass long and wild really, and full of flowers, not short and full of sheep droppings.'

I laugh. 'I didn't realise you have fields as well.'

'Well, only two small paddocks at the end of the garden. I like to watch the wildlife and birds. Come, bring your tea and I will show you.'

I tripped along behind him, wishing I could take off my heeled sandals as they are beginning to pinch and are not designed for a garden adventure. How the children would love a garden and a pool? I dare not think on it, but my mind gallops ahead of me. We are all entitled to fantasise after all, there is no harm in imagining a future for ourselves. I could give up the day to day drudgery of the shop and live here in this scented peacefulness. The meadow is wild and unspoilt save for the path he has roughly mown across the centre to reach the opposite boundary fence. Taking my hand he pulls me down into the grass, drawing me back to reality, spilling my tea and his own in the process. *'Nous pourrions faire l'amour ici,'* he says, 'no one would see us.'

'I think not,' I say, scrambling to my feet. I'm definitely not taking off my shoes or any other item of clothing now as he might think I'm encouraging him.

'Do you not want to make love to me?' he asks.

I brush the question aside, putting it down to his Latin descent, a Frenchman through and through. 'I should be on my way home: the children will be wondering where I am. I've been away longer than I said.'

'Come back into the house first then, I need to talk to you about more concerts.'

The contrast of the light from outside to in is so strong that I can hardly see for a moment as we go inside. He picks up a brochure from the table. 'There is a list of concerts for the next month in there. Can you come with me?'

'To all of them?' I say aghast, 'maybe to one or two, I don't know, I can't promise. I have the shop and my family to organise.'

'I'll take you home then.' This was the last thing he said to me right up until the moment when he deposited me back at the end of my street. It strikes me that he's sulking like a grumpy child who hasn't succeeded in having his own way.

'*Merci pour cette après-midi,*' I say to him, and he nods, his face unsmiling. He watches me seriously as he turns the car around and drives away.

Turning back toward my house I catch a glimpse of Patrick hurriedly jumping into his van parked at the other end of the road near the market. 'The bastard has been waiting and watching for me,' I say out loud, in shock and disbelief. I run quickly to my door and let myself back in to hear the joyous cry of, 'Mum's back,' from Ben. My first thought is how wonderful to be home! Why did I ever go out? The notebook, I must write down the time and the circumstances before I forget.

The concert was a treat, it made me wake up to the world outside my work and children. Sometimes the walls of my house trap me and close me in, making me forget how it feels to walk away from everything for a few hours. My thoughts are a stream of contradictions. I must finalise our holiday plans in the next few days.

Jean Paul stirs something inside me. I daydream about him constantly while I work; his private retreat surrounded by flowers, the scrunch of the gravel under my feet and the tick of the wooden clock in his kitchen, the sound that emphasises the incredible stillness of his abode. How does he spend his days? He left message for me on my answer machine after I'd gone to bed, asking me when I will be free again. I replay the message several times, relishing the timbre of his voice, his accent so much more pleasing than the local southern dialect I'm used to hearing. Sometimes I find it difficult to understand him so I have to concentrate hard. I believe he was brought up near Paris. He begins to telephone me repeatedly while I'm working and stubbornly refuses to understand why I'm too busy to talk to him.

'*Tu ne veux pas me parler?*' he says, petulantly.

'*Écoute!* I'm trying to make coffee and sandwiches, so I have no time to talk now, you could call me later when I finish.'

'I might be busy later,' he replies, which is the most infuriating thing he could possibly have said and I wonder why I bother. Why are men so difficult? Generalisation is justifiable, as all the men I become involved with do appear to have faults in their personality with which I struggle to come to terms. Obviously it's my judgment of character at the outset which is lacking as on each occasion I fall headlong into disaster, like a skater, confident at first, then crashing onto the ice. All the time, energy and potential grief that a fresh relationship inevitably entails, could I possibly go through all of that again? Middle age has brought nothing but anxiety, when my vision for my future years was one of the contentment that accompanies stability; a boat reaching the still waters and protection of a port after the stormy days of one's youth at sea, tossing on the ocean.

'He is keen then, this new friend of yours,' Stephanie observes.'

'Annoyingly so, especially when I'm busy, he must have forgotten what life is like having to earn a living, and he has never had children to provide for.'

'He may just not be the man for you then.'

'Oh don't say that, or I shall give up now and I like him. There is something about him.' I finish with a blush. Stephanie nods her head slowly, the perspicacity of age on her side.

I ring him back in the early evening, thinking this must be the best time. If he's out, I've already prepared a message ready to leave a smooth communication on his answer machine. Why do I feel so nervous? A simple telephone call is an easy undertaking and not worthy of such worry.

I dial his number and wait. I nearly chicken out and replace the receiver before giving him a chance to respond.

'*Ah, oui ... Elle.*' My confidence falls further with each of these three words and the tone with which they are delivered. '*Je mange, à plus tard*' he says and quite simply puts the phone down, leaving me at a complete, but slightly angry, loss. After all the times he's called during the day, expecting me to drop everything to speak to him, and then he can't talk to me because he's eating? I would put aside any meal to listen to him but not, on the other hand, my work. Was that his problem? Is he merely highlighting my determination to put my customers higher up on the scale of importance than he? He baffles and confuses me. And what should I do next? Luckily my pride steps in to prevent me from ringing him back again, so I wait all evening for him to call and he does not.

I hear nothing from him then until following Saturday evening when he calls and asks me to watch cricket with him on Sunday afternoon at his local club. Nothing could hold less appeal for a girl who never takes any pleasure in sport involving a ball, excepting tennis at Wimbledon, which is a joy of quintessential Britishness. I explain to him how I have a build up of paperwork that I've set aside for Sunday, but I invite him for a glass of wine on his way home from the cricket. He is obviously disgruntled about the afternoon, but agrees to call by in the early evening.

'Who is this man anyway?' demands Frannie. 'Does it mean we are banished from the living room?'

'No, of course not,' I say, 'you live here, just be normal and polite, the same as I am when you have friends round.'

'All right, point taken,' she fires back at me. I've registered the beginnings of teenage back chat from the twins; they are improving with practice at this irritating skill of late. Do I need to feel self conscious about someone visiting *me* for a change? I have to welcome anyone they chose to bring into our home. For the second time in a week I feel the constraints of motherhood.

Jean Paul doesn't like being around the children I can tell, and his obvious discomfort encourages the children's suspicions of him. I usher him through to the back of the house and pour our drinks in the kitchen. What happens next is worse than I could have possibly have envisaged. Glancing out of the window I can see Patrick, I must have left the back gate ajar or somebody had, because he's peeping in through the courtyard and twisting round in order to have a better view through the window. I meet his eyes to his surprise, perhaps he thought I would't notice him? He disappears so quickly I wonder if I've imagined his startled face. There's always a possibility that my worst fears had somehow summoned him from my sub-conscious to distress me still further, than he has already managed to in reality. But Ben ran into the kitchen and saw him at exactly the same moment as I did.

'There's someone spying into our house Mum, did you see him?'

Luckily Jean Paul seems to be completely oblivious to Ben's remark having chosen to adsorb himself in the magazine lying open on the table.

'Just pop out and lock the back gate for me would you,' I say quietly to Ben, 'one of us must have forgotten to bolt it.' Ben runs outside without a word and slams the gate shooting the bolts home noisily, both top and bottom. I was shaking and desperately trying to be nonchalant. This time he's gone too far, I'll go back to the Gendarmerie tomorrow. He's destroying my life, like some pathetic peeping Tom, at least Jean Paul hadn't noticed nor understood my exchange with Ben.

'Can we sit and drink our drinks in the shop?' he asks. I thought this to be a rather strange request but I led him through and we sat woodenly at one of my tables in the empty shop. I have to admit that with the blinds pulled down on the north facing room it's cooler than the rest of the house, although I suspect he made his choice to put distance between himself and my children. I'm jumpy now because of Patrick spying on me so our conversation is stilted. He finishes his drink quickly feigning tiredness from sun and cricket and takes his leave. I'm relieved, I need time to think what to do about Patrick.

22

'There is a considerable difference between knowing what to do and doing it, I suppose one spends most of one's life in this gap.'
Elizabeth Jane Howard, *The Sea Change*

I believe I can see deeply into a person's character by studying their hands and also, more particularly their feet. If I encounter a person whose feet are bare or encased in sandals I've developed a habit of always looking down to their toes. I imagine, if they're bendy and lacking in uniformity, with uneven gaps between, that they reveal a quirky, disorganised person, whereas those with perfectly straight digits hide a tidy, strict, intelligent mind. I can tell a brutish or stupid man immediately with just one glance. Women are trickier, but the colour of varnish (which French women always wear) is a strong clue to their level of sophistication, self care, and the boldness of their nature. If I lived in a cold climate my bizarre observations would of course, be impossible.

As I sit outside with Jean Paul on matching steamer chairs in his garden, luxuriously sipping cold champagne, while he reads the paper, I am studying his bare feet, which like his hands are soft and brown. In fact all of his limbs look as though he has never walked far or done much manual labour in his life. I decide that his feet are definitely those of a rather delicate, highly intelligent man. I have already surmised that he suffers from some inner turmoil by his finger nails, which he has bitten down irretrievably.

'What are you thinking about?' he says.

'Nothing,' I lie, 'just enjoying the champagne.'

The second part is no lie, I'm loving the ice cold sensation of the bubbles hitting the roof of my mouth. It's easier to spend some time with him now the children have gone back to school, I can at least have a couple of hours at his house sometimes on a Monday, although I know he wants more.

Sexually he's greedy for me, so much though that I have my suspicions that he is obsessed with our lovemaking. I worry about his exclusivity. How does he survive when he is away or we are unable to see each other? I've never in my life had such an enthusiastic lover. He requested, on the first day that we slept together, that he make love to me in every room of his house. I was extremely attracted to him but I found I'd tired of our vigorous games long before he was satiated. He makes love to me at every opportunity, in the garden, in the field, even on the cliff top where we frequently go for a walk. I'm closer to him at times than I've ever been to anyone, even my first love, Peter, pales in my memory compared to Jean Paul. We have virtually nothing in common, except maybe a love of good food and wine and he's interested in cooking. He has expressed a fear of being out on the water so we'll never go sailing together. His conversation is stimulating when I can distract him away from the physical side of our relationship. I hate the way he's prone to sulk when I leave him, like a child deprived of a favourite toy, he always wants me to stay the night with him and I never can. It's just not possible, I would never leave the children, perhaps for a few hours, when I know they are safe and cared for, but not overnight. He has plainly shown his discomfort when in their company, so he will never stay at my house either.

After one such episode when he had ignored my departure, he didn't contact me again for two weeks, causing me to ask myself if I need such heartbreak, for that's how I was … heartbroken. Every time he turns his back on me after a day of loving intimacy, I feel his punishment as one who suffers a hard slap across the face. He leaves me reeling. He holds me so close to him I drown in his love and then, as soon I say I have to go, he pushes me away with a cruel coldness. I need reassurance: I want him to care for me, and to be consistent in his attention to me. What is a relationship after all without such minimum requirements? I would do anything for him, except I won't desert my children or neglect my duty to provide for them. He's offers me nothing, no talk of a future together or of permanence and he's shown that he can't tolerate to be near children, anyone's children, not just mine. He wants to possess me, on his own terms, and oh, he's a master of charm when he needs to re-seduce me after we've drifted apart during one of his periods of moody silence. For a few hours he changes and becomes the man I want him to be until I fall into to his arms again. His heart stopping smile and deep blue eyes hypnotise me, and I'm lost. Standing in my room I breath in a feint trace of him from my t-shirt before putting it to wash, just a lingering hint of lavender. He comes to me in my dreams, a perfect being, an Adam to my Eve, but I can see the transparence in his vapoury form . When I look more closely there's a curled creature in the core of him, some horrible, slug-like mollusk, a harbinger of harm.

Just over two months into our affair I make a decision and dial his number hoping he'll be at home.

He answers immediately. 'Jean Paul.' This is always the way he answers a call, simply stating his name.

'*C'est moi, Elle.* I need to talk to you seriously.'

'Oh?' he says, surprise in his tone and I can see him in my mind's eye with his eyebrows slightly raised in question, and my courage ebbs.

'We can't go on like this, I find you blow hot and cold towards me and our relationship is unsettling. You leave me for days at a time with no communication, and I don't know where you are, or who you're with. It isn't right, or fair or normal.' I'm stumbling, searching desperately for the right way to express myself.

'*Tu m'insult,*' he says, just that. How could he possibly see my comments as insulting when I'm just stating the facts, without condemnation? I haven't called him childish, scheming or cruel or any of the other words that jumped into my head when I was preparing my speech. I'm the one who has been insulted, by his obvious use of me when he wants, and his brutal abandonment of me when I have to care for my children and work.

'I am not trying to insult you, I am trying to tell you how you make me feel,' I answer. 'You make me unhappy.'

'Are you seriously suggesting that you don't want to see me anymore.' He sounds incredulous.

'I suppose I am,' I say, heady with my words.

He cuts me off.

The next day he calls my mobile when I'm late shopping with the twins for clothes. His voice is kind and his words imploring, determined to win me over again. I stoop among the rails of clothing removing myself from the world around me, listening intently.

'Please, Elle, don't think like that, I will come and see you tomorrow, I'm sorry, I never mean to make you unhappy, I will try.'

My head spins and I want to cry. I give in again, his sweet beguiling tone banishes all that has gone before. 'Yes, please come and see me tomorrow.' My heart lifts. He's back with me again.

'Who were you talking to Mum?' Frannie asks me across a rack of dresses.

'Jean Paul,'

'Oh him …'

'We really don't like him Mum, he's weird,' Florence has her say now.

'Okay,' I say, I've no intention of discussing Jean Paul with them in the middle of a boutique. 'You can form your own opinions and I mine, you needn't worry he won't be moving in or playing happy families with us,' I conclude harshly and the subject is closed.

Patrick is rearrested following my detailed account of his antics. Since he had been cautioned on the previous occasion, this time he will have to appear in court, a serious and far more complicated affair for him, but not for me. I'm not even expected to attend. I had a letter informing me of the details, the case number and the date; short, exact sentences in black and white. Sexual harassment and trespass. A few stark words, on one single piece of paper, hiding the enormity of my concern and emotion, as a small grey cloud conceals a thunderstorm. How can his family possibly understand this latest development? I foresee I'll take the blame in the end. They will close ranks around their own, and I'll be the "devil in the woodpile", as my mother used to say, the proven witch.

As I tuck the sheet away in a pile of correspondence on my desk, a letter from my father slips forward and I ease it out from the bottom, without destroying the heap. How I love him. My mother is blind to anything outside her own life, worry for her children is something set aside and forgotten in a distant past (if she ever did worry). She had come to stay after the twins were born which had not been of any help at all, quite the opposite. She was intent on her own system of disciplinary measures before they were even five weeks old. I was amazed I'd survived my own childhood; the reason being that myself and my brother had nannies and au-pairs until we were shuffled off to boarding school. My mother had often been heard to proclaim that she'd only produced children because it was part of her marital duties.

But my father clings to me, his eldest daughter, in his letters, revealing his deepest thoughts and his constant concern for my future. Thank goodness he knows nothing of the problems of the last few years, only that Philippe and I no longer live together as man and wife, but he had never liked him anyway. He encourages me to embrace my single status, until I find the right person to share my life again. After a turbulent decade during the failure of his second marriage, he has last found his soul mate and is settled and happy. He's proud to be a grandfather, adoring the girls but more especially Ben who can do no wrong. He implores me to move back home so he can spend more time with them. He's adept at casting a gloom over my French life, continuously finding fault with the climate and the people, and pointing out all the good things about British life. If the children and I were with him every day he would undoubtedly tire of our proximity.

"I am longing to spend time with this remarkable, handsome, brainy, advanced grandson of mine. We promise that if you come it is comfortable here and peaceful and the garden is starting to look lovely. The climate is so much cooler and more relaxing. Business opportunities are much improved this year and you could still have a little shop, near us, so we can help and spend time with the children."

In spite of this gentle persuasion, I'm absolutely sure it would be a mistake for me to go back to my roots. France is my home and England having only made me unhappy as a child, I can't believe that anything will have changed with the passage of time. Sometimes I force myself to picture how life would be back there, the cruel frosts, and Sunday roasts with my father, unconvincingly admiring my mother's small flock of sheep and striving to be convivial with my stubborn step-father who grows more cantankerous with age. Damp beds, roaring fires and a discouragingly short burst of summer, when, amongst the roses and sweet peas, I could almost forget the bone chilling cold of wicked, winter days. But I love the idea of him wanting us near, he's there in the dark places of my mind, a strong wall to which I can attach a line when times are difficult, and the tide and wind turn against me.

Who was it who said age brings wisdom? The years truly give us a better understanding of ourselves, we learn our own failings and weaknesses of character, but the trenches still open wide before us and we continue to fall, headlong to the depths. On each occasion clambering back out on the other side is harder than before. I'd managed to escape from the grasp of Philippe, and Patrick's hold over me is loosening, why then have I *chosen* to love, (no, that's not the right word for a feeling I find unavoidable) such an unsuitable, and at times, disagreeable man like Jean Paul. In my race across flat turf, I've flattened two hurdles and must rise over a third standing tall in my path. I've reached the conclusion that independent, creative women can rarely be happy in love, as they have extreme difficulty in bending to the will of a man. I have to be at the helm and in control of my life in order to be content, and so far I've not met any partner who truly understands this and loves me for the way I am. I'll never change; I've tried and failed.

Jean Paul went to Spain on holiday, he omitted to tell to me he was going; I just noticed the complete lack of any communication and presumed I'd done something wrong again. Sometimes he calls or texts me perhaps twenty times a day while I'm working and then, bizarrely, I hear nothing. The postcard that comes from central Spain is the first clue of his absence. There's no information on the card just a signature. No 'how are you' or 'I wish you were here.' Another stab at my heart. I wish I didn't care. I begin to suspect him of having a personality disorder, for I don't understand him at all, and puzzle over his actions again and again in my head. Distracted, I study the picture on the front of the card. I thought at first it was a close up of a hill with trees. The name of a Spanish town is inscribed across the photo in flamboyant writing. But then with another examination, my brain reorganises the image in front of me and I reach a conclusion, by turning the card completely the other way up. I'm looking at a part of the female anatomy cleverly photographed to resemble a view of the Spanish landscape. Astonished and disgusted, I tear the card into tiny pieces and throw it into the bin, for fear that the children might see. How can such an intelligent man be so obsessed by sex. Of course he might have someone with him for all I know, for he never tells me anything. I'm full of jealousy and resentment, my life is an open book and his is nothing but blank pages, the information that I'd like to read is invisible. I'm not even allowed a hint and I dare not ask. The worst thing of all is that every time I try to end our relationship, he talks me round with his silken tongue, becoming again the man I adore, charming and attentive.

I reluctantly agree to fetch him from the airport, (as he's arriving on a Monday, I can't truthfully find an excuse why I'm not available) and to drive him to his home in Grasse. I'm excited nevertheless as I see him walking through the arrivals area and he looks relieved to see me. A convenient taxi driver perhaps? How can I think so badly of him? The sting of his departure without a word still pricks me.

'Do you only have that one small bag,' I ask after our initial hurried embrace. Why did I always feel so nervous around him? Waiting for another axe to fall perhaps?

'*Oui,*' he says, '*toujours une seule petite valise.*'

The damned sexual solicitation hangs like a hot cloud around us. There's no need to speak of it thereby stating the obvious. I know he will want me as soon as we arrive at the villa, perhaps even before.

'I brought you something Spanish,' he says.

We drive in silence then, with me concentrating on the road and he with his eyes closed. Once or twice he tries to sneak his hand between my legs but I push him way. 'I'm driving,' I say, longing to feel his hands on me.

As we turn into the drive, there's a man strimming on those terraces that are wide enough to sustain wild, yellowing grass. I marvel that any growth is possible with such a heat and the burning, dry wind. Seeds and insects decorate the screen as I drive slowly down the track, a living summer pattern.

'*Arrête ici,*' orders Jean Paul. I stop rather more abruptly than I intend, exaggerating my surprise at his intention. '*Reste là.*'

I stay where I'm told and watch his progress as he jumps down the ledges to talk to the man. I've never seen anyone around the villa before. I was completely unaware that he has an arrangement at all with such an individual. He has a gardener in his employ. Strange then that the land and the garden around the house appear so unkempt.

Jean Paul was talking and gesticulating as the French always do. I'm too far away to hear what he's saying. Speaking with his hands, reinforcing his message, he slaps the man on the back, a final friendly gesture towards his gardener who, lifting his machine to his shoulder, wanders off in the direction of the boundary gate.

Jean Paul has sent him on his way before his work is finished. I see. He doesn't want anyone around the house or garden whilst I'm here. The reason for this is not at all clear to me. Is he embarrassed to be seen with me? Can I not fit in and be a part of it all, even make the man a cup of tea perhaps so to be acknowledged as the woman with Jean Paul. Evidently I'm not to be so included. I'm just some person he has brought home to entertain him, someone not even worth the bother of making himself accountable to, or sharing his whereabouts with in-between our assignations. He cheapens me. Despite this, I can't resist him, and when he pushes me down upon the old wooden table in the porch, he has not even unlocked the door to the house. I give myself to his eager body with a gasp of pleasure. His desire for me consumes and thrills me and when the calloused surface of the wood grazes an old wound upon my lower back, I fail to notice neither the hurt, nor the bleed.

'What did you bring me from your holiday?' I ask him as we drink the tea he's made.

Out of his bag he produces a small, soft parcel. I open it carefully. Inside there's some sort of garment of cream cotton and when I spread it out on the kitchen table I recognise it to be a short apron of the type I never wear as the size of it would provide little or no protection. It bears the same disgusting printed picture as the postcard he had sent me.

'I thought you would like it,' he says, giggling at his own joke, a crass display of pathetic immaturity. I fold it without saying anything and replace it roughly in the wrapping. He doesn't deserve a false show of gratitude for his insulting gift. He's taken another square parcel from the bag and for one bizarre moment I'm reminded of Mary Poppins, and the way she'd produced all sorts of weird and wonderful things from one small bag. But this unpacking held no such magic.' It's perfume,' he says, 'for my sister, do you think she will like it?'

'I'm sure,' I say, my face reddening. Why had he not brought *me* a bottle of perfume, a normal gift for a lady who you cared for, instead of the other sexually provocative rubbish.

And in that instant, I finally begin to dislike him. The children and I are going away on holiday soon,' I say. l would have done better to have remained silent, to have left him in ignorance of our departure. Too late, I had told him now.

23

'All men will be sailors then, until the sea shall free them.'

Leonard Cohen, *Suzanne*

I trip along on buoyant feet on my way to collect the airline tickets for our holiday to the Caribbean. I break into a steady jog, completely oblivious to the busy street around me, as if my urgency will somehow relieve the pressure of all the arrangements I have to organise before our departure. I round the final corner and simply run into him, too late to take evasive action, and he catches me squarely, a hand on each of my arms as I face him. 'Patrick,' I say, my voice sounds cold and empty. I look into his face with a mounting fear of the anger he might now voice against me.

'*C'est toi,*' he says sadly and then, 'why did you send that horrible gendarme woman to take me away in the car, in front of my family, Elle, in full view of my children, can you begin to imagine what that was like? Is it against the law to leave flowers for someone as a gift? What else did you tell them? What other crimes have you convicted me of? We used to be friends, we were more than that, we were lovers.'

'You broke into my property to spy on me and leave your wretched flowers.' I state my case calmly but my voice shakes. 'There was nothing caring or loving about that. You tried to drive me off the road, never mind harassing me with endless messages when I'd made it clear I did not want to communicate with you at all after the awful business with Marguerite. Do you have any idea what any of that was like for me? How they all treated me? And the names I was called in front of my children? After *all* of that, you still wouldn't back off and leave me in peace. What *is* the matter with you? *Tu es malade.*' My final statement brands him as ill, the only possible explanation I can find for such unreasonable behaviour. Suddenly overcome with fatigue, I want to go, to walk away from him and carry on to collect our tickets and return home and share the excitement with my children as they begin to pack.

'I've moved on,' I say determined to make my situation clear with no open cracks he could squeeze into with soft words he might yet find. 'I'm seeing someone now, a happy, loving relationship, so you are wasting your time and your flowers.'

'Him? That old man? You are not telling me that you love him? I know him and I know where he lives, I've followed you there and seen you in his precious garden. What are you thinking of? He will never make you happy.'

'That's my choice and has absolutely nothing to do with you. How dare you spy on me! If I see that you are following me, or him, I shall inform the gendarme because you have no right to interfere in my life. You are just playing a selfish power game, without a thought for your family or for me and mine.' I was becoming agitated and if I let my fury overcome me, I risk to lose the thread of my reasoning in my argument with him. I disentangle myself and push past him to continue down the street, aware that his eyes are following me as are those of others who slowed their steps to witness our furious exchange of a few moments earlier. I didn't look back.

Standing at the airport check in in Nice, I begin to feel better than I have in a long time. I can sense the strain seeping away from my tired muscles and bones, and the nervous cough that has clung to me these past few weeks isn't bothering me any more. I've been rushing around too much, determined that everything at home, in the shop and the house, will be refreshingly clean and tidy when we come back, ready to pick up our lives again. Although Christmas is still months away I've begun to start stockpiling puddings to allow them time to mature. Our last holiday in the Canaries was such a long time ago and everything about my life has changed since then. I'm a single woman again now, alone with my three, wonderful children.

Philippe drops us off at the departure entrance, home from his tough summer long cruising. He is sad and wistful that he's not accompanying us. Tempted as I was to have some company, he might have drawn hope of some sort of reconciliation from my invitation and I couldn't risk that scenario. It would be unfair on him. We'll never be a couple again, although there is a bond between us, a thick solid rope of familiarity, with all the bitterness gone, leaving only affection, but nevertheless, hollow and shaded by sadness.

I held and kissed him briefly, as a sibling would, at the entrance to the departure lounge. The children's excitement carries me through and onto the plane. Arguments about window seats and discussions of films to watch become the most important things in our lives, everything else we shall leave behind us for two whole weeks.

I gaze out of the window of the plane, above the head of my son as he rearranges all the in flight magazines. He's been trying to shake off a sore throat for the few days preceding our departure. I hope, like my annoying cough, that it will disappear, carried away by the soft, warmth of the trade winds. It's wonderful to be together, just the four of us, without all the distractions of everyday life, to reestablish our relationships with each other and bond tightly as a family unit. I'd always dreamt of taking them to the Caribbean before they grow too old to want to go away with their mother. I wish we were going to St Lucia. The island where I'd found my grandfather would have been my first choice, but holidaying there is just too expensive, so I'd decided to try somewhere new, Hopefully I can go back to the Windward Islands when I only have myself to worry about.

The flight is not too arduous, the children, who immerse themselves in films and food, hardly moan at all. I'm able to switch off completely, flicking through the first of the novels I'd chosen to bring; I doze the time away. We're scheduled to land at nine in the evening, local time, and as we begin to descend, it's dark beneath us with the lights of the Dominican Republique winking up from far below. This is the part I'm not so keen on, but I close my eyes and reassure myself we will soon be down.

The dense heat and the smell of the Caribbean engulf us as we walk across the tarmac to the airport buildings. The air-conditioning is hardly noticeable in the stuffy hall as we wait to have our passports checked. They appear to need to study every word on each one, I'd forgotten how pedantic these islanders can be. We pass through to another hall for our baggage. We're held up for almost another hour, spent with the children fading fast upon some steps, (the only place to sit). Their excitement and capability for patience are both long gone. Ben's face is as pale as a ghost.

'How long before we go to the hotel Mum,' he moans.

'Just as soon as we have our stuff.' I try to sound cheerful and bright, although I, too, am longing for the hotel bar and a sniff of sea air. 'You can put your phones away girls, you won't need those until we are home again.' With bored faces the twins tuck their phones back in their hand luggage. I reach in my handbag and touch my new phone resting snugly in a special pocket. I'm free.

The baggage carousel begins to grind with an awful broken sound. One suitcase appears through the rubber hole at the end followed by another and then another. 'There's my rucksack,' says Ben, suddenly awake like a toy rewound, and he runs to grab hold of it before it disappears to the other side. Shortly, with all of us reunited with our bags, we make our way wearily to look for the transport, which is to take us through the dark night to the hotel. The bus is as disheveled and worn as the passengers inside with too many people for seats. I have to stand until the first drop-off point where I'm able to grab a slot opposite my children.

'They didn't show this in the brochure, did they Mum,' Frannie remarks and Ben giggles.

'Try to see it as an adventure,' I say, 'I know you're tired now, we all are, but we will soon be there.'

Although the information had stated that the hotel was twenty minutes from the airport, the final part of our journey takes almost an hour, along bumpy roads, in suffocating heat. The nights are never as hot in the South of France. Perhaps its just because we've never taken an uncomfortable midnight bus ride to the back of beyond at home. Either way we're all relieved when we emerge from a banana plantation to find ourselves at the entrance to the hotel. I wake Ben gently as he has managed to doze on my shoulder for the last part, if he hadn't grown so heavy I'd have carried him to his bed. We're checked in by welcoming faces and a man with a sort of electric cart loads us and our luggage for the last part of our journey, across the hotel grounds to the block where we will find our room. I've never stayed in such a place in my life before, the hotel is enormous, comprising of a complex of blocks of rooms and pools, surrounding the main building. I can hear the sea at last, although I'm not sure yet in which direction it lies. I notice the high fences that surround the perimeter and I wonder if they're to keep the guests in or to keep invaders out. I finger the coloured band that's had been attached to my wrist, a sign that I'm an inmate of this strange compound, a prisoner for my own pleasure. Of course, I remember the border with Haiti isn't so far away, and the other part of this same island is an altogether different place, rife with poverty, disease and crime. I try to put this thought from my mind but it makes me a trifle uneasy all the same.

Up some wide, tiled stairs, next to a glistening, clean pool we find our designated holiday home. The room was large enough and had a sign on the door with a date of recent fumigation. Fumigation from what exactly, I wonder. Cockroaches? I shiver involuntarily at the thought.

The stifling heat fills our accommodation and I quickly find the air-conditioning controls and set them to maximum. It's quite noisy but I suppose we'll all get used to the steady rumble of the machine. Flo goes to open the balcony doors but I stop her. 'Leave them shut, darling, give the air-conditioning a chance, otherwise we'll just be letting the heat back in. You can open them in the morning for a while when we wake up. You can't see the view now anyway: it's too dark. I suggest we go down and find something to drink while the room cools down.'

We wind our way through illuminated pathways, amongst palm trees and bougainvillea and I have to admit the grounds are beautiful. There are four pools, two with swim up bars, where you can climb half out onto a stool and remain partially immersed in the water to drink. Several snack bars thatched with palm, are dotted around, obviously only for daytime use as they are closed and locked. We pass through a cavernous open foyer with a cocktail area and four or five different restaurants next to the main dining room. I would never in my life have considered an all-inclusive holiday for myself, but for the children it means they can roam, graze and drink, without pestering me all the time. This will be a perfect rest. No shopping or cooking for two whole, blessed weeks. And there's an endless supply of entertainment on offer, wind surfing, sailing, tennis, beach games with other youngsters, bikes we can hire, and a pool table in the bar. For me there's the sea, where I can swim to my heart's content and walk along the beach. I can see the waves, glinting in the dark alongside the outside beach bar and taking my children's hands I run like a child myself, kicking off my sandals, longing to feel the warm water of the Caribbean sea once more around my ankles.

A restraining hand falls on my shoulder, and I turn to see a uniformed guard. 'It is forbidden to enter the water at night Madam,' he says.

'We only wanted to paddle,' I say, and then as if to justify my enthusiastic behaviour I add, 'we have only just arrived.'

He shakes his head, 'Not after dark. There are dangers,' he says.

I look back at the sea, as if searching for any menace that can possibly be hiding there.

'Come on Mum,' says Flo suddenly, our roles reversed, she's the adult now taking control of her mother, who has become the child, 'Let's go and find that rum punch you've been talking about for days.'

Seated at the bar, I relax a little, admiring my children, I'm so proud of them. Ben has gone to a seat in front of a small stage where there's entertainment of sorts, a woman singing anyway. The girls are drinking pineapple and banana daiquiris, their brown legs swinging from the high bar stools. No one seems bothered about their age but evidently there's no rum in their punch. I've ordered a Pina Colada having high hopes of rediscovering the drink I loved at the Admiral's Inn in Antigua all those years ago. But the rum they pour for me is white rum, it has none of the flavour of the golden rum of the islands, and the coconut blend is watery.

'Not nice Mum?' Fran looks worried on my behalf.

'Just not what I expected that's all,' I admit. I should've known better, it's always a mistake to try and recapture the pleasures of one's youth. Memories are precious treasures. A hopeless challenge set for later years to try to find the same. We wander our way back to our room and it's cool as I had promised, and we fall on our beds with, unusually, no argument about who sleeps where. The grumble of the air-conditioning drowns all thoughts and dreams.

I'm woken in the small hours, by a desperate need for the bathroom for I had drunk copious amounts of water during the journey knowing that dehydration exacerbates fatigue. I slid out of bed and having no idea for a moment where I am, I walk into the wall between the bedroom and the bathroom. Stunned I fall back on the bed, next to Flo who is stretched out beside me. (We have to share a double bed as we are all squashed into a family room designed for two adults and two children).

'Are you all right?' mumbles my daughter.

'I bumped my head that's all.' With my fingers I can touch the large bump that's already grown out of my forehead. 'Its fine, just a bit of an egg there, I'm sure it will be gone tomorrow.' I try another attempt at reaching the bathroom, successful this time and make myself a compress with a flannel soaked in cold water for a while, which relieves the smarting pain between my eyes. The first sign of light is beginning to filter through the shutters of the verandah doors and I've an overwhelming urge to go outside and see. I open one door as quietly as I can and swiftly glance back in the room, to check that no one has stirred. Stepping out I pull the door shut behind me, for the heat outside, although it's early, is dramatically different to the chilly temperature of the room I've left.

Sometimes we have moments that make our eyes fill with tears, it can happen in the cinema, (slightly embarrassing) and often at weddings, not the full blown tears of some terrible sorrow, nor tears of joy exactly, just an uncontrollable shift of emotion that somehow triggers the unmentionable when we would prefer not to show such feelings. This was just such a moment for me, as I breathe in the Caribbean air and look across to the palm trees, and see the dawn breaking over the mountain beyond. I'm weeping, a little at first and then wiping away the tears that fall, freely down my cheeks. I can see large, coloured birds amongst the trees and when I manage, hard as it is to focus as I cry, I recognise them to be parrots. There are horses (or mules) drawing carts full of workers, bound for the banana fields, and men walking in the same direction too, with machetes, dangling low at their sides. This procession moves along outside the boundary fence, separated from us, the idle holiday makers cocooned in our world of swim up bars and fresh towels. I'm crying for the joy of returning to the islands, and the respite from work and all the troubles I've left behind. Patrick, Jean Paul and even Philippe, they've all shrunk into the distance with no importance at all in this, the bigger picture of me with my blessed children in a faraway land with the sea, the birds and the mountains.

24

"He saw her whole – her promise, her dangers, her degree of life, what moved and what slept in her, what shape, what colour, what sound of a woman she was now."

Elizabeth Jane Howard, *The Sea Of Change*

I go down in bare feet and a thin robe intent on finding a cup of tea in this hotel wilderness where I've awakened. Everywhere there are natives cleaning, washing the huge marbled floors, polishing windows, sweeping the pools with nets for any creepy crawlies or foliage that lies on the surface. A group of small black birds, not unlike British blackbirds but slightly longer in the leg, are taking their early bath on the edge of the pool, ignoring the presence of the pool boy, tamed by regularity and the absence of threat. There are four loungers near the pool under a shady tree and I shall go back to the room for towels to reserve them, as soon as I've found a cup of tea. Across the far side of the immense hall, I see a boy pinning up a sign next to a large coffee machine. I tread carefully over the glistening wet floor to reach him. Everything needed for a take away hot drink is neatly presented on a tray, and the sheet the boy has put up is the weather forecast for the day. 'It will surely be a lovely day?' I ask.

'Today yes, but not always,' he says in that West Indian drawl that I love, 'somedays we have strong winds and big seas and then we fly a red flag on the beach to tell you it's not safe on the water, no sailing, or wind surfing on those days, and swimmers must take care.'

'It's hard to imagine those conditions today, thank you.' I head off with my cup of tea, not that special but hot and wet, and at least it resembles tea in colour. I might become accustomed to what is on offer after two whole weeks, even the rum.

I take the towels to the loungers, the girls still sleeping soundly but Ben is flushed and feverish, tonsillitis threatens, as I'd initially feared before we left. I dress quickly and with purpose.

'I want you to stay in the room with the girls until I come back,' I tell him. 'I'm going to see if I can find you some antibiotics. They must have a doctor at hand somewhere in a big hotel like this.'

I give him water, paracetamol and leave him there, and rush out again, full of my worry and duty as a mother.

Down at the reception desk, the staff are surprisingly bemused and disinterested that anyone could possibly be unwell in their hotel. I gather that if I leave the complex and walk into the small village that serves the hotels surrounding ours, there's a medical centre where I can make an enquiry. I set out immediately following the directions I've written on a scrap of hotel paper from the desk. After a fifteen minute walk, the centre lies in a small backstreet. I find a plaque on the wall that tells me I have found the place. It really bears no resemblance to my idea of a medical centre at all. A shabby front door and a dark corridor lead me to another door where a notice says that the centre won't be open until nine o'clock. It's only eight. How stupid of me, I'd completely disregarded the hour, driven by the urgency of my quest and now I'm forced to wait. It's not a good idea to go all the way back to the hotel in the heat, I'll have to find a shady place to sit outside. I've no hat to protect me and the day is already fearsomely hot. A spot under a tree affords me little shade but it's better than nothing. A few people pass, casting me strange, sideways glances but otherwise I'm undisturbed and the hour passes quickly enough although I'm haunted by an image of the girls coming to look for me, leaving Ben alone in the room. The West Indies always seemed a safe place to me when I was alone but now I have a family I see danger on every street corner.

I explain Ben's symptoms to an elderly pharmacist, whose medical training is probably doubtful but I don't care, I can see a familiar yellow bottle of Amoxicillin on the shelf and I know Ben has been prescribed that before for tonsillitis. I point this out to the man who appears content that I've made the diagnosis and treatment on his behalf and I hand over far too many dollars for my purchase. I wonder on the way back if I should have bartered for the drug because he has, quite obviously swindled me. As long as Ben is better does it really matter?

I jog on my way, in spite of the heat, eager to be reunited with my brood. They're in the room, thank goodness, why had I worried so? Next I realise I've no teaspoon for the syrup so back I go, down to the snack bar outside which is just opening and they begrudgingly lend me a spoon which I promise to return. I'm exhausted before the day has even begun, and I'm supposed to be on holiday. My shoulders are burnt to a crisp as I'd left on my mission without applying any sun lotion and the bump on my head is formidable. Ben, on the other hand, perks up immeasurably as soon as I administer the syrup, so much so that I wonder if the punishment I've endured in the last couple of hours has really been necessary. Better to be on the safe side though, as now I'm sure we can continue our holiday without the worry of him taking a turn for the worse.

No sun for me for the rest of our first day, I nurse my burn under the tree with a book, while the children are free to roam the hotel and amuse themselves. I venture out to walk to the beach with the girls in the late afternoon, leaving Ben under our tree and we plunge into the clear water, which is better than any swimming pool. The girls, however are not so sure there won't be a shark lurking beneath on the hot sand, although I point out the reef at the entrance to the small bay which will have prevented any large, dangerous fish from coming close to swimmers. They're still not confidant and desert me for the pools, leaving me to swim alone and think about my grandfather John and his daily swim from the beach in St Lucia, followed by his glass of rum on the way back up the hill. He had life worked out, a wonderful way to spend one's last days, for his last days they surely were, for cancer had taken him just months after my visit.

Ben improves quickly and begins learning to windsurf, while I take the girls out in a sunfish dinghy, which they hate, unanimously swearing never to attempt such a dangerous sport again. I have to placate them afterwards by allowing them to have their hair braided on the beach by West Indian girls, at enormous cost. That's the trouble with the beach, sellers, pushing their wares, plague us. They carry beaded necklaces, carvings, all sorts and most of the traders aren't even local, they are Africans. They aren't allowed in the hotel so they lurk on the sand ready to pounce on unsuspecting visitors who need a change from the hotel grounds. I can't remember this sort of badgering down in the Windward Islands, not on the beaches anyway, only in the towns, except for the boys who sailed out to sell us fish, a practice that suited me for I often bartered for their catch to feed my guests.

We book an excursion to fulfill the girls' ambition to swim with dolphins. The marine centre is a long bus ride from the hotel but I'm eager to see more of the island. To my horror, as soon as we take our seats in the bus, the driver walks around pulling all the blinds down so we can't see anything at all of the countryside. 'It's the rules', he says, with a West Indian glare that defies discussion and I can't understand why. Surely with the windows closed the air-conditioning can function perfectly well, without the blinds being pulled down. I wonder if for some reason these people don't want tourists to see their island. What are they hiding from us?

We wander around the vast aquariums lost in an under-sea world. First we go to the dolphin pool, which is a touching experience for all of us, although I am not allowed to use my camera. We are apparently restricted to buying the professional images at the end of our visit.

The children are able to snorkel in one of the tanks that simulates a reef full of tiny multi-coloured fish and I find a bench in the shade to sit and wait for them to tire of swimming round and round. They look as if they have been transformed into underwater creatures. A safe way to look at marine life in close-up I can't deny. A man comes and sits on *my* bench. There are other seats, why can't he sit elsewhere and leave me in my space?

'Yours in there?' he says amicably nodding towards the tank. I detect an accent, Dutch, Swedish, something like that.

'Yes, mine are in there,' I answer looking at the tank and not at him.

'Are you on your own?' he asks. His question both direct and intrusive takes me off guard.

'No, I have my children,' I say.

'I meant is your husband not with you,' he smiles, 'but I think you know what I meant.'

'He's not here, no,' I say, not really wanting to chat about such personal issues with a stranger, but then what harm could come from a conversation by a fish tank, miles from home. I've no reason to be unfriendly. We'll probably never see each other, ever again.

'Erik,' he said suddenly, jumping to his feet in front of me and stretching out his hand, a formal introduction. He's not tall, probably only half a head taller than me.

'Elle,' I'm suddenly shy, taking his hand for a second but not moving from the bench. 'Is that a Swedish name then, Erik with a k, instead of the English Eric with a c?'

'Yes, that's right and Elle must be short for something,

although I know Elle can stand alone as a name, just 'she' in French, isn't it?'

'Yes, it's short for Eleanor in my case, but we do live in France.'

I warm with this soft, meaningless conversation and to his gentle way. He looks at me with deep green eyes that tell me he understands the loneliness of a holiday resort full of couples with, or without, offspring. He recognises the effort needed to make decisions and to stay in control when feeling lost inside. We share the unspoken knowledge of our lives left on hold and problems temporarily set aside, while we escape to entertain our children and sooth our weathered souls with carefree sunshine and rest; to boost positive strength and compose ourselves before returning to face what we must.

He begins to speak of time and places and how the world of the islands is so far removed from his own. We can stand back, strangers together and try to make sense of all.

I'm half listening and half thinking about Philippe, Jean Paul and Patrick and how distant and unimportant these three men have become since I've been away. All I had needed was the Atlantic Ocean between us to bring everything into sharp focus. Patrick is no real danger to me, just an infuriating nuisance with an obsession for me, if he truly loved me he wouldn't be so cruel, and Philippe? I should've never married him, as simple as that. I'd not known him long enough nor understood how it would be to take on someone else's children. Finally Jean Paul, for whom I thought I'd developed the deepest feelings, now that I'm so far removed from him, even he seems to fade into insignificance.

Our wet, excited children come to interrupt us, his two boys chattering with my three with the camaraderie that only children can discover so quickly with strangers. We move on down past several, huge aquariums. We gaze at giant ray that flutter against the glass and appear to look at us, looking at them. Finally we swim in a pool with waterfalls surrounded by hibiscus, where a pacing tiger watches us through impenetrable glass. Erik and I join in and swim behind the fall to sit upon a rock, a cool, secret place hidden from the harsh heat of the sun, sprayed by escaping tendrils from the falling water. A romantic spot better suited to lovers, than a couple who barely know each other.

We talk of aspirations, goals and dreams, of husbands and wives, of laughter and sadness and our unburdening leaves us fresh; we try to listen, one to their other in our haste to tell our own tales.

With small goodbyes we leave on separate buses to return to our hotels with images of sharks and dolphins, piranhas and tigers all muddled in our heads. Our faces are aglow with too much sun and the surprise and colour of marine life. Our clothes are stiff with salt, and skins itchy. I no longer care that the blinds are closed for we all doze on our bumpy way into the sunset and the cold, local beer tastes better on arrival in our temporary home than on previous days, as I drink it down, greedy for the soothing icy chill.

25

'Juliet says, Hey, it's Romeo, you nearly gave me a heart attack
He's underneath the window, she's singing, Hey, la, my
boyfriend's back
You shouldn't come around here, singing up at people like that
Anyway what you gonna do about it?

Juliet, the dice was loaded from the start
And I bet and you exploded in my heart
And I forget, I forget the movie song
When you gonna realize, it was just that the time was wrong,
Juliet?'

Dire Straits

We fly back through a dark night, like a ball thrown by a giant hand, from a wild, sandy beach set in an emerald sea, to land in a cold, black London; our return flight involves an unwilling change for sleepy youngsters to another plane to take us on to Nice.

'Why can't we go and see Grandpa,' says Ben.

'Not this time,' my guilt swells, large, like something I can't swallow, the bruise of tears unshed. 'We have to go home.'

The second week of the holiday was different from the first. The red flags flew along the beach, the wind blew and the sea bore a menacing grin challenging beach goers to enter at their peril. No more wind surfing, dinghy sailing or the delicious bathing along the shore line that I'd become accustomed to every day. We were blown along the sand by an all consuming wind, the sand tossed in our faces and the sun burning hot with a ruthless strength, augmented by the gale. The rain fell fiercely but only during the night, leaving then, to allow us to awaken each day to a world washed clean, scent rose steaming from hot flowers to hang in the breeze. The black birds found it hard to hold steady on their spiky feet at the corner of the pool, for the wind threatened to carry them quite away.

The children became fractious and Ben in the tactlessness of youth, frequently announced his desire to return home, loudly and with a whine in his tone.

'We only have a few more days to enjoy the pools and the weather and Mum has paid a small fortune for this holiday, so why don't you just shut up,' Florence had said to him. I thought I couldn't have put the case better myself and I didn't intervene to protect my youngest as I usually would have done. The twins hadn't made any real friends until, fatefully, the last night, which is always the way of things, for then there was sadness at their imminent departure.

The flight was delayed for an hour or two and we'd sat, wide-eyed and stunned as only travelers can. Our bags had lain forlorn on the scruffy airport floor, and our small group watched in fascination as the largest moths we'd ever seen, battered themselves to a sure death on the glass of the windows in a futile attempt to reach the light inside.

Ten hours later, we arrive and Philippe bears his silently grateful ex-family home as arranged, sulky faced with lack of sleep and confusion for the hour. He leaves us, with few words spoken, on our chilly, autumnal doorstep.

When I recover from the journey, which does take a few days, I fly about my tasks with a lightened heart and wallow in the improvement of my spirit and well being following our holiday. The children are happy and even enthusiastic to resume their studies. I am equally content to return to work and reopen my shop, greeting my customers gratefully, receiving from them the measured affection for one who has been missed.

I bump into Jean Paul in a side street, and the unmistakable excitement that he never fails to awaken inside me, is almost overpowering and threatens to leave me stupid and speechless. Somehow I manage to speak first, after kissing him fleetingly on each cheek, as is customary in France for a public greeting between two friends.

'Jean Paul, c'est bien de te voir,' I say. This is the truth for it's extremely good to see him, and I'm glad I'm wholesomely tanned with freshly washed hair and happen to be wearing a dress I consider to be pretty. He stands back a step or two and I can tell he's impressed.

'When can I see you,' he says, his mind sadly, is as predictable as ever.

'I'm not sure, I'm rather busy this week, as we're only just back from holiday, but give me a call, next week maybe?' And so it was with us, always the same, we will drift apart when I become infuriated by his incomprehensible behaviour and then, after time we'll find each other again, drawn by our irresistible attraction, one for the other. But that is all it'll ever be, nothing more, and at last I understand that the choice is always mine, to take opportunities or to leave them lying on the pavement of my life, and walk away.

I awake on Sunday morning as light hearted and happy as I'd ever been when sailing my precious *Galuette* out of the port on a sunny autumn day. But this day is to change quickly and become something strange and ugly. I still have no idea as I potter about in my kitchen, sweeping the floor, unloading the dishwasher, all the jobs I'd not had the energy nor the inclination to complete at the end of a busy Saturday baking and serving customers. I always stir early, even on a day off, more willingly than on a working day because the day's my own and I can fill the hours however I choose. Clearing up first makes the house feel fresh and means I can spend the rest of the day doing pleasanter things without a trace of guilt, or thoughts of having left things undone. I vacuum the hall, not caring if I wake the children, they should learn to follow my example and not waste the day. Grabbing the empty milk carrier I open the front door to replace it upon the step. I almost fall over Patrick for he's lying there, spread-eagled on the stone, I hadn't realised how big a man he was until I see him flat, his boots upon the pavement. A bunch of cellophane wrapped freesias lie partly squashed in his right hand, as if he'd somehow tried to save himself from harm with them, as he fell. There's no one else in sight as I look up the street in desperation now, with the thought that I must call for help. Having ascertained that he does have a pulse I realise that he must have tripped on the step somehow and knocked himself out. It's then that I see the ugly wound around his temple and it begins to dawn on me that someone has hit him with something hard and that I need to call an ambulance quickly.

How can I possibly explain to the children that a man they don't know lies beaten upon our doorstep, while obviously delivering flowers? I take the freesias indoors with me, throwing them on the kitchen table, before grabbing the phone to call for help. No sign of the children, thank goodness.

'Il y a un homme,' I start to explain, confused at what I should say, 'a man who I know and he's unconscious on my doorstep, he has a wound on his head, please come.'

Of course when the ambulance arrives the siren awakes not only the children but the whole street. Claude and Amelie stand huddled in their doorway in their dressing gowns exchanging knowing glances with each other and shaking their heads. I go to them, 'I hope you don't think I hit him,' I say, the truth will out now, 'he's been stalking me for some time but I would never have done anything like this,'

'No of course not,' says Claude, 'but somebody did.'

Á LA FIN

A few months have passed since that terrible Sunday morning and there are never any flowers outside my door anymore. There is just a feint stain where Patrick's head had lain, bleeding, before I found him. Stephanie has scrubbed the whole step with bleach but the mark refuses to budge.

Béatrice has only been given the French equivalent of a short suspended sentence, on the grounds that her children need her and of course, she had been pushed to the limit to commit what the French recognise as a domestic crime of passion. Although Patrick wasn't fatally wounded, he has, I believe, taken some time to recover.

I know for certain that I'll never have a problem with him again. This is something to thank Béatrice for at the end of the day. Apparently she'd struck him with the broken end of a garden tool, which was later found, nearby, on the pavement. She had certainly hit him hard enough to stop him in the act of delivering flowers, but she hadn't, the *juge de proximité* had ruled, delivered a blow with the intent to mortally wound. She'd followed him, having seen the flowers and guessed the truth, so long denied to her, at last. She'd wept for it was never her choice to believe the unbelievable.

As I stand at my door and watch the market stalls awaken, I remember the film Patrick and I had joked about at the beginning of the whole affair. So much had passed and changed for all since we'd glibly discussed the out come of the extra-marital relations portrayed in "*Bridge over Madison County*". I tip my head back to feel soft moisture as it caresses my face. I'm the one left standing alone in the rain. Freedom embraces me as only freedom can, and I'm glad.

The Warmth of Waves

★★★★★

Lynette Fisher's first novel is beautifully crafted with several stories running through it, binding together to make a strong, un-put-downable read.

★★★★★

Entrancing read. I absolutely loved it. I was carried away into the warm climes of her sailing travels. I was simply transfixed and had to pace myself so that I wouldn't finish it too fast!

★★★★★

Immediately delighted by the writing style, this book was hard to put down. The intended journey amidst the real journey. The author was not frightened to make her heroine a real live character, however gritty, putting this book in the realm of actual female equality.

★★★★★

What a beautifully written and atmospheric book.

Other titles by Lynette Fisher

Born in Hampshire and educated at Godolphin School in Salisbury, Lynette spent the first twenty years of her adult life pursuing a successful culinary career on the ocean. With at least five Atlantic crossings under her belt, she still has a passion for old, wooden boats having owned and restored three, before finally succumbing to bricks and mortar, in 1991.

After the birth of her son, Lynette opened her patisserie, Le Vieux Four, in Dorset where she has been trading for 25 years.

Lynette has recently published two cook books, the first, *Recipes from le Vieux Four, The Secret Culinary Adventures of a Dorset Pastry Chef* follows her journeys with recipes collected along the way. The second, *Special Cakes from the Old Oven* is (as the name suggests) all about the cakes found at Le Vieux Four, with the individuality of Lynette's own recipes and photographs.

The Flowers that Bloom on a Dark French Night is her second novel continuing the story of her heroine who leaves her ocean life behind her and settles in France.